FIRST FANGS CLUB

SUCK IT UP BUTTERCUP

USA TODAY BESTSELLING AUTHOR

# KRISTEN PAINTER

**Suck It Up, Buttercup:**
**A Paranormal Women's Fiction Novel**
First Fangs Club • Book Two

Copyright © 2020 Kristen Painter

Published in the United States of America.

At 49, Belladonna Barrone's life has taken some interesting turns. She unwittingly married into the mob but managed to get free when her husband died in a car accident. Most recently she was attacked and turned into a vampire, something else she never intended. As with everything, she's made the best of her situation.

She just didn't know this newest situation would also result in her becoming the vampire governor of New Jersey. It's cool, though. The perks are great, the penthouse is spectacular, and the salary couldn't have come at a better time. Vampire politics, on the other hand, might be more complicated than she anticipated.

She's handling it all pretty well, including dealing with another governor who thinks she ought to do his bidding and telling her kids that she's now one of the immortal, when a new wrinkle from her old life complicates things in ways she would rather ignore. But Belladonna isn't the kind of woman who runs from her problems.

Instead, she makes a plan and attacks. With her friends at her side, everything goes off without a hitch. Or at least she thinks so until a note shows up telling her the one person who's been instrumental in making sure her past life stays in the past is in serious dangerous. Belladonna suddenly fears she's bitten off more than she can chew.

But she's not about to sacrifice a single one of her friends, so there's nothing left to do but suck it up, buttercup.

# CHAPTER 1

There was money. And then there was wealth. The penthouse apartment Belladonna Barrone had just entered was all about wealth.

She took a few steps and stared at the spectacular space before her. The Wellman Towers was prime real estate on the New Jersey side of the Hudson River. *Prime.* If she had to guess, she'd estimate these units—at least this one, the penthouse—went for about seven or eight million. Without furnishings. This place—and this view—proved exactly why.

Through the wall of windows and beyond the river, Manhattan sprawled across the horizon like an enormous beast of steel and glass, glittering with lights that outshone the stars in the night sky. The vibrant hum of life emanating from the city was almost audible. If she stepped onto the expansive balcony, it probably would be.

"That view is unbelievable." Donna breathed out. "This place is amazing."

Pierce, the attorney who was also Donna's new assistant, let out a low whistle. "Spectacular."

Artemis, vampire queen of the United States and Donna's grandsire, nodded. "It is. But it needs to be impressive. It's the governor's quarters, after all."

"Right." And Belladonna was now the vampire governor of New Jersey, something that had yet to fully sink in. But then, she'd earned the title barely twenty-four hours ago during a sudden and unexpected trial that had almost cost another vampire her life. That vampire, Claudette, was Donna's sire and the previous governor. Winning the trial (thanks to Pierce's litigation skills) meant Donna had taken Claudette's place, but also, thankfully, she'd been able to pardon Claudette and spare her life, as losing had earned the woman a death sentence from the Immortus Concilio, the vampire ruling council.

"I know what you're thinking," Artemis said.

"You do?" Donna had suspected before that Artemis could read minds.

She nodded. "Claudette will have forty-eight hours to move her things out."

"Oh. Good." Donna hadn't been thinking that at all, but she wasn't going to correct Artemis. The woman was a little too scary for Donna to cross that bridge. Although it was nice to know the woman hadn't read her mind. Really nice. Artemis was powerful enough as it was. Fortunately, Donna's time as a mob wife had taught her a lot about when to speak up and when to stay quiet. "She can have longer if she needs—"

"No, she cannot." Artemis frowned. "You have a

6

week to settle in and get your staff up to speed, then you can expect visits."

"Visits?"

Pierce started jotting things down on his iPhone. Donna appreciated how thorough he was without her having to say anything. But then, the man was a world-class attorney. His skill set was a little wasted on being just an assistant. His choice, however. And one she greatly appreciated.

"At minimum, there will be one from the New York governor. And most likely the governors from Pennsylvania, Maryland, and Delaware as well."

"I see." Crap. This was actually turning into a job. She hadn't really counted on that. She had no clue what a governor did. Impostor syndrome was setting in fast. "They'll call ahead of time, right?"

"Maybe. Probably." Artemis shook her head. "Fitzhugh can be a bit of a loose cannon. He pretty much does what he wants, when he wants. He may just show up."

"And he is?" Donna asked.

Pierce kept tapping away. Donna assumed he was taking down names. She hoped so. Although she wasn't likely to forget a name like Fitzhugh.

"Hawke Fitzhugh is the governor of New York." Artemis's gaze held detached amusement and the slightest hint of bitterness. History between her and Fitzhugh, perhaps? "He considers himself quite the gift to vampire society. And females in general. You'll see."

"Hawke? That's really his first name?"

"It is. This century, anyway."

"Well. Can't wait." She could handle a man who was full of himself. She'd spent twenty-seven years married to one.

"You may also get petitions for things others need or want done or would like you to grant. You're under no obligation to see those vampires, or grant anything, but if you continually turn them away, you won't be popular." Artemis shrugged. "Ask Claudette if you don't believe me."

"I believe you."

"Good. Find a balance, but make time for your constituents. That's my best suggestion."

"Thank you. I'll do my best."

Artemis looked a little bored, but Donna supposed she probably was. Giving a tour of the governor's place was pretty menial work for the queen. "This penthouse has five bedrooms, five baths, an office, a conference room, a salon, kitchen, dining room, two lounges, and a private elevator. There's a gym and indoor pool on the first floor of the building. If something isn't to your taste, or you need to repurpose a room, that's perfectly fine."

A salon? Donna smiled. "I think it all sounds wonderful."

"Additionally, there is access to the roof and to the apartment below, which the governorship also owns. Rest assured, both floors have been fortified with iron. The windows have all been coated with UV film too. Although that's meant as a precaution, not a lifesaving measure. Understood?"

"Perfectly." Donna nodded with great seriousness, but the truth was, she didn't need protection from the sun so long as she was wearing the blessed crucifix she'd had on when she'd been turned. The crucifix, a gift from her nun sister, Cammie, had been purchased at the Vatican and blessed by the pope. Donna wasn't sure what part of that was keeping her safe from the sun, or if it was just her belief in a higher power, but whatever the reason, the cross's protection was her secret. It would stay that way as long as possible too.

Artemis went on. "The apartment below is where your driver and administrative assistant live. There's more living space available, should you like to install additional staff. The driver and admin are available to you at any time."

"Good to know." Donna gestured to Pierce. "And my assistant?"

"You can put him up in the apartment below, but most governors have their assistant in-house."

Donna nodded. "That's what I thought."

Pierce smiled politely. "I'm happy to live wherever you'd like me to."

"Thank you." Donna would have to think about that. Having Pierce close had benefits, but she was just getting used to being alone. And liking it.

Instead of giving an immediate answer, she walked through the living room, which she imagined qualified as one of the lounges, and into the kitchen, which had enough space for a breakfast bar and a table that sat six.

Lots of polished concrete and clean lines with touches of charcoal, slate, bronze, and rose gold. It was darkly modern and sleek and very sophisticated. More androgynous than full-on masculine, but not so much that it felt oppressive. And not at all like the kind of place she would have pictured the vampire governor might call home. But then, she wasn't sure what else it should look like. And it didn't much matter, because she didn't really plan on living here.

Did she?

A new question popped into her head. "Is it mandatory that I live here?"

"You're the governor. It's expected that you're here occasionally. Well, more than that, I suppose. Enough to be considered regular." Artemis frowned. "If something isn't to your liking, there's money in the budget to make changes."

"It's not that, it's just… Wait, there's a budget?"

"Yes. How do you think you and your staff get paid?" Artemis shook her head. "Don't get too caught up in being here, though. Your schedule is yours. As long as you're fulfilling your duties, you're good. Like I said, you must find a balance."

Donna was still focused on one of the first things Artemis had said. "I get a salary?"

Artemis laughed. "I did mention that before. Did you forget? This is not a volunteer position."

"I completely forgot. Remember, I've been a vampire for less than a week. And it's been a pretty crazy week at that."

Artemis's expression softened. "Forgive me. It has been. But you're still much more...together than most at this stage."

"I appreciate that."

Pierce leaned in. "You're doing very well."

She smiled at him. She was glad he was here. "Thanks."

"Yes," Artemis said. "There is a salary for you and your assistant. And obviously, whatever staff you need besides your admin and your driver, who is also your head of security. Like I said, there is also room for you to hire more staff. The governorship of New Jersey has deep pockets. Your admin can provide you with the budget. Bear in mind, my office audits every governor at the end of the fiscal year."

"So don't be foolish," Donna supplied.

"Yes. This isn't your personal bank account." Artemis smiled. "I doubt this will be an issue for you. But I tell you these things because I must."

"I understand." Claudette's downfall had come about because she hadn't told Donna all the things she should have. There was no way Artemis would follow the same pattern of behavior. Otherwise, she wouldn't have become queen.

Artemis waved a hand. "If you have questions, you can reach out to me, but your staff can help you as well. They've been at their jobs for a while."

Which meant they'd worked for Claudette. Donna instantly wondered if they'd resent her for what had happened. Or would they be happy to have a new boss?

"Is there anything you'd like to know right now?" Artemis asked. "Otherwise, I'm done here. Feel free to tour the rest of the penthouse and stay as long as you like. It's your residence now."

"I..." Donna was sure she ought to have a thousand questions, but none came immediately to mind.

Pierce cleared his throat. "The elevator has a fingerprint scanner. Who will take care of getting us set up with that?"

"Good question." Artemis's smile didn't entirely convey that sentiment, however, making Donna proud of Pierce for being willing to ask. "Either Donna's admin or driver can handle that." She looked at Donna. "Anything else?"

"Not immediately. No." Donna took a breath. "Wait. Yes. This building. Everyone who lives here, they're okay with having such interesting occupants? All the late-night comings and goings?"

"They are." Artemis's eyes narrowed. "Because everyone in this building is either a supernatural or engaged in supernatural-related business."

Donna blinked. "Good to know."

"Your admin can give you a list of your neighbors, if you desire." With another wave, Artemis nodded and headed for the door. "Be well. I hope you succeed."

"Thanks." Donna frowned as Artemis left. The door closed, leaving her and Pierce alone in the apartment. She raised her brows and looked at him. "So. I'm sure the rest of this place is equally amazing, but it feels weird to look around while Claudette's stuff is still here."

He nodded. "We'll have plenty of time to look around tomorrow. We have other things to do anyway."

"That's for sure. We should get back to my house. I need to pack enough to allow me to stay here for a few days at a time."

"Or," Pierce started, "you could do some shopping and just stock this place accordingly. I believe that would be in the purview of gubernatorial spending."

Donna bit her lip. "You think?"

"We can ask your admin."

"Right. And we still haven't met her, or him, as the case may be. We should go do that."

"And meet your driver. Both introductions Artemis should have made."

"You would have thought so. Well, let's go meet them." She put her hand on his arm and grinned like a schoolgirl. "This place, though."

He laughed. "It's amazing. Do you like the way it looks, or are you going to redecorate?"

"I like it. It's got a very strong vibe. Like the person who lives here has it all going on and isn't to be messed with."

He nodded. "I think that describes you very well."

She shook her head, amused. "You have a very high opinion of me."

"One you earned."

The words of her therapist, Dr. Goldberg, about

trusting in her own strength echoed in Donna's head. "Well, thank you. I need to own that more. So the reminder is appreciated."

She took another look around. "It could use a few things. Some pictures of the kids, definitely. A few plants, maybe. A litter box for Lucky." She slanted her eyes at Pierce. "I should have asked about the pet policy."

He typed something on his phone. "Your admin will know. And what are they going to say, that you can't have your cat? You're the governor. You make the rules."

"True." She put her hands on her hips. "What do you think of this place? Would you change anything?"

He gave it an appraising glance, then shook his head. "Like you said, maybe a few personal touches, but it suits me just fine." Then he chuckled softly. "But I will be happy to take a room in the apartment below."

"I think...I'd prefer you here."

His brows lifted. "You're sure?"

She nodded. "I realize we're still getting to know each other, but you've proven to be an incredible ally. And since I routinely drink your blood, we're already intimately acquainted."

"There is that."

"The truth is, right now, you're part of my very small circle of trust. Having you close seems like the best idea. I don't want to have to run downstairs every time I want to talk something over with you."

"That would be less than convenient."

She tapped her index finger against her chin. "Although, there is some value in having you in the other apartment, getting to know the admin and driver. But I suppose if they worked for Claudette without issue, they should be fine working for me. I hope."

"I can still get to know them." A more serious expression crossed his face. "You know I will do everything in my power to keep you safe."

"I do know that. You've already shown me that by defending me to the council." She ran her hand over the kitchen countertop just to feel the stone under her fingers. "I wonder what your salary is. And if I have the power to give you a raise in case it's not sufficient."

He grinned. "Probably something else your admin will know."

"Then let's go meet her. Or him."

"Artemis said there's access from the penthouse to the apartment below. Do you want to look for it?"

"I think for our first meeting, it's better we show up at the front door and not suddenly appear in the living room or wherever."

He nodded. "Good call. First impressions and all that."

# CHAPTER 2

They rode the elevator down one floor, and Pierce knocked. An older woman with silver hair cut fashionably short and spiky opened the door immediately. Her trim navy pantsuit was accented by a fuchsia blouse and flats and sculptural silver jewelry. She smiled at them. "Hello there. You must be Belladonna Barrone, the new governor."

"I am," Donna answered. "Hello to you. This is my assistant, Pierce Harrison."

"Pleasure to meet you both. I'm Charlene Rollins, your administrative assistant. You can call me Charlie, if you like."

"Nice to meet you, too, Charlie." The woman had a competent air about her. And her outfit was great. Donna liked her instantly. "Anyone ever tell you that you give off a Jamie Lee Curtis vibe?"

"I get that a lot." Charlie took a few steps back. "Come in, please. Temo is in the kitchen. He's your driver and head of security." She hesitated. "Unless you'd like a tour of this apartment first?"

"No, there's time for that later. Like tomorrow."

This apartment had the same spectacular views as the penthouse, but the decorating was much more comfortable. Oversize burnished brown leather couches, fluffy white area rugs, lots of pictures, soft lighting, and a crackling fire in the fireplace. The scent of baked goods lingered in the air.

Donna smiled at the photos on the mantel. "This place is a lot homier than the governor's apartment."

"I hope that's okay," Charlie said.

"It's perfect," Donna answered. "You live here, after all, so it should be to your tastes. Assuming it is. Did you decorate it?"

"I did. Mostly. I've been here longer than Temo, so it was up to me anyway. Thankfully, he's fine with it. He's added a few touches of his own too."

"Well, you did a great job." Donna looked at Pierce. "I want some of these fluffy rugs. Lucky would love them."

Pierce looked at Charlie. "Will you let me know where you got them?"

"Sure." Charlie smiled. "Come in. I'll introduce you to Temo. And get you your welcome packet."

"There's a welcome packet?" Donna glanced at Pierce and mouthed the words, "Who knew?"

They followed Charlie through to the kitchen.

A large man with twinkling eyes and black hair scraped back into a long braid was stirring cream into a cup of coffee. Nearby on the counter was a plate with a stacked sandwich and the ingredients that had gone into it. A tray of cookies was on the stove. Sugar, maybe.

"Temo," Charlie said, "this is Governor Belladonna Barrone. Our new boss. And this is her assistant, Pierce Harrison."

Temo nodded. Black tribal tattoos swirled out from under his rolled-up shirtsleeves, wrapping his arms down to the wrists. They peeked out from the neck of his dress shirt too. "Nice to meet you, Madam Governor. Mr. Harrison."

"Call me Pierce, please."

Donna wanted to tell him to call her by her first name as well but refrained. Would that be a breach of protocol? She wanted to be friends with these people, but at the same time she had to maintain a professional relationship with them. At least until she got to know them better. "It's great to meet you both."

Charlie stood with military stiffness. "I have a master's in business management, and before coming to work here, I was the executive assistant to the CEO of Rothchild's Antiquities in London for fourteen years. Before that, I was a concierge at the Regency Hotel, also in London. I hold dual citizenship in the UK and the US."

"Wow, very impressive." Donna's brows rose a little. That was quite a résumé.

"My background's not so fancy," Temo said. "I was Special Ops, did two tours I'd rather not talk about, then got out and went to work as security at a club in the city. I've done some high-end private security too. Besides my tactical mobility training in the military, I've been to evasive-driving school and racing school." His smile was bright and broad. "I'm pretty good behind the wheel."

"Sounds like it," Donna said. "I think your résumé is just as impressive as Charlie's, but for different reasons." Then came the big question. "How did you both like working for Claudette?"

Temo glanced at Charlie.

The older woman picked up a manila envelope from the counter as she laughed and shrugged. "She's not our boss anymore, so I suppose it's okay to be a little honest. She was fine as a boss for me. For Temo, not so much."

He frowned. "She didn't like me."

Donna thought he seemed pretty likable. "Can I ask why?"

He sipped his coffee but didn't make eye contact until a second later. "I'm sure she had her reasons. But she almost never used the car."

Donna thought he was holding something back. If he didn't want to speak ill of Claudette, Donna respected that. She might be in Claudette's position someday herself. "She told me she ran everywhere. I guess that was her way of not needing you. It struck me as weird when she said it, but hey, to each their own, right?" Donna smiled at him. "I *will* be using the car."

Temo smiled back. "Good. Because I don't like feeling like I'm being paid for nothing. Is there anywhere you need me to take you this evening? Or any security concerns you'd like to discuss?"

"No. I have my own vehicle here, and we're

heading back to my house soon. I wasn't prepared to stay here tonight. It'll probably be a day or two before that happens. Plus, Claudette needs to move her things out."

"That won't take much doing," Charlie answered. "She has a studio in the Village. Most of her possessions are there. Here's your welcome packet, by the way." She held out the envelope.

Charlie knew a lot about Claudette, more than Donna had known, but the woman had been Claudette's admin, so it made sense. She took the packet. "Well, that's good about Claudette. I'm glad she's not homeless. Say, if I have some things sent to this address, will you take delivery of them if I'm not here?"

Charlie nodded. "Absolutely. And if you're buying anything for the apartment, please use the credit card in the packet. It's paid by the governor's account. Use it for all your expenses from here on out. And just so you know, when you're not here, I do a daily check on the apartment, bring the mail in, that sort of thing. I actually work out of the office on this floor. Unless you'd rather I not."

"No, that's great. I'm probably going to add some plants. I suppose those might need watering on occasion. And I have a cat. Lucky. I hope having him here will be all right?"

"You can have any pets you like," Charlie said.

Temo chewed the bite of sandwich he'd just taken, then swallowed. "I like cats. I can't wait to meet him."

"You'll like Lucky," Donna said. "He's a sweetheart. I'm not sure how he'll like the change in his environment, but hopefully it won't bother him too much. Good to know he's allowed in the building too."

"I haven't been a good host." Charlie took a mug down from the cabinets. "Would you like some coffee? Or something else?"

"No, thanks. I'm fine. Pierce?"

He shook his head. "I'm good. And we only have a couple hours before sunrise."

"Thanks for reminding me," Donna said. Even though the sun wouldn't affect her, she had to keep up the ruse that she was as vulnerable as every other vampire. "We should get going. I look forward to working with both of you. I am very new to all of this, so I hope you'll be patient with me."

"Of course," they both said.

She looked at Charlie. "Can I ask you to do something for me?"

Charlie smiled. "You can ask me to do anything. That's what I'm here for. What we're both here for."

Donna nodded, laughing softly. "Right. That's going to take some getting used to. Can you put together a little dossier on the governors of the surrounding states? Artemis told me there's a good chance they'll drop by. Governor Fitzhugh especially."

"Oh, he'll be here." Charlie pulled out her phone. "I'll get them to you by sunup. I keep files on all of them. I can email them to you, in fact. Which reminds me, we need to exchange contact information with both of you."

They all got their phones out and took care of that detail, then Donna was about to say goodbye when the lights flashed.

Charlie looked up. "There's someone at your door."

"Is that what that means?" Pierce asked.

She nodded. "Part of our system. Helps us be ready in case we're needed, but it can be turned off if the governor wants more privacy, although it's only activated in the common areas."

"I'm okay with it, I guess."

Charlie's brows rose slightly. "Are you sure? Because it's very easy to turn off. Claudette never wanted anyone sneaking up on her."

"I'm kind of surprised visitors aren't buzzed in or announced or something."

"They are, unless they're on a vetted list."

"Oh." Donna tucked her phone back into her purse. "Maybe it's Claudette coming to get her stuff."

"This close to sunrise?" Temo asked. "I don't think so." He rolled his head around, audibly cracking a few vertebrae like he was prepping for a fight. "You want me to see who it is?"

"No, I'll do it," Donna said. "I'm the governor, right? It's my job. But good to know you're available for such things if necessary."

Temo grinned. "Happy to assist as muscle when needed."

"Nice," Donna said. She'd never had her own

lunk before. Although, Temo was too nice to refer to by that term. Still, being the vampire governor was starting to feel a little like being back in the Mafia. But without the dark underbelly of criminal intent.

"Technically," Pierce said, "getting the door is my job."

She shot him an amused look. "Well, then, I should let you do it."

He headed upstairs and toward the door while Donna, Charlie, and Temo followed, out of sight several yards behind. He opened it. "Can I help you?"

"I'm looking for the new governor," a man answered.

"Who's calling?"

"Governor Fitzhugh," he said.

Pierce glanced back at Donna and silently mouthed the words, *that didn't take long.*

*No, it didn't,* she mouthed back. There was no other option. They couldn't take the chance that Fitzhugh's hearing would pick up their conversation. *I'm not ready to meet him.*

Mostly because her casual outfit of leggings, boots, and oversize sweater wasn't really the first impression she wanted to make. When she met the other governors, she wanted to wear something like a power suit and good heels. Something much more woman-in-charge than woman-on-a-Starbucks-run.

Pierce nodded but didn't open the door any wider. "You can make an appointment. Tomorrow at 10:00 p.m. is open."

"I've come all the way from uptown Manhattan."

"Without an appointment," Pierce pointed out.

Donna grinned.

A moment of silence followed. "Fine. I'll be back tomorrow evening."

"Very good." Pierce shut the door and faced Donna. "He must really want to see who's taking over for Claudette."

Charlie clucked her tongue. "He just wants to know if he can intimidate you. He's counting on being able to. He talked Claudette into co-sponsoring a few things that did a whole lot for New York and nothing for the state of New Jersey except make a dent in our budget."

Donna frowned. "Doesn't he have his own money to spend?"

"Sure, but why do that when you can get someone else to kick in?"

Donna snorted. "That's not happening on my watch. Claudette doesn't seem like the pushover type. How did he talk her into doing those things?"

Charlie crossed her arms. "Simple. He's a good-looking guy and very persuasive. Claudette wanted him to like her. They might have…actually, it's not my place to say."

"Say what?" Donna asked. "Come on, I need to know what kind of relationship my predecessor had with him."

Charlie sighed. "Call it intuition, but I always got a feeling when they were together that they'd been… intimate. Just a feeling, though. Nothing I can substantiate."

"I can," Temo said.

Everyone looked at him, but Donna spoke first. "How do you know that?"

He made an odd face. "Because it happened in the car. That's why she didn't like me. I just didn't want to say anything earlier, but since we're being straight up, why not? When it happened, the privacy screen was up, but I knew what was going on. She was embarrassed by the whole thing and didn't want to see me after."

"Wow. That explains that," Pierce said.

Donna snorted. "If Fitzhugh thinks we're going to have that kind of relationship, he's going to be very disappointed."

Charlie pursed her lips for a moment. "Fitzhugh probably wants to meet you to suss you out. You've only been a vampire for a short period of time. Your rise has been a little meteoric, and I'm sure he's curious to see what kind of woman survives a council trial and becomes governor a week after she's turned."

"Is that whole situation common knowledge, then?"

"It is," Charlie answered. "You're a little bit of a celebrity in the local vampire world. I'd say you can expect a lot of appointments in the coming days. Mostly from vampires who want to meet you, but also so they can try to get on your good side."

Temo chuckled. "Doesn't hurt that people also know about your human history. Adds to your street cred, if you know what I mean."

Donna had a pretty good idea. "You mean that I was married to a mobster?"

He nodded. "That would be the history I'm talking about."

She pressed her fingers to her temple. "You know, that isn't really history in the sense that it's behind me. I mean, Joe's dead, but I haven't fully extricated myself from the Villachi family. And there's some complications with the Russian mob too." She shook her head. "I do hope to take care of all of that as soon as possible."

Temo's brows lifted. "You need help, boss, you just ask us, okay? Again, that's what we're here for, you know? Not just helping you keep appointments and protecting you and driving you places. Think of us as your personal soldiers. I can't speak for Charlie, but I'm down to crack skulls together if need be."

Yep, her very own lunk. "That is very kind of you, but—and not to be indelicate—aren't you human?"

Temo laughed. "Not entirely. I'm a descendant of Mafui'e, the Samoan god of earthquakes."

Donna blinked. "Wouldn't that make you a demigod? My driver is a demigod?"

He shrugged one massive shoulder, but he was still smiling. "The bloodline is a little too dilute to call myself a demi, but I have enough of my family's powers to be effective as muscle when needed."

"But you're working as a driver and security. That doesn't seem like a job befitting your obvious skills."

"I was a bouncer in Manhattan when Artemis found me. I like this a lot better. And not just because the pay is about fifteen times what I was making at Spotlight."

She looked at Charlie. "And you? Are you also something more than human?"

"Half banshee on my mother's side with a smidgen of fire mage on my dad's side." Flames crackled in her gaze. "It's a very useful set of skills in the right situation."

Donna shook her head. "Wow, this is all good to know. Especially if the Russians come calling. And on that note, I think Pierce and I should head home before the sun comes up. I'll see you both tomorrow night, and we can talk some more."

Charlie nodded. "I look forward to working with you, Governor."

"Same to both of you." A banshee and a demigod. Things were certainly getting interesting.

# CHAPTER 3

Pierce was driving, something he'd told Donna he thought he should do as her assistant. She'd let him, only because she wanted to see what kind of driver he was. People who lived in the city weren't always great on the road because they drove so infrequently, but he was doing fine.

Okay, he was also driving because he had an Aston Martin. She'd never ridden in one before, and now that she had, she was a little bit in love. It was a gorgeous piece of machinery.

Didn't hurt that James Bond drove one.

But she was letting her mind wander, and she had something important to talk to him about. She watched his face now to see his reaction. "I think...I should move into that apartment."

"Okay." His brows went up a little, but he nodded. "What changed your mind?"

"A couple things. The security. The freedom from Big Tony and his cranky wife dropping by. Making it harder for the Russians to find me. And I'm suddenly feeling like I should fully embrace this new life. I mean, go feetfirst into the deep end. And just to keep the whole foot metaphor going, how do I do that if I still have one foot in my old life?" She took a deep breath. "What do you think?"

He nodded, a slight smile on his mouth. "I'm all for it. If that's what you want, then by all means, go for it. Your reasons are all valid and great points for making the move." He glanced over. "You're going to be amazing as governor."

"Thanks for the vote of confidence." He was so good to have around. Good for her ego and her confidence, but also great company. He was the kind of level-headed sounding board she'd always wanted in a partner. Instead, she'd ended up with a man who thought everyone was out to get him. Or he'd been working on a way to get them. "I want to sell the house anyway. It's too big for me and has too many memories I'd rather let go of."

"You'll have to buy a second place at some point."

She let out a little laugh. "You mean in case I'm suddenly not governor anymore like Claudette?"

He shrugged. "I don't think anything remotely similar is going to happen to you, but you should still have a place that's exclusively yours. Just so all your eggs aren't in one basket. And so you have a place to escape to if the need arises. There might come a time when you don't want to be as accessible as the governor's estate makes you."

"Good point. And I agree. I was going to buy a condo in the Florida Panhandle, but I think something closer makes more sense. Something I can get to in a couple hours, tops."

He nodded. "Exactly. You'll easily be able to afford it, too, when you sell the house."

"And Joe's cars, which I'd like to get rid of as well."

"That should be easy to do. They're nice cars. I could take care of that for you, if you want. Did he keep them well maintained?"

"Yes. He was anal about it. Especially the Ferrari. If you want to handle that, I'd be grateful."

Pierce's fingers drummed the steering wheel. "You know, I'm pretty sure I could get more for those cars than they're worth."

"How?"

"Make a big deal about who they belonged to. If you're all right with that."

She thought about it. About cashing in on her husband's status as an infamous mobster. "I guess that would be okay."

"I don't have to. I just thought—"

"No, it's a good idea. And why not? About time Joe did something positive for me."

"I'll get to work on it first thing in the morning."

"Thank you. And speaking of money, I don't even know what my salary is. Or yours." She looked at the welcome packet on her lap. "You think that info is in here?"

"Open it and see."

She slipped her nail under the flap and opened the envelope, then slid the contents onto her lap. A welcome letter was on top of a small bundle of papers. She scanned it. "Blah, blah, blah, nothing here about salary. Let me dig."

She found what she was looking for on the next piece of paper. And gasped. "This can't be right."

"What's it say?"

"My assistant makes three million a year." She looked at him. "I hope that's enough. I'm sure you make more than that as an attorney."

"Actually, that's a little above what I cleared last year." He was smiling. "And I'm okay with that. But I don't think that's what made you gasp."

"You're right, it wasn't." She stared at the paper in front of her, at the number there in black and white. "I get ten. Ten million. A year." The words didn't mean anything. The sum was too large to grasp.

She'd thought the five million she'd found in her late husband's stash room had been a fortune. But this was twice that. And it was all clean. Unlike the cash Joe had squirreled away, which she'd come to find out had been given to him by the Russian mob for a deal she knew nothing about.

This was legit. A salary.

"Wow," she whispered.

"You'll earn it, I'm sure," Pierce said. "And I'm glad for you. You won't have anything to worry about this way, which is probably the point of that money. Artemis doesn't want you to struggle. She wants you to focus on being governor."

"I don't think I'll earn ten million. I mean, how

many meetings would you have to take to even come close to them being worth that amount? It's crazy. But amazing. I'll be set for life. Or immortality, as the case may be." She shook her head. "This just isn't sinking in. I'm sure it will. But wow."

"You'll be able to buy yourself a place in Florida and a second place nearby."

"I will. You're right." She took a breath. "For that kind of money, moving in full-time seems like the right thing to do. The only thing to do. I can't be part-time and accept a salary like that. Not with any kind of clear conscience."

"I agree." He glanced at her quickly before looking back at the road. "Are you sure you want me in the same apartment as you?"

"I think you should be. Sure, there might be occasions when I need some alone time, but we'll work that out."

"Maybe we could set up a schedule with a day off for me each week. That would build in some alone time."

"Maybe." She appreciated how concerned he was with her well-being. "Let's figure out a routine, see how busy I'm actually going to be, and then we'll tackle that. Not that you can't have time off when you need it. I know you still have to take care of your own place."

"I do, but in light of this, I might sublet it."

They rode in silence for a few more minutes, giving Donna time to think. Living with Pierce wouldn't be hard. She'd had a few days of that already since he'd stayed with her to help her prepare for the trial. They'd been together constantly, too, and he'd been very easy to be around.

But keeping her secret about being immune to the sun might get tricky. She didn't necessarily want to have to hide it. Not in the place she was going to call home. "Do I have attorney-client privilege with you?"

He made a funny face. "Yes, but why are you asking?"

"I'm thinking about telling you something, but it's the kind of secret that vitally needs to remain that way." They were nearly back to her house. "It could be a life-or-death thing for me."

"Belladonna. I am willing to protect you with my life. You are my queen. I would never reveal to anyone something you told me in confidence, but a secret of such magnitude? I'll take it to my grave."

"You swear?"

"On my life." He turned onto her long, winding driveway and headed for the house.

"Okay. So here's the thing—" She leaned forward. "Hang on. There's a strange car parked on the curve in front of the house."

He slowed. "Any idea who it might be? Rico?"

"No, he would have told me he was coming by. And that Chevy Tahoe?" She shook her head. "That's a lunk car. Could be the Russians again. Or worse." It was difficult to see through the vehicle's heavily tinted windows. Even vampire eyes had limitations.

The Tahoe's brake lights came on, then it peeled away in the opposite direction down the other side of Donna's horseshoe drive.

The driver was wearing a hat and sunglasses and had his hand on the side of his face. Donna whipped around in her seat to follow the vehicle with her eyes as it sped off. The light above the license plate was out, making the numbers impossible to read. Probably on purpose.

"Anyone you know?" Pierce asked.

"No. But definitely a man. And he clearly didn't want to be recognized. Kind of firms up my decision to move into the governor's crib."

Pierce pulled into the driveway. "Who do you think it was?"

"My best guess is another Russian. They have to be curious since the lunk they sent never came back. And I'm sure Boris wants his money."

"Boris is the equivalent to Big Tony, right?"

"He is. Boris Reznikov. And he and Tony aren't what you'd call best friends, which makes the fact that Joe was dealing with the Russians so odd. The idea that Joe, and possibly his sister Lucinda, would work a deal with the Russians behind Big Tony's back is crazy. Although that's the first word that comes to mind when I think about Lucinda." Donna sighed. "I really don't want anything to do with all that."

Pierce turned the car off and looked at her. "So why don't you just return the money? With your new salary, you can afford to."

She thought about that for a moment. "True. It would take a little time. I don't have it all anymore. I donated a significant amount of it, so I'd have to come up with a million to replace that." There was enough cash on hand to cover the shopping spree she'd been on, but it would leave her with very little. Except she now had the governor's credit card.

"Maybe you could broker a deal. Not that I want you dealing with the Russian Mafia, but you're a lot less vulnerable as a vampire than you were as a human. If you could get them to agree to, say, half the money in exchange for leaving you alone…" He shrugged. "That would be worth it."

"It would be. Except I'd still like to know why they gave my husband the money in the first place. And what my ex-sister-in-law, Lucinda, had to do with the deal. Whatever it was."

"I bet if you offered them the money, they'd pony up some information."

"I don't know. If they still think they can work something out with Lucinda, they aren't going to tell me what was going on." She sighed. "I never thought I'd say this, but I guess I need to meet with the Russians."

"I could probably take care of setting up the meeting. But you need to bring backup with you. At least me and Temo. Because you know Boris isn't going to come alone."

"You're right about that." She pondered the idea and who else she might bring. "Backup is a necessity."

"Are you thinking about Charlie or the First Fangs Club women?"

"Neither, but that's not a bad idea about reaching out to the girls. A little more vampire backup couldn't hurt. Although of that crew, I think Neo would be the best choice. I can't see rolling into a meeting with Francine and Bunni." Although her new friends from the therapy group would probably love to meet the Russian Mafia. They were crazy like that.

"If not them, then who are you considering?"

"Rico."

Rico Medina was the FBI agent she'd been working with to bring down the Villachi family. He'd been a pretty important part of her plan to safely escape the mob life. That plan had changed a bit after Joe was killed in a car accident, but the end goal of taking the Villachis down remained the same. And Rico was the key to that.

Pierce shook his head. "As your attorney, I'd advise against involving him. The less he knows about your contact with the Russians, the better. I realize he's a werewolf, so you think of him as a supernatural ally, but his position as an FBI agent means he's going to abide by human laws first."

"You realize he's the one who helped me out when I accidentally killed Yuri." Yuri was the Russian lunk who'd been sent to collect the outstanding five mil she'd found. The same Russian lunk she'd inadvertently drained to death when the hunger of being a newly turned vampire had gotten the best of her and driven her to the point of no control.

36

Yuri was the pivot point upon which all her vampire troubles had turned, too, because killing the first human she'd ever drunk from had severed the psychic tie between her and Claudette and given Donna the ability to see the memories of those she drank from. All of which the Immortus Concilio, the vampire ruling council, considered against the rules. Like, big-time.

Hence the trial.

"I do," Pierce said. "I also realize that if we don't go inside soon, the sun's going to come up. And you might attract the fae."

She grimaced. "Good point. Let's get inside. I could use a glass of wine." She'd seen one fae so far in her short vampire life. Based on that experience, she'd be fine never seeing another one again.

# CHAPTER 4

Pierce fed Lucky, then got the fireplace going while she opened a bottle of red and poured two glasses. They settled in front of the gently crackling fire and stared into the flames, both quiet and seemingly content just to be.

Donna certainly had a lot to think about. Despite the incredible upheaval of the last couple of weeks, things were somehow looking up. She'd wanted her life back for so long, and she'd started to think the freedom she'd gained because of Joe's death was slipping away again due to becoming a vampire, but now…now she saw a bright, shining light at the end of this new and interesting tunnel.

Being governor was like a fresh start. Sure, it was a whole new set of responsibilities, but only the responsibilities were new, not the weight of carrying them. That part was nothing new. She'd raised children, essentially by herself. She knew how to balance work and family duties with social obligations.

What came with the job of governor—the salary, the staff, and the penthouse—was life-changing.

Those things would allow her to truly shed her connections to the Villachis. It would take some doing, but she wasn't in it alone.

She smiled at Pierce. He was quite the find. She owed Neo, one of her new friends in the First Fangs Club, for that meeting.

He caught her looking at him. "What?"

She shook her head. "Just thinking how amazing it is the way things work out. You, especially."

He laughed and smiled. "I'm glad you think of me that way."

"I do." She sipped her wine as she pulled her feet up underneath her. "When I was first turned, I thought it was the worst thing in the world. Now, I'm starting to see it as a gift. Not the whole vampire bit so much as the life that comes with it. Being governor, in particular."

He nodded. "I can certainly understand that." His brows bent. "Say, what were you about to tell me before you saw the strange car?"

"Oh right. That." She stared into her wine. Should she tell him? She felt like she had to before he found out accidentally. She also didn't want there to be secrets between them. "You confirmed that whole confidentiality thing, so here goes."

He waited with obvious interest.

She took a breath. "Sunlight doesn't affect me."

His eyes narrowed, and he stayed silent for a moment. At last, he spoke. "What happened that makes you think that?"

"I had to run out to my car to get something one

morning, and I hadn't parked in the garage. It was just a quick dash. I figured if I suddenly burst into flames, I'd duck back into the garage and put myself out. But nothing happened."

Lucky walked in and jumped up onto the hearth to clean himself in front of the fire.

She shrugged. "Then I tested it out for real on a bright sunny day. And I was fine." She was keeping the part about the crucifix being the source of that protection to herself for now. That was the most important part of the whole thing and the one secret she wasn't ready to divulge.

"That's amazing." He scooted forward on his chair. "But you're right to keep it a secret. I don't think you should tell another living soul. Or nonliving. This gives you a serious advantage over other vampires. It could make you a target."

She nodded. "I know. And I don't plan to. But I figured you'd find out sooner or later once we're living under the same roof."

He nodded. "That would be a hard thing for you to hide. Especially when that penthouse has rooftop access." He laughed. "A vampire who's impervious to the sun. I'm sure it's happened before, but wow, that kind of makes you a superhero."

"I don't know if I'd go that far."

His grin remained. "Any idea why?"

She knew exactly why, but she shook her head all the same. "The planets were all aligned in the right way at the right time? Who knows?" She shifted a little, tucking her legs under her even more. "No one knows. Not even my sister the nun, who knew about vampires before I did, by the way."

"Your imperviousness to the sun has to be a difficult thing to keep from her, but considering the Church produces more vampire hunters than any other organization, it's probably also wise. Not that Cammie would turn you in. It's just probably better she doesn't have to keep that secret for you."

"I agree." Donna watched the flames flicker over the ceramic logs. "That reminds me. I still haven't told my kids what's happened. About me becoming a vampire."

He nodded slowly. "Are you going to do that in person?"

"I'd like to. But traveling isn't easy. Not when I'm supposed to only move at night."

"So bring them here. After you get moved into the penthouse. Bring them for a weekend."

"That's a good idea." It really was, even if her response didn't convey much enthusiasm.

He swirled the wine that remained in his glass. "But you're still worried about what they're going to think."

"I am. Can you blame me?"

"Not in the slightest."

She leaned back. "Their mother is a vampire. How do you begin to process that? And right after their father died. It's a lot."

"It is. But they're adults. And even though I don't know them, you've told me a lot about them, and they sound like very well-adjusted kids."

41

"They are."

"I bet they'll take it better than you think."

She sighed. "I hope you're right. But I have to tell them. Putting it off doesn't help anything. Maybe I should just call them."

"I support whatever decision you make." His gaze shifted to a point behind her. "Sun's coming up."

"I can feel it. Hard to explain. It's kind of like when you're being watched." She drained the last sip from her glass. "I'm going to bed."

"I'm turning in too. Lots to do when we get up."

"That's for sure." She looked at the cat. "Lucky boy, time for bed." He didn't budge. He had one leg over his face, something she referred to as the paw of invisibility.

Pierce laughed. "I don't think that cat's going anywhere."

"Not while that fire's on."

"You want me to turn it off?"

"Nah. Let it be. It won't hurt anything. It's behind glass, and it's making Lucky happy. You could probably turn it down, though."

"No problem." He used the fireplace remote to lower the flames, then got to his feet and drank what was left of his wine.

She got up and took his glass, kissed him on the cheek, and headed for the kitchen. "Night."

"Night."

She put the glasses in the sink and padded up to bed. She wasn't super tired, but she had the feeling she'd be out as soon as her head hit the pillow.

She was. But a man's voice urgently speaking her name woke her up. She blinked and found Pierce at her bedside.

He frowned. "Sorry to wake you, but you have a visitor."

"Cammie again?" She looked at her phone. Almost nine.

"No. A woman I've never met. And she won't tell me her name."

She sat up. "Russian?"

"Not by the accent. She seems more like one of the Villachis' associates."

"Great. One more reason to move. Did you let her in?"

"Yes, but just into the foyer. Do you want me to throw her out? Call the police?"

"No, no. I'll be right down." She was probably one of the wives, just coming by to see how she was doing. Big Tony's way of checking up on her without doing the deed himself.

Pierce left, and she pulled herself together. One of the best things about being a vampire was always looking pretty good. So long as she kept herself fed, there were no bags under her eyes, no deep lines, no bleary first-thing-in-the-morning look. All she really had to do was run a brush through her hair and throw on clothes. She went with jeans, a sweater, and Gucci loafers. She added some jewelry, then, as an afterthought, a swipe of mascara and a nude lip gloss.

Wouldn't do to have one of the wives think she wasn't looking her best. Old habits died hard.

She went down the back steps that went into the kitchen, then went through the kitchen and out into the living room, where Pierce was at the ready. She stopped cold at the sight of the woman standing in her foyer. Donna was really glad she'd taken the time to fix herself up a little. "Why on earth are you here?"

Lucinda Villachi had a loaf pan in her hands. And she was smiling. That alone was enough to make Donna cringe. "Hello, Donna. You look well."

That didn't answer the question. And it wasn't a compliment Donna could truthfully return. At best, Lucinda looked a little ragged around the edges. Stressed, even. "Thank you. Really, though, why are you here? I know you don't like me, and after our little visit the other night—"

"About that." Lucinda shifted uncomfortably. "I'm sorry. I want to make amends." She held out the loaf pan. "I made you another banana bread."

Pierce held his hands out. "How kind. I can take that."

Once again, Donna was infinitely grateful he was there. He'd answered so she didn't have to. "Thanks, Pierce."

He took the bread. "I'll put this in the kitchen." He left, giving Donna a distinctly sympathetic look as he walked past her. "Call me if you need me," he whispered.

"Thanks." She took a few steps toward Lucinda. "It surprises me that you want to make amends. That you even care after all these years. Especially with your brother deceased. You realize we don't need to be friends. We don't need to be anything. We're not really family anymore."

Lucinda put a hand to her heart. "Donna, you will always be family to me. You're the godmother to my children."

"Who are grown and couldn't care less." Not to mention, Alberto was in jail for running a chop shop, and Sofia had married and moved to California.

Lucinda persisted. "You're my sister-in-law, even if Joe is gone." She crossed herself. "May he rest in peace." Then she sighed. "I haven't been the best sister-in-law to you. I know that."

Big Tony had either set Lucinda up to do this, or she was working her own angle. Donna didn't know which it was, but something was up. "No, you haven't been. What is it you really want?"

"For us to be friends. Or at least civil."

Sure. That would happen. Donna crossed her arms. "What else? Because I know that's not really what you came here for."

Lucinda frowned. Then she sniffed like she was still deeply grieving. Which maybe she was. But the woman was normally as phony as a three-dollar bill, so it could all be an act too. "I was hoping for something of Joe's. A keepsake. Would you let me look in his office for something of his that I might have? There was a picture of us as kids that he used to keep in there. I was hoping I might have that."

There were some family pictures on one of the shelves in Joe's office, but Donna hadn't spent much time in there and couldn't really recall the one she described. Although lately, she'd been in there more than she had been in years, mostly due to discovering the secret room behind one of the bookcases. The stash room. Where all the Russian money had been stored. Along with a hoard of guns, boxes of drugs, and a bunch of other paraphernalia. Most important, after the money, were ledgers detailing Joe's years of working for the Villachi family.

And now Lucinda wanted to get into his office.

Right. That seemed logical.

Donna shook her head. "I'll look for it. If I find it, I'll drop it off at your house."

A little spark of anger danced in Lucinda's gaze, then she smiled. "That's kind of you. But if I could just grab it now, then you wouldn't even have to think about it."

On a whim, Donna decided to indulge her. "Fine. Let's go get it."

Lucinda's smile suddenly became real. "Great. I'll just be a second."

"No worries." Donna let her mouth curve upward ever so slightly. "I'm going with you."

Lucinda laughed. "What's the matter? Don't you trust me?"

Donna kept her smile in place and spoke as sweetly as she could. "No, I don't."

Then she turned on her heel and marched off to Joe's office. She prayed that she'd remembered to close up the stash room the last time she'd had it open.

She flipped the light on and exhaled in relief when she saw that everything was in place.

Lucinda pushed past her to stand in front of Joe's office. She shook her head. "I don't see the picture." She looked at Donna. "Did you move any of his things?"

"Nothing on these shelves. Although I really do need to clear this room out."

Lucinda paused, then it was almost as if a light bulb went off inside her fetid little mind. "You know, I'd be happy to help you with that. I'm sure Tony would love a memento of Joe's too."

The need for sleep tugged at Donna. She hadn't had nearly enough. "I'll let you know. I guess the picture isn't here, but we looked, right?"

Lucinda turned back toward the bookcases behind Joe's desk. "It's so nice to be in this space. I miss my brother so much."

"I'm sure you do."

She coughed suddenly. Donna wasn't sure if the woman was supposed to be choked up with emotion or coming down with the croup. Lucinda cleared her throat. "Could I get a glass of water?"

"Sure. Come into the kitchen." Donna started to move toward the hall.

Lucinda stayed put. "Do you mind if I just spend another moment in here? I feel like Joe's spirit is still here. Like I'm close to him in this room."

It was an office, not a chapel. And Donna wasn't Lucinda's to push around anymore. With a frustrated sigh, she decided to cut through the crap.

Whatever the consequences. "Enough with the games. Why do you want so bad to be alone in this room? What are you after in here?"

# CHAPTER 5

Lucinda's mouth fell open in shock. "What are you accusing me of? I just want something of my brother's to remember him by. I'm trying to extend an olive branch here, Donna, and you ain't being very nice about it."

"Right. An olive branch. That must be why I feel like I'm being poked with a stick." Donna stepped into the hall. She had an idea of what Lucinda was after, and it wasn't a photo. "It's time to go."

In a huff, Lucinda stormed out. "I told my brother not to marry you. That you were trouble. That a woman like you would only bring him—"

"Stuff it, Lucy. He's dead, and I don't have to take your crap anymore. Not under my roof."

Lucinda choked on her words but quickly found new ones. "The roof my brother paid for? The roof you're shacking up with some guy under? My brother's not even cold in the ground, and you've already got someone new in your bed."

Donna's palm itched to make contact with Lucinda's face. But that was only going to stir a pot she had no desire to eat from. "That *guy* is my attorney. He's helping me take care of the estate. But always good to know where your sick little mind goes first." She pointed toward the door. "Get out of my house and don't come back. Whatever you came here for, you're not going to get it. Ever. Capisce?"

Lucinda's eyes narrowed, and Donna imagined she could see smoke rising off the woman. "You will regret this."

"More than I already regret marrying into this family? I doubt it. Now start walking, or I'll remove you myself."

Lucinda snorted. "As if you could—"

Donna grabbed the woman's arm and started pulling her down the hall. She did her best to keep her emotions under control so that her eyes wouldn't glow. "When I say something, Lucy, I mean it. Best you understand that."

Lucinda yelped but had no immediate option except to move. She tried to pull away, but Donna's strength was far superior.

So Lucinda started swinging with her free arm. She connected a right hook with Donna's rib cage. Lucinda's fist bounced off like she'd hit rubber. "What the—"

"I work out," Donna quipped as she dragged Lucinda into the living room and toward the foyer. She released Lucinda, shoving her at the door. "Let's go over this now. Do you understand that when I say don't come back, I mean don't come back?"

Lucinda was fuming. Her chest heaved with the

exertion of her impending meltdown. "You have no right to do this. Joe is my brother. I should be allowed something of his."

Donna put her hands on her hips. "How about this? You tell me what you really came here for, and maybe I'll reconsider. But it has to be the truth, and you only get one shot. I have way too much to do to fool around with your sorry self all morning."

Lucinda didn't look convinced. At least not enough to speak up.

Donna shrugged. "Okay, get out."

"No, wait." Lucinda took a deep breath, and the heaving subsided a little. "The truth?"

The muscles in Donna's jaw tensed in frustration. "Yes, obviously. The truth."

"I want that picture. I know it was in his office. I'm sure it's still in there. Just be a decent person and let me look for it."

Donna stabbed her finger into Lucinda's airspace. "Don't tell me to be decent. That passive-aggressive crap is not going to fly."

Lucinda held her hands up in implied surrender. "Fine. Sorry. Just let me find the photo. I can't imagine what you'd want with a picture of me and Joe as kids at the state fair."

Donna still mostly believed that Lucinda was full of crap. Past history supported the validity of that belief. But Lucinda's answer actually had the ring of sincerity to it. Not a big, clanging ring. More like the little ding your phone makes when a nonessential text message comes in. But still. Maybe she really did just want something of Joe's. And the only value a picture like that could have was sentimental.

Donna sighed. "Listen. I get it. But the best I can do right now is think it over. I had a long, eventful night, and I need a few more hours of sleep before I can decide this. I'll call you." That was a lie. Donna had no intentions of talking to Lucinda ever again, if she could help it.

"Hmph."

"Don't push me."

Lucinda rolled her eyes but headed for the door. She left without another word.

"Thanks would have been nice," Donna muttered.

Pierce emerged from the other side of the house, where his guest room was. "Everything cool?"

"Yes. But she's up to something. I just don't know what." She glanced back toward the kitchen. "What did you do with that banana bread?"

"It's on the counter. I was going to throw it away, but I figured I'd let you decide."

"Nope, you were right. Pitch it. No way I'm eating anything that woman made."

He nodded, chuckling. "Will do. Are you going back to sleep?"

Donna yawned without meaning to. "And there's your answer. Yes. I need a few more hours. You need anything before I go?"

"No." One side of his mouth quirked up. "But I should tell you, you have a date tonight with Boris Reznikov."

She stared at him. "I do? When?"

"Midnight at the Russians' club, Pravda, downtown."

"Meeting on their turf, huh?"

"I know that's not a good idea, but it's all I could get them to agree to. Do you want me to cancel?"

"No. I want this over with."

"Is that enough time for you to meet with Governor Fitzhugh at ten? I figured if you were going to be dressed to impress him, might as well knock out Boris too."

"It should be plenty of time. Good thinking." She put her hand to her stomach as nerves started to tangle it in knots. "Tonight, huh?"

"Too soon?"

"No, it's fine. I wasn't expecting it to happen so quickly." When Pierce said he was going to do something, he did it. Night and day from Joe, who'd only jumped when Villachi business was involved. "I'll be done with Fitzhugh in plenty of time. I don't plan on entertaining him long, not if everything Charlie said about him is true. Which I'm sure it is. That's great. I really appreciate it."

"That's what I'm here for. At least until Charlie takes over." He laughed. "Rest well. I'll see you in a bit."

"Thanks. I'll call Neo and see if she wants to go along." She started for the stairs, then stopped. "Hey, is Boris going to expect me to have the money tonight?"

Pierce shook his head. "He shouldn't. We're only going to negotiate."

"Listen, about that. If he wants the whole lot back and won't budge from that, then I'm ready to give it to him. I just want to be done with this whole thing."

Pierce nodded. "I completely understand."

"Good. Thanks." She gave him a little wave, then jogged up the steps. She stripped off her clothes, shoes, and jewelry, fell onto her bed, and was about to go back to sleep when a different urge struck her.

She picked up her phone and dialed.

Cammie answered on the second ring. "Hey, sis. How are you?"

"Better. Just wanted to see how you're doing."

"I'm having a blessed day. How are *you* doing?"

"Well, Lucinda was just here."

"Ew. And I mean that in the holiest way possible. Is that why you're not asleep? Because you should be at this hour."

"Yep." Donna rolled over onto her back. "I'll go back to sleep in a bit. I just wanted to talk to you first."

"You sound like you're pondering something."

"I'm always pondering something these days."

"Anything specific?"

Since she had Cammie's attention, Donna figured, why not ask one of the questions that had been rattling around in her head? "Have you ever heard of a crucifix giving someone special protections?"

"It wouldn't be outside the realm of possibility. Does that answer your question?"

"Enough, thanks." Donna's free hand went to the crucifix, the metal warm and comforting. "Hey, I need to tell you. I'm moving out of the house and into the governor's penthouse in the Wellman Towers."

"Wow, that is quite the step up. Sadly, it'll be a bit before I can visit. A few of us are leaving tomorrow for a trip to the orphanage that we support in Nicaragua. I was going to call you tonight to let you know."

Cammie was so good. "Well, good timing on my part then. I hope you have a safe trip. Call me when you're back, okay?"

"I will. Be good while I'm gone."

"I'll try."

"That's all I ask. Love you."

"Love you too." Donna hung up, closed her eyes and went back to sleep almost immediately.

Four hours and some minutes later, she woke up feeling infinitely better but very hungry. Even so, she lay on the bed for a few moments, staring up at the ceiling. Then she glanced around the bed. Lucky had left. Probably hanging out with Pierce.

She had too much to do to lie here any longer. Plus, there were several hours of sun left in the day, which energized her to get things done. She scrubbed a hand over her face and got up. She was still in her underwear from stripping down earlier, so she pulled on some jogging pants and a T-shirt, then sat back on the bed to call Neo.

She answered immediately. "Hey, Mama. Good timing. I just woke up. What's happening?"

"All kinds of stuff. How are you?"

"I'm good. How's life as the governor?"

"It hasn't really started yet. I have a meeting with the governor of New York this evening, though. I also have something else going on, which is why I'm calling. I need some help."

"Hit me. I'm listening."

"You want to tag along with me and play gangster? The short of it is, I need to meet with some heavy hitters, and while I have two people going with me already—"

"You want some vampire backup."

"It's like you're reading my mind." Donna chewed on her bottom lip. This felt like a big ask. "You in?"

"That depends. Who are these heavy hitters?"

Donna hesitated. "Russian Mafia."

Neo laughed as she let out a curse. "Straight up?"

"Yep."

"Oh, I'm in. I'm so in I'm already there. What do you wear to a meeting with the Russian mob?"

"I'd say dress tough but sharp. If that makes sense."

"Sure thing. Like I'm part of your personal security detail, right?"

"Exactly."

"Hey. Are you inviting Bunni and Francine to this too?"

"No, just you. Why? Do you think I should?"

"Bunni will be bent out of shape if you don't. Francine won't care, but she'd get a kick out of it. But Bunni could be a liability, so…your call."

"Hmm. I guess I could reach out to them."

Frankly, Donna was surprised Neo had brought Bunni up. Neither woman liked the other much.

"Well, like I said, your call. It's your meeting. What time do you need me?"

"We'll pick you up at eleven thirty. Meeting is at Pravda. You know it?"

"Yeah. That's not my scene, too human-y, but I'm aware of it. I'll see you then."

"Call if anything comes up."

"Like I'd miss this. Later."

Donna hung up, then dialed Bunni.

The young woman answered right away. "Hiya, Donna. How are you?"

"I'm good. How are you?"

"I am fantastic. I'm packing for a quick trip."

"Oh? Where are you going?"

"Home to Puerto Rico for two days. Just to see my abuela to surprise her for her birthday, then I'll be home in time for Francine's party."

Donna had completely forgotten about Francine throwing a party in her honor. But Bunni's trip made everything else easier. "That sounds so nice. I hope you have a safe trip and a great time. I'll see you at the party, then."

"For sure. Is that what you called about?"

"I was going to ask if you wanted to do something with Neo and me tonight, but you're obviously busy. Another time."

"Neo? You know I don't like her."

"Well, it was her idea I call you, so maybe you should rethink that."

"It was? Huh. Maybe next time, okay?"

"You got it."

They hung up, and Donna dialed Francine next. Her voicemail picked up, so Donna left a quick, vague message and hung up. If Francine was planning a party, she probably didn't have the time—or the desire—to go out tonight. Besides, she might be a vampire, but she still looked like a senior citizen.

Not really the standard Pravda patron.

With the calls made, Donna stuck the phone in her waistband, then went down to start her day for the second time.

Her hunger pushed her toward the kitchen and the supply of blood in her refrigerator. She'd have to cancel the regular shipment she'd set up. Or have it sent to the penthouse. Although she supposed the penthouse had its own supply, but then, how much was she going to need? She had Pierce now. She just wasn't sure how often she could feed from him without doing him harm. But then, as long as she was feeding him in return, didn't that balance things out?

She didn't know. "Pierce?"

"Yes?" He answered from another part of the house.

"Where are you?"

"Gym," he called out.

"Okay." She stuck the bag of blood in a bowl of hot water from the Instahot to warm, then went to the exercise room at the back of the house.

He was using the lat pulldown machine, his

sweaty T-shirt stuck to his broad back. She leaned against the door, admiring the view. He took very good care of himself.

He caught her watching in the mirrors and smiled, then finished his set and got up. "Feel better with some more sleep in your system?"

"I do. I have a question."

He toweled off his face. "Shoot."

"How often can I feed from you if I'm feeding you in return?"

He shrugged. "Daily, pretty much."

"Really? That seems like a lot."

"It's a symbiotic relationship." He scrubbed at his hair next. "Are you hungry? I can take a quick shower."

"I am, but it's all right. I already have a bag warming in the kitchen."

He shook his head. "You have two very important meetings this evening. You need to be as sharp as possible."

She loved how he looked after her. How he always thought about what was best for her. It was so drastically different from her life with Joe, but then their relationship had certainly been unbalanced. She smiled. "Then I'll feed again."

He smiled back. "Deal."

"I'll let you get back to it."

"I'm mostly done. I need to get back to actual work anyway. Speaking of, do you have the titles for the cars? I've been researching what they're worth and sending out a few teasers to some car auctions I know. I think you're going to be surprised at how much they bring with Joe's name attached."

That reminded her of the picture Lucinda had been going on about. "I have the titles in the safe. As far as getting back to work, I'd say you've been busy already."

"That's what I'm here for." But he looked pleased. "Speaking of, I already pulled the cars out of the garage and took pictures of them in the sun and sent those along too. Do you need me to do anything for you right now?"

"No. I have to figure out what I'm wearing tonight, and I have to look for something in Joe's office, but then I'm going to work on packing some items for the penthouse, since I guess tonight is our first night officially in residence there." She put her hand to her face. "That's actually a lot to do. I guess I could use some help with the packing later. But only when your stuff is done."

"Just tell me when you need me, and I'm there."

"Okay." She grimaced. "Actually, I can't pack without boxes."

"Already handled. I went out and got some this morning when you were sleeping. Four wardrobe boxes and a slew of smaller ones. Probably not enough, but it's a start. They're out in the garage. What do you want me to pack first?"

"Awesome! You really do think of everything. As far as packing, maybe you could start with the family photos on the piano? Those with Joe in them can be left behind."

"Sounds good. I was thinking we should use Joe's Escalade. At least for the first load. It has more room than your sedan. Temo offered to come over and get some things too. Or I can run a load over before the sun goes down. That will mean less work for your trip over."

"Having Temo come over is probably not a bad idea. I think I could fill the Escalade with clothes alone. Well, maybe not. I don't have nearly as many clothes since becoming a vampire required me to get a new wardrobe."

"You should probably do some shopping, too, then."

She grinned. "I'm never opposed to that. Especially if the governor's credit card is paying for it. Have Temo come over. The more we can get out of the way, the better. That will make the last trip over easier since I'll already have my hands full with Lucky and all his stuff."

Pierce smiled. "I called Charlie and gave her a list of everything Lucky needs. His favorite foods, his brand of litter, all of that. All you'll have to do is put him in his carrier and bring him and his toys."

Her brows lifted. "Wow, you are definitely earning your salary. Thank you."

He gave her a little bow. "I also gave her a list of some of the other things I know you like. The kind of coffee you drink, the creamer you use, your favorite wines, those sorts of things. Pretty much you just need whatever clothes, toiletries, and personal items you want."

She shook her head. "I could kiss you on the mouth."

His eyes darkened with obvious desire. "I'd let you. But I really do need to shower."

She blushed as she realized that he'd let her off the hook graciously when her words had come out before she'd thought them over. "Thanks. I should get to work."

"See you in a bit, then."

She went back toward Joe's office. Her attraction to Pierce was there, for sure, but she just wasn't ready to pair up again. Even if Pierce was basically perfect.

And she knew Rico was never going to happen. She'd resigned herself to that reality. A relationship with him would be too complicated, and even if those complications went away, she'd learned enough to know that all he could ever be was a fling. Werewolves and vampires didn't end up together, because werewolves mated for life with their own kind.

Not that a fling would be so bad. But then again, she could feel herself changing, wanting different things, and something about becoming governor made her think that one-night stands weren't the way forward.

She wasn't looking for a new husband either, though. Her job was the only thing she planned to be married to for a long time.

There was a lot of responsibility in a job like that. Maybe second only to her job as a mom. She was determined to do her absolute best.

She slipped into Joe's office. The lights were still on from Lucinda's visit. That woman was one crazy piece of work. Could there really be a picture? And if there was, was it just a picture? Or was there something else to it?

Donna would have to answer the first question before she could answer the second. But after a good half an hour of digging through Joe's desk and riffling through the cabinets that made up the bottom half of the bookcases, she'd found nothing. If there was a picture, it wasn't in this room.

Just for good measure, she pulled out the copy of *The Godfather*, pressed the little button beside it, and opened the bookcase to double-check the stash room hidden behind it. Still empty.

Everything in here, except for the cash and a couple of small odds and ends, had gone to Rico and the FBI. The back wall had housed an arsenal of guns. Now it was bare, and only their outlines remained in the niches where they'd been stored.

She did a slow turn, checking every inch. There was no secret stash within the stash. So whatever Lucinda had wanted to find, it wasn't in here.

Could it have been in this room? Had Rico taken it without knowing? Even more interesting, had Lucinda known about this hiding spot? If so, how? Because Donna found it incredibly hard to believe that Joe would have told his sister about this secret room when he'd had ledgers in here detailing his years of criminal behavior on behalf of Lucinda's husband.

Or were those ledgers what she was after? Was she trying to protect Big Tony? That was plausible. Lucinda would kill to keep him in power and thereby secure her own position. But again, how would she know about those ledgers? Or this room?

Donna couldn't figure it out. And honestly, she no longer cared. She tipped her head back and pinched the bridge of her nose. Lucinda was such a giant pain in the—

There was an access panel in the ceiling.

# CHAPTER 6

No more than twelve by twelve, the small panel was painted the same white as the walls and ceiling. It was framed out with simple molding and looked like nothing interesting.

Except, in light of Lucinda's visit, even the uninteresting was worth investigating.

How had Donna not noticed it before? She probably had and just thought nothing of it. Had Rico seen it? Had he already opened it? If so, he hadn't said anything to her. And she hadn't noticed him doing it.

She ran to the kitchen for a step stool and a flashlight, then propped the stool under the panel and climbed up.

The first good push, and it gave way. She moved the panel to the side, then flicked on the flashlight and poked her head up to have a look around. What on earth could need this much hiding?

A few things, apparently.

The first was a bundle of cash. The same size as what had been stacked on the shelves in the stash room, so Donna knew it was fifty grand. Chump change compared with the five million she'd already found. She tossed the money down and went back in.

The second was something bundled in an old rag.

The moment she picked it up, she knew what it was. A gun. She lifted enough of the fabric to confirm she was right, careful not to touch it. There was only one reason a gun would be hidden like this. It had been used in a crime and could incriminate someone.

She climbed down from the step stool and put the gun on a shelf. That was definitely going to Rico.

Back up and she found the third thing. A small, yellowed photograph in a cheap little gilt frame. And it fit the description of the one Lucinda had been looking for. Why that would be up here, Donna hadn't a clue.

She took one last look to make sure she hadn't missed anything, then put the panel back in place. She'd left her phone upstairs, which was where she needed to go anyway. But as soon as she got up there, she'd send Rico a text.

She put the step stool and the flashlight away, came back for the cash and the photo, then went upstairs to focus on something much more enjoyable. The right outfit to show Governor Fitzhugh who was boss.

First, however, the cash and the photo went into the big safe in the walk-in closet. She wasn't sure what she was going to do with either, but this way she didn't have to worry about them.

Except, she was essentially moving out of this house tonight.

She stood there for a moment, just looking into the safe. Really, everything in there needed to be taken to the governor's penthouse. But was there a safe over there? There had to be, right?

She found her phone and sent Rico a text first. *Found a gun I want to turn over to you. Can you come by today?*

Next, she looked up Charlie's number and sent her a text. *Is there a safe at the penthouse?*

Charlie's response came back so fast, Donna figured the woman probably never walked away from her phone.

*Yes, there's a safe. Will this do?*

A pic followed. The safe was large and looked a lot more high-tech than what Donna had in her closet.

Donna responded, *Thank you! That's perfect.*

Now she just had to remind herself to clear this one out before she left for the penthouse. A single small box would do it.

But first, she had to deal with her closet. She started looking through the assortment of clothing she had that fit her new vampire frame. The turning had changed her in ways she'd never imagined possible. For one thing, it had given her an instant, full-body makeover.

Breasts lifted, waist trimmed, arms firmed, thighs toned. It had done what all her years of yoga and running and Pilates and spin class and barre class and every other freakin' class had failed to accomplish.

It was as if every carb she'd ever eaten had been forgiven overnight. And they continued to be forgiven, which was the real miracle.

Then there was her face. The fine lines had disappeared. Her eyes had brightened, as had her skin. Her pores were invisible. Her jowls, one of the worst things about aging, had returned to the same shape they'd been in during her thirties, meaning her jawline was just as firm as could be. The Botox and fillers she'd come to think of as a necessary evil were no longer on her beauty-regime menu.

Not much was, really. Sure, she still cleaned off her makeup before bed, but that was about it.

Best of all, however, was the internal change. She wasn't just stronger and faster. As best as she could tell, her hot flashes were gone. So were her night sweats. All the joyous changes that came with approaching the big Five-O had vanished.

That alone was enough to make her smile. And she did that a lot lately. Mostly thanks to Pierce. He'd saved her from death at the hands of the Immortus Concilio, and she owed him for that.

She hoped she could repay him properly one day.

He seemed happy in his new position as her assistant. Maybe even more so now that she was governor, but she didn't feel that prestige or place meant much to him. After all, he'd left his job as a highly paid Manhattan attorney to be at her side.

He genuinely seemed to be in it for her. That was a concept so foreign to Donna, she hadn't fully wrapped her head around it.

Life with Joe had been…well, all about Joe. And the family. Not *family*, as in her and the kids, but rather, the Villachis. The Mafia family she'd unwittingly married into.

But since Joe's death, she'd finally begun to pull away from that dark life. That's what she wanted. What she'd always wanted. Freedom.

It was the whole reason she'd been willing to turn state's evidence for Rico and go into WITSEC.

Freedom from the threat of everything bad the mob brought with it. Not just for herself, but for her two children. Christina and Joe Jr. understood how awful their father had been. They'd done everything they could to distance themselves from him.

Donna didn't blame them either.

She just hoped that they'd understand about her new situation. She hadn't chosen it, but with every passing day, she realized what a strange and unusual blessing this new life was.

Not for all the great physical reasons, but because she now had the power to defend herself. And some amazing new people had come into her life. And with her rise to governor, she was finally in a position, literally and financially, to do good things.

Things that would balance out some of the terrible things Joe and the Villachis had authored.

That alone was reason to get up and get moving.

With that buoyant thought, she dug into her reduced wardrobe to see how best she could present herself to the governor of New York. And then, the head of the Russian Mafia.

Several outfits later, she was standing in front of her mirror looking at yet another option when someone knocked on her bedroom door.

"Pierce?"

"Yep. Do you want any packing help up here?"

"I'm okay there, but I could use an opinion. Come on in."

He found her in the closet. "Wow."

"You think?" She did a quick turn.

He nodded. "Classic black suit is always a good choice. Especially when it's cut as well as that one is. Armani?"

"Alexander McQueen."

"Excellent choice. Strong shoulders."

She stepped aside so he could have a better view of her shoe wall. "What shoes?"

His brows lifted as he took in the selection. "Okay, Imelda. You are definitely going to need help packing all of those."

She laughed. "Hey, I like shoes. And good shoes are kind of a Mafia wife thing."

"I see." He approached the wall, hand on his chin, pondering. Then he reached out and snagged a pair. "Try these."

"Bold choice. I like it." She slipped on the wine-colored snakeskin Louboutins and presented herself to him for comment. The shoes had a spray of matching wine-colored crystals across the toes, giving them a little sparkle.

He gave her the once-over, then nodded. "Those are truly amazing. Sexy, powerful, a little bit of dark red, which is very vampirey, and they give you enough height to probably put you at eye level with Fitzhugh. Or maybe taller. I like them."

"I do too." She narrowed her eyes. "You're pretty good at this."

He laughed. "All I did was pick out a pair of shoes."

"But they were the right pair the first time."

He leaned against the center island that served as her dresser and a little display area. "I've studied appearances for a long time. When I get someone ready for court, I do more than prepare them with what to say. I prepare them with how to act and how to look. Clothes and grooming can make a dangerous person look meek, a weak person look strong, and a guilty person look innocent. And vice versa. Appearance is everything."

"You're right. Although I don't know if I ever gave it that much thought."

"Most people don't." He shrugged. "But I also like nice things. And it's not hard to see what looks good on a beautiful woman. Which, in your case, is just about everything."

His gaze was arrowed in on her so intently that she felt her cheeks heat. "Pierce, I—"

He held his hands up. "I know. We are not going there. Not soon, anyway. But I'm also not going to lie about my attraction to you or how you make me feel. You can rest assured, however, that I won't act on it until you give me a very clear signal that it is appropriate to do so."

She smiled. "Thank you."

"You're welcome. Now let's figure out what other accessories you need."

That ended up being a simple pair of diamond earrings and a wide diamond band. She spread her fingers so she could have a look at the ring on her hand. "I should probably get a manicure."

"I bet Charlie could arrange that. Want me to text her?"

"I can do it."

"I know you can, but it's not your job." He pulled out his phone. "I'm guessing whatever services you need can come to you. Hair, nails, massage, yoga instructor, probably anything. Why else do they have a salon in that penthouse?"

She tipped her head. "Good point. Go ahead and text her."

He finished the text and looked up. "Done."

"It will be nice to have all those services come to me. And it would certainly make keeping my little secret easier."

His phone chimed. He read the screen, then said, "She can arrange a manicure for eight p.m., if that works for you."

"It does. Great."

He started texting. "I'll let her know. I'm also having her get a hairstylist. I'm sure you can do your own hair very well, but a good blowout will be a confidence booster too."

"You're not wrong about that. How do you think I should wear my hair?"

Text completed, he tucked the phone into his

pocket. "Blown out straight and sleek. The end goal is to make you look like the baddest boss on the planet. I'd suggest adding sunglasses when we go to see Boris. They won't affect your vision as a vampire, but they will give you a mysterious air."

She laughed. "I think you're going to be my stylist from now on. I like the idea of being a boss. It's not a position I've ever really held."

"Well, you do now." He winked, then surveyed the closet again. "How much of this is going to the penthouse? Temo will be here in an hour. I figured that was enough time to get the first load sorted."

"It should be. I need to grab some boxes, though."

"I brought two wardrobe boxes up with me, but I'm guessing you're going to need all four. And several more for shoes. And purses."

She put her hands on her hips. "Not all of this has to go. My taste is changing. Some of this is way too Mafia wife for me to ever wear it again. And a lot of it doesn't fit. You can help me decide on some of it."

"Happy to. How about I go get some more boxes, and you start separating out what's going?"

"Deal. I'm going to change out of this suit first."

When he got back, they went to work. It was liberating to get rid of the clothes that had been part of her old life, and the sorting got easier with that thought in mind.

About an hour into the packing, the doorbell rang.

# CHAPTER 7

"It's probably Rico," Donna said as she hung a few more tops on the bar of the wardrobe box. "Or Temo."

"You want me to check?" Pierce asked.

"Maybe. Hang on." She pulled out her phone.

There was a text from Mr. FBI himself. *Here.*

She held up the phone. "It's Rico."

Pierce put the shoes he was holding into the box on the floor. "I'm coming with you anyway. Not saying I don't believe you, but better safe than sorry, right?"

"Right." She smiled but tried not to let him see. His concern was commendable, but if it wasn't Rico at the door, she wasn't sure what Pierce could do exactly. She had more strength and power as a vampire than he did as a human. Even one who had the benefits of her blood. She wasn't about to stop him from coming, though.

Together, they went downstairs and headed for the door. She let Pierce answer it.

Rico gave him a nod. "Hey."

"Hey," Pierce said back. Then he looked at Donna. "I'm going to put more boxes together in the garage. Yell if you need me."

"Will do."

He left as Rico entered. She closed the door, noting he'd arrived in a standard black SUV and not the usual undercover plumber's van.

He faced her. "So. You found a gun?"

"I did. And some cash." No point in mentioning the photo. Rico wasn't going to be interested in baby pictures. "The gun was wrapped in fabric and hidden away. I think it either has incriminating prints on it or can be connected to a crime by ballistics. Either way, I want you to take it. And I didn't touch it."

He grinned. "Look at you, deducing away like an agent."

She laughed. "Well, why else would it be hidden away?"

"Nope, I agree. There's something going on with it. What about the cash?"

"No idea, but if it's mob money, I don't want it. Can't you run the serial numbers or something?"

"We can. We can check the money for prints, too, but that will only tell us who touched it."

She shrugged. "I just thought I'd give it to you and see what you could do with it."

"Happy to take it." His smile widened. "Speaking of happy…"

"What?"

"We've pulled some pretty damning stuff from

those ledgers you turned over. Unfortunately, there are no names, so no one's really implicated. It's all times, places, amounts, what the job was, that kind of stuff. Hopefully, that will change once we finish working out the code Joe wrote them in."

She exhaled. "Nothing on Big Tony?"

"Not yet. But we did find something else of interest."

She leaned in, listening hard.

"Lucinda Villachi has an LLC that Big Tony has nothing to do with. We need to do more digging in that direction, but she's definitely up to something."

"She was here this morning."

"About what?"

Donna filled him in. "She was acting oddly nice, which was obviously hard for her because she isn't that good at it. She brought me banana bread. Can you imagine? Like I was going to eat that."

"She had to want something."

"She did. A memento of Joe's. She was all weepy and whiny about how she wanted something to remember her brother by. She kept talking about this picture of the two of them from when they were kids at the state fair. She said it was in his office and that she just wanted to run in there and get it."

"I'm guessing you didn't let her."

"No freakin' way. We went into the office together. She didn't find anything, and I didn't remember seeing a picture like that, but after she left, I went looking again. In the stash room. That's how I found the gun and the money. Oddly enough, the picture she described was with those two things."

He frowned. "You didn't mention that earlier."

She lifted one shoulder. "I didn't think you'd be interested in a family photo. It's old and yellowed and must have been important to Joe. Or he was hiding it from Lucinda for a reason I can't fathom. Anyway, all three things were together."

"Where in the stash room? We cleaned that out."

"There's an access panel in the ceiling. I popped it open, and there they were."

He sighed and shook his head. "I can't believe I missed that."

"I missed it too."

"Are you turning the picture over to the Bureau?"

She made a face at him. "No. Is there a reason I should?"

"Not that I can think of, but if Lucinda wants it—"

"If anything, the picture was a ruse to get into Joe's office. There had to be something else in there she was after."

Rico nodded slowly. "You think she knows about the stash room?"

Donna considered that. "She might. As brother and sister went, they were very close. I don't know that he confided things like that to her, but then again, there was a lot I didn't know about Joe."

"Like the Russians?"

"Exactly." But if her meeting went well tonight, they'd be out of the picture.

"Have you heard from them since the incident with Yuri?"

She shook her head. "No. Maybe the fact that they haven't seen him again was enough for them to leave it alone."

"When there's money and an inter-Mafia deal at play? I doubt that." He glanced back toward the driveway. "Maybe they're watching. Waiting for the right time. It has been a little busy around here lately."

She threw her hands into the air. "Oh, thanks. That's a happy thought." Then she thought for a moment. "You know, there was a strange car sitting outside the place when we got home last night. The plate light was out, and the windows were tinted, so I couldn't get any kind of info on the vehicle or the driver. Could have been Russians. Could have been anybody."

Rico's expression turned serious. "Might be time for us to start surveilling this place again."

"Have at it. I'm leaving. As of tonight, I'm moving to the governor's penthouse at the Wellman Towers."

Rico let out a long whistle. "I've heard about that place. Totally swanky."

"No one says swanky. But yes, it's very swanky." She smiled. "Come over anytime. I will gladly give you a tour."

He tucked his thumbs into the front pockets of his dark jeans. "I forgot for a second there that you're governor. Moving to the penthouse makes it sound like you're taking this pretty seriously."

"I am. And why not? It's a chance to get away

from this life and start my new one with a purpose."

"Becoming a vampire really suits you."

"Thanks. I think."

"It was a compliment."

"Well, I appreciate it. Let me go get that gun and the cash, and then you can be on your way. I have a lot of packing left to do."

"Sure thing. Would you bring the picture too? Just so I can have a look at it?"

"Yep." Letting him look at it wasn't going to hurt, but he was definitely not taking it. Not when it might be the leverage she needed over Lucinda.

"Great. While you get them, I'm going to grab some evidence bags."

"Okay. Back in a minute." She jogged upstairs, retrieved the items, and jogged back down as he was coming back in the front door.

She held out the items. "Here you go."

He opened the first evidence bag. "For the gun."

She placed it carefully inside, then held out the wrapped bundle of cash.

He opened the second evidence bag. "Thank you."

She dropped the money in, then showed him the small, framed photo. The picture was in color, but faded and yellowed by time. The frame was cheap gold metal, and the backing was brown felt that was molting away in spots. "It's nothing special."

He took it from her, turned it over once, then again. "No, it's not. Did you open up the frame?"

"No."

He handed it back to her. She slid away the two little metal tabs holding the frame's back in place. The felt was uncut on one side, acting as a hinge. She opened the frame carefully, thinking it might disintegrate in her hands.

Two little initials in wobbly script decorated the back of the photo. "L and J. Lucinda and Joe."

She showed it to Rico.

He seemed nonplussed. "Why was it hidden away, then?"

"Maybe he was secretly sentimental? Although that doesn't sound much like the Joe I knew." She shook her head as she closed the frame. "I have no idea. Maybe he knew Lucinda wanted it, and he was keeping it from her. For another reason I don't know."

"I suppose it's possible. People do weirder things for lesser reasons. Are you going to give her the picture?"

"I don't know." Donna looked at the faces of the children. So innocent. Hard to believe they would grow up to be two giant pains in her backside. "Lucinda hasn't ever really done anything for me to feel kindly toward her."

"Don't you feel bad that she lost her brother?"

Donna raised her gaze to him without moving her head so that she was looking at him through her eyelashes. She stared at Rico for a moment like that, calming herself down so that she wouldn't yell. "Don't you think a good sister would have told her brother to get out of the life of crime he was in?"

She finally raised her head to match her gaze. "The life that was destroying his family?"

Rico took a step back. "I can see by the glow in your eyes that I've struck a nerve. I know you don't like her. But you said yourself you're leaving this life behind. Why not give her that and get her off your back?"

"If I thought it was that simple, I'd do it. But I don't believe Lucinda will ever truly leave me alone. She blames me for a lot. And an old photograph isn't going to make that go away." She was miffed at him for not seeing her side of things more clearly. "I hope I hear some good news from you soon. The kind where people have been arrested."

"We're working on it. I promise."

"Great. Thanks for coming out. You know how to reach me if you need anything else."

He nodded, his hand on the doorknob. "I didn't mean to tick you off."

Her mouth twitched, almost achieving a smile. "It was bound to happen while talking about Joe and Lucinda." She took a breath to calm herself. "I really do appreciate you coming out on short notice. Now, if you'll excuse me, I have packing to do."

He opened the door. A black Land Rover was pulling into her driveway. The day was waning, giving the sky that hazy, just-before-sundown look and pushing the shadows out so they were long and thin and reaching.

He glanced at the car as Temo parked and got out. "You know that guy?"

"My new driver and head of security."

Rico's brows went up, but that was his only response. "Talk to you soon."

She nodded and waited at the door for Temo.

He greeted her with a big smile. He had an Amazon box with him. "Hi, boss."

"Hi, Temo. How was the drive?"

"Nice." He looked up. "Quite a house you got here."

"Don't be too impressed. It was bought with blood money."

He nodded. "Right. Mafia husband."

"Right. What's in the box?"

"Security cameras. Pierce thought it might be a good idea with you out of the house. They're pretty easy to set up. Once I have them done, I'll get the car loaded."

"Hey, that's awesome. Come on in."

He came in. "I don't want to interrupt. I'm sure you have plenty to keep you busy."

"Just packing, mostly. In fact, I should get more of that done so you can take those boxes back with you. I'll show you where the boxes are that are ready, then I'll let you get to work." Pierce had started a grouping in the living room, so she took him there first. "These can all go."

"I'll get to work."

She left him and went back upstairs, her mind turning to the two meetings that lay ahead of her. Governor Fitzhugh and Boris Reznikov.

Which man was going to give her more trouble? Which meeting was going to be more fruitful? She had no idea. But she knew one thing for sure.

Both meetings would test her in some way. She just prayed she would pass.

# CHAPTER 8

Donna changed into a robe before sitting down with the manicurist. Each nail was filed into a short, blunt-ended shape the woman told her was called coffin. Seemed fitting, all things considered. Then she painted them the same deep, rich wine as the stilettos Pierce had picked out.

In the kitchen, where he was getting ready to make steaks for dinner, Donna splayed her fingers, showing him her nails. The hairstylist had just arrived and was setting up in the salon room, which Donna had to admit was a very cool thing to have. She wondered if Claudette had put it in or if it had already been here.

Charlie and Temo were in the living room. After Temo had helped her set up the security camera app on her phone, she'd asked them both to stay. Even though she was in the midst of getting ready, she wanted them around. Not just for the company, but in the hopes of getting to know them better.

She'd also asked the manicurist to do Charlie's nails after she finished with Donna's. Charlie had made the visit possible, so it seemed like a kind thing to do.

Pierce glanced at her hands, then nodded. "They look great. I like that you took my suggestion and matched the shoes. The color reminds me of drying blood. It should be a good reminder for Boris as well. Do you have a lipstick that color?"

"Nice image. And yes, I do. You think I should wear it, obviously."

"If you're not opposed to it."

"I'm not. What do you think about a smoky eye? Or should I go simpler?" She hadn't had someone to talk to about clothes and makeup since Christina had gone off to college. Joe couldn't have cared less if he'd tried, so she'd never asked his opinion on what she was wearing.

If he'd hated something, he'd tell her. That was as much input as he'd given.

Pierce sprinkled sea salt over the steaks. "A smoky eye would be great." He traded the salt for the pepper. "You're going to turn heads like no one's business. I'm glad we're taking Temo with us to Pravda. I know you can handle yourself, but he'll be a good visual. And an even better deterrent for anyone thinking it's all right to approach you."

"Plus, we'll have Neo." She liked the idea of backup. If things went poorly with Boris, which she was praying they didn't, having extra help would be important. Especially because they were going to be on Boris's home turf. His club. His advantage.

Temo came in. "I heard my name."

She looked at him. "Just talking about going to Pravda tonight."

"Should be interesting." He grinned. "I've never seen Russian mobsters. That I know of."

Pierce adjusted the heat on the grill pan. "Donna is going to attract attention. I want to make sure none of that attention goes further than looking."

Temo nodded. "There's not a chance anyone will touch her." He narrowed his eyes, and his mouth firmed into a hard, tight line as he clasped his hands in front of him, widening his stance. The transformation almost caused her to step back. Instead, she pulled her robe a little tighter. Like a few yards of chenille were some kind of defense.

He tipped his head ever so slightly as he looked at Pierce, then Donna. A second later, he burst into a smile again. "What do you think? That's my big-trouble look. As in, make a move and you're in big trouble."

She laughed. "Well done. I hope you never look at me that way. You and my friend Neo are going to be all the muscle I need."

Pierce laid the steaks in the pan, filling the room with the sizzle. "Indeed. Very effective."

India, the young woman who'd come to do Donna's hair, stepped into the kitchen. "I'm ready for you now, ma'am."

"All right." She patted Temo on the arm. "Thanks for agreeing to go along this evening."

"Anything you want, boss."

With a smile, she followed India back to the salon and got settled in the chair.

India started to put a cape around her, but Donna held up a hand. "I don't think we need that. I don't want a cut. Unless you think I need a trim?"

India took a look, mostly at the ends. "No, it looks pretty good." She hung the cape back in its spot. "What would you like me to do?"

"Sleek, straight blowout. Very smooth and sophisticated."

"Same part you have now or in the middle?"

"Which do you think? I want to look as boss as possible."

"Middle," India said without hesitation.

"Okay, I trust your judgment." Donna closed her eyes and let the woman do her thing. Having someone work on her hair, in combination with the heat from the blow dryer, put her into a state of deep relaxation. For a fleeting moment, she wondered if that's what Pierce had intended.

Then she drifted off.

When Donna woke up, India was smoothing some kind of serum on the ends of her hair.

She looked in the mirror. "Oh. That's incredible. My hair has never looked so good. I didn't even know it could be that straight and sleek. I really like it parted in the middle too. It's different. Makes me look a little mean. In a good way." Laughing, she turned toward India. "You're like the hair whisperer."

"Thank you. That's kind of you. I am very happy to be of service."

Donna hopped out of the chair. "Let's go make sure Charlie has you on speed dial."

She went straight for the kitchen, but Pierce and Temo were in the living room, watching what looked like rugby on the TV. The steaks had apparently been devoured. Charlie was sitting with them, but she was typing away on a small laptop and giving the game no attention.

Donna put her hands on her hips. "What do you think?"

All three looked at her. Temo whistled. Charlie smiled.

Pierce nodded. "Gorgeous."

"I think so too. Charlie, add twenty percent to India's tip and make sure we have all her contact information." Donna stuck her hand out to India. "Thanks again. I need to go get dressed, but I know you'll be back."

India shook her hand, smiling broadly. "I'd like that."

Donna gave the group a little wave, then headed off to her bedroom, which was easily her favorite room in the penthouse. She hadn't bothered to look at it when she'd been here earlier because she'd figured Claudette's stuff was still in it, but when she'd finally seen it, she'd been as impressed with it as the rest of the place.

It still had all the same shades of gray with touches of white and crystal, but the bedroom was plush, instead of sleek, and decidedly more feminine. The wall behind the king-size bed was upholstered and tufted in a charcoal velvet that had a silver thread running through it. At certain angles, the fabric seemed to dance with light.

Thick, fluffy carpets, like the ones she'd admired in the staff apartment, lay on most of the polished concrete floor, overlapping in some spots so that the paths to the bathroom and closet were completely covered.

A sitting area just inside the door had an absolutely indulgent chaise done in the most breathtakingly bold fuchsia silk Donna had seen. The lounge chair was angled to take full advantage of the river view, and now that it was dark and the city lit up, she could see herself sitting there just taking in the beauty of that scape.

The closet wasn't as big as Donna's old one, but then, she'd shared that space with Joe. This one was all hers. And still large enough to have a center island like she was used to. It also had a lighted three-part full-length mirror and a pretty chandelier made from shards of crystal that looked like icicles.

The bathroom was all iridescent glass tile and white marble with the same polished-concrete flooring, but there were no rugs in here other than in front of the shower and tub. She figured out pretty quickly that the floor had radiant heat.

She liked the feel of the warm concrete underfoot. She also liked the spa-like feel of the bath. And the size of the shower. And that the space in the closet was all hers. She liked the whole place immensely.

She was getting used to the idea of being

governor. But the meetings she had to get through were giving her some nerves, that was for sure.

Time ticked ever closer to Fitzhugh's arrival. She expected him to be early, so she wasn't going to leave anything to the last minute. She planned to be completely ready by a quarter till.

Not that she was going to actually see him until ten. If he was early, that was on him. He could wait.

Or maybe she'd greet him a little early. Just to prove she was ready. She hadn't quite decided that yet.

She kept her robe on as she did her makeup, complete with the deep-red lip Pierce had suggested, then got dressed, slipped her shoes on, and added jewelry as well. Done, she took a long look at herself in the triple mirror.

This wasn't the Donna she'd known for the last twenty-some years. This woman was brand new in so many ways. Older, but infinitely wiser. Smarter. Stronger. Bolder.

And thanks to becoming a vampire, she looked better than she ever had. India's transformation of her hair had done something too. The middle part had somehow brought her features into sharper focus and given her an edge she'd never had before.

She liked it. She'd always thought about how she might reinvent herself when she got free of Joe. She'd never imagined it like this, though. This was *good*.

A knock at her door called her attention away from the mirror. "Yes?"

Pierce answered her from outside the open bedroom door. "Would you like a glass of wine? You have twenty minutes before Fitzhugh is set to arrive."

One glass wouldn't do much. Her vampire metabolism took a lot more to get buzzed. "No, I'm all right."

She stepped out of the closet and into his line of sight. "What do you think?"

He took a breath. "Total boss. You look stunning. I'm a little afraid of you right now."

She laughed softly. "I doubt that, but I'll take it."

The doorbell rang.

She and Pierce looked at each other, their eyes widening at the same time. He shook his head. "It can't be. Twenty minutes early?"

She frowned. "I am *not* going out there this early. I don't want him to think I'm at his beck and call."

"Agreed." Pierce held up a finger. "Let me go make sure that's actually him. Be right back."

"Okay." She stood there for a moment, then walked over to the windows to take in the view. As she looked out, she realized that was Fitzhugh's territory she was admiring. That made her grimace. She'd never been much for politics, and now she would be stuck in the middle of them.

The muted sounds of conversation drifted in from the other room, but with the television still on, the words weren't clear. They sounded oddly happy, though.

A few more seconds and Pierce returned. Before she turned toward him, she knew by the sudden wash of scent that he was holding flowers. And indeed he was. An extravagant bouquet of black roses, lavender roses, purple orchids, and bold greenery.

He peered around them. "It wasn't Fitzhugh."

"I see that. Who are those from?"

"We didn't open the card, but Charlie says they're from Fitzhugh. She said he did the same thing before meeting with Claudette, sent over a big flashy arrangement."

"Is that so?" She came over and plucked the card from the overwhelming spray in his hands, taking a moment to sink her face into the blooms and inhale. "The roses smell amazing. I have to give him this much, he does flowers well. Not sure these would have been my color choices, but they're very pretty."

"They're very vampirey."

"That they are." She opened the card and read the brief message out loud. "To our future endeavors and a wonderful new friendship. HF." She lifted her gaze to meet Pierce's. "He sure thinks a lot of himself, doesn't he?"

Pierce rolled his eyes. "He sure does. Where do you want me to put them?"

She tapped the card against her hand as she thought. "Powder room."

Pierce snorted. "Oh, that's good."

"When he leaves, we'll move them out to the dining room table, because they really are lovely. I just don't want to give him the slightest bit of upper hand here."

Pierce was still chuckling. "I really had no idea how mercenary you could be. If I wasn't already mad about you, I would be now."

She grinned. Pierce always had a way of making her feel like she ruled the world. "You know what? I think I will take that glass of wine after all."

"I'll bring it right back."

But by the time he'd put the bouquet in the half bath and returned with her wine, the doorbell had rung again.

"It's got to be him this time." Pierce handed her the wineglass. "Charlie's going to take him into the sitting room and offer him something to drink."

"Good. That's perfect. We don't want to be inhospitable. Even though I'm going to let him stew for five or six minutes before I go in."

"Do you want any of us in there with you?"

She thought a moment. "Go see if he brought anyone with him. I want an even playing field."

"On it." Pierce left.

She sipped her wine, careful of her lipstick.

He returned momentarily. "Other than his driver, who's still downstairs in the car, it seems he came alone."

"Then I'll meet him that way. Don't go far, though. I'm fine with you guys listening in."

Pierce rubbed his hands together. "I'll discreetly let Charlie know."

"Thanks." She glanced at the time, her nerves kicking in suddenly. That had to be her need to make a good impression. And not get swayed by

Fitzhugh's games. Or allow herself to be intimidated by him, although she was already a little intimidated. He had far more experience being governor than she did.

Impulsively, she downed the remainder of her wine in one big swallow.

It was symbolic at best because the alcohol wouldn't do anything. She knew that. But maybe it would have a little placebo effect. She blew out a long breath and shook herself, loosening up.

So what if the wine didn't work? She didn't need it. She'd spent the last twenty-seven years of her life living with the Mafia. She'd faced down Big Tony, one of the most notorious criminals on record since Al Capone. She'd handled Lucinda just fine this morning.

And she was a vampire. An actual killing machine. Not that she could ever see herself going on a rampage, but she was certainly capable of it.

Fitzhugh wasn't a man to be intimidated by. He was her peer. Nothing more. He simply had more experience, which didn't mean he was more capable.

She lifted her chin, stuck her chest out, and headed for the sitting room.

# CHAPTER 9

He stood in front of the windows, staring out, his broad back to her as he mimicked the pose she'd just held a few minutes ago. "The city is very beautiful at night, isn't it?"

"It is," she answered.

His dark pin-striped suit was impeccably cut, as was his hair, although it had been left just long enough to run your fingers through. His hands were clasped behind him, showing off an ornate silver ring set with a dark green gem polished into a cabochon.

He was taller than her, but shorter than Pierce. Built like Pierce, too, with the kind of lanky ease that came with natural athleticism.

In her heels, they'd be eye to eye.

Finally, as if he'd been allowing her time to take him in, he turned. "Very beautiful," he repeated.

Charlie hadn't lied about him being exceptionally good-looking. He was Hollywood handsome. Too pretty, maybe. Everything about him seemed deliberately meant to look unplanned. From his crisp white shirt left unbuttoned at the throat to his casually arranged pocket square. Even his stubble looked artfully cultivated.

His thick, dark brows twitched ever so slightly higher as he appraised her. "But perhaps not as beautiful as the new governor of New Jersey."

Flattery, she thought. Nothing more. She offered him the same smile she used to give her children when they'd failed at something despite their best attempts. "Good evening, Governor Fitzhugh."

He bowed slightly. "Governor Barrone."

"Please, call me Belladonna."

"And you may call me Hawke." He extended his hand, the one with the ring. "It's a pleasure to meet you. I understand your transition has been rather swift and unexpected. If there's anything I can do to help you settle in, please consider me at your service."

She shook his hand. So far, so good. "That's kind of you. My team is all the help I need at the moment, but it's always nice to know the offer exists."

He smiled. "You're very fortunate to have a better team around you than I had when I was appointed."

That intrigued her. "Oh? Was your transition not smooth?"

He glanced to the side as if remembering and stuck his hands into his trouser pockets. "'Smooth' is not the word I'd use to describe it, no. I took office much the same way you did. After a dispute. You'll hear rumors that I started the thing, but I promise you those are false. Time has a way of exaggerating the truth for effect."

"I know that to be true."

"I imagine you do." He touched his chest. "I would like to add that I am not the scoundrel I am often made out to be."

"Is that so?" She took a seat in one of the chairs, crossing her legs carefully. There was no wineglass on the coffee table. No drink of any kind. He must not have wanted anything when Charlie offered.

"It is." His gaze never strayed from her. "May I join you?"

"Of course." She gestured toward the chair across from her. This was going better than she'd anticipated. Although she expected him to say or do something at any moment to prove what she'd been told about him. Even if he claimed that wasn't the case. "May I ask you a question?"

"Certainly."

"If you're not who everyone says you are, why, then, do you have the reputation you do?"

He unbuttoned his suit coat and sat where she'd indicated, filling the chair with his form. "I suppose people like to talk about me. They like to talk about anyone who's in a position of power."

She couldn't argue with that. Not with her history. "So it's just because you are who you are and not because you give them any reason to?"

He nodded. "Exactly. I knew you'd understand."

He needed to hold his horses. She wasn't Team Fitzhugh just yet. "You knew that about me? That I'd understand? How is that?"

"Because you are... What's the word? Mafioso?"

The small hairs went up on the back of her neck. Using the Italian word for Mafia didn't make it any easier to take. Her irritation was instant, and so was the change in her mood.

The look of surprise on his face seemed artfully constructed. "You didn't like that, if the glow of your eyes is any indication. If I offended, I didn't mean to."

"*If* you offended?"

"Poor word choice. Obviously, I did. My apologies."

Be that as it may, she was about to nip this in the bud. "To be crystal clear, I'm not Mafia or Mafioso, nor was I ever. Marrying a man who was didn't make me so. To be even more transparent, I didn't know what he was when I married him."

"I see." But his eyes still held no remorse for his words.

"No, I don't think you do. The Villachi family and their criminal behavior disgust me, and it's my sincere hope that they all pay for the terrible things they've done. I believe they will, Hawke, because I also believe that justice does eventually win. No matter who has to mete out that justice."

Fitzhugh stopped smirking. "Again, I apologize. And thank you for correcting me." But his repentance was short-lived as he smiled again. "You see? This is how rumors begin. So easily. And with an unwitting misunderstanding. But I promise you won't hear another mention of your Mafia connection from my lips."

Despite his promise, he'd used *that* word again.

She stifled the urge to verbally assault him. Or physically. At this point, either one was an option. "Good. And yes, I understand how rumors begin. I also know they're best dealt with immediately, which is why I gave you the background that I did." She didn't believe for a second that he'd spoken unwittingly. He'd deliberately said what he'd said to see how she'd react. She'd bet on it.

Joe had always done that too. Dropped little bombs into a conversation to find the weak spots of the person he was speaking with.

Fitzhugh was going to have to be more original.

"I understand." He nodded slowly, a new look of admiration creeping across his face. "I like you. You're not afraid to say what you think, are you?"

"Not most of the time, no. But then, you don't survive twenty-seven years of my life by being a delicate flower."

"I suppose not." He raised his finger. "Although you are named after one."

Like she'd never heard that before. "I'm pretty sure the Belladonna plant is more known for its deadly qualities than its pretty foliage."

"Is the same true of you?"

"I guess you'll have to figure that out for yourself."

"I will endeavor to remember that."

She smiled. She hoped he would. "Good. We should get along just fine, then." She glanced at the time.

"Am I keeping you?"

"Not yet, but I do have another appointment this evening."

He nodded like he understood, but she was pretty certain whatever he was imagining, it wasn't a meeting with the Russian mob about five million dollars. "You'll be very busy these first few weeks, I'm sure."

"I'm sure."

"Has anyone else come to see you?"

"Considering this is pretty much my first official day as governor, no. You're the first one." He might think he was making himself seem important, but she just thought he was a suck-up.

For the second or third time, he looked around the room. "I hope you got the arrangement I sent."

"I did." She wasn't going to tell him she'd had it put in the powder room. Let him wonder. "Is there anything else you want to discuss while we have this time? Anything you think I should know about governing this area? Words of wisdom? I'm open to talk about whatever you'd like."

He leaned forward, resting his forearms on his knees. "Now that you mention it, there is. I've been thinking about putting on a grand event, something to bring in vampires from all over. Maybe even make it an annual thing if it goes off well."

"Oh? What kind of event?"

He sat back, grinning like he'd just discovered fire. "A masquerade ball. Very grand and old school. The kind of ball that was commonplace in days gone by."

"That sounds interesting." And like a lot of work. And expense. "What would the purpose of this event be?"

"To bring our kind together. To have fun, of course, but also to encourage networking. We're a rather solitary species, you know."

She'd heard that. "Where would this event take place?"

"I could hold it at my estate. Or perhaps at one of the big hotels in the city. We'd co-sponsor, of course. I think it would be a grand way for you to introduce yourself as the new governor too." He snapped his fingers. "In fact, that's exactly what should happen. You would be the guest of honor. We can call it the Governor's Ball."

She almost laughed. She was sure there was nothing *sudden* about his sudden idea. No doubt it had been his goal all along. As if she were that gullible. "So you'd pay for everything *and* do all the organizing?"

He stared at her.

When he didn't instantly respond, she smiled sweetly and dug in deeper. "That is very kind of you. I'm truly honored. Have your admin reach out to mine about availability."

His brow furrowed. "I wasn't... That is... No, we'd co-sponsor. We'd share the cost and the planning."

"In that case, I know a few places right here in New Jersey that would be happy to host a large event."

He frowned. "The city has better—"

"No," she cut him off. "Anything the city has, Jersey has too. If we're co-sponsoring, and I'm the guest of honor, the event will be held in New Jersey. If you want to pay for the whole thing, I'd be happy to remain the guest of honor and allow you to have the event in New York. Otherwise, you can certainly host your own event anywhere you please."

He opened his mouth to respond but seemed to be searching for words. Finally, he found some. "I can be useful to you. You've been governor for what? Two days?"

"Nope. Just to repeat, this is my first day, but thanks for listening."

His rant continued as if she hadn't spoken. "You can't possibly know what you need to do, how to do it, who to contact, what friends you need to make. I can answer all of that for you. I can mentor you. But for me to do that, you need to meet me halfway."

"I'm good."

His expression held total disbelief. "How can you possibly think that?"

With a smile, she stood so that she was gazing down on him. "Sharks are born swimming, Governor Fitzhugh. I'll be fine."

He closed his mouth, looking very frustrated.

She was done with the conversation and felt very much like it was time to end the meeting. "Thank you for coming. It was nice to meet you face-to-face. Let me know what you decide about the masquerade ball, will you?"

His frustration remained, but he got to his feet. "Belladonna, I don't think you understand the opportunity an event like this could be for you. A chance to network with the upper crust of vampire society. That would be very good for your future."

"Future?" She wondered if her amusement showed in her eyes. "I don't think we look at being governor the same way, Hawke. I see this as a chance to do some good. Not as a stepping-stone to bigger and better things."

He looked incredulous. "You're telling me you don't want to be queen?"

"Artemis's position? Oh my, no. Not even remotely." Then, just because she could, Donna decided to status-drop. "I would never do that to my grandsire."

"Artemis is your—"

"Grandsire. Isn't that what you call it? She was Claudette's sire, and Claudette was my sire, so—I thought you knew that."

He swallowed. "I assumed that was a rumor."

"Nope. That part's true." Apparently, he hadn't talked to Claudette in a while either. She checked the time. Now she really did need to get moving. But the talk about rumors had gotten her a little wound up and feeling frisky. Might as well leave him with something to talk about. "If you'll excuse me, I have a meeting with the head of the Russian Mafia."

Once again, he had no words.

She almost laughed.

"You have a safe ride home, now." She patted his

arm, then with a bright smile, she stepped around him and left the room.

She was shaking just the tiniest bit from the rush of adrenaline. She'd met with the infamous Hawke Fitzhugh and come out on top. At least she felt like she'd come out on top.

When she walked down the hall into the kitchen and saw Charlie, Temo, and Pierce grinning wildly, she knew she'd done what she'd set out to do.

She'd held her own against Fitzhugh.

Charlie seemed to be barely keeping from laughing. "I'll just go see Governor Fitzhugh out."

"Thanks."

No one said a word, but Temo's and Pierce's expressions said they were bursting to talk. Finally, they heard the door close, and Charlie came back in a few moments later.

She shook her head. "That was some meeting. Good for you!"

"You think he's mad?" Donna asked.

"Not mad, no," Charlie said. "Probably more stunned that his charm and good looks didn't get him anywhere. He didn't say a word on the way out, which is *not* his style." She giggled. "Poor Hawke."

Temo put his hands on the counter. "Way to go, boss."

"Thanks." She was feeling pretty good. Which was a nice way to head off to meet the Russians.

"Are you ready for me to pull the car around?" Temo asked.

"Yes." She looked at Pierce. "We should go, right?"

"If we're still picking Neo up, then yes."

"We are."

Temo headed for the door. "Give me five minutes."

"You got it," Pierce said before glancing at Donna. "You did great with Fitzhugh. You're going to do great with the Russians."

"I hope you're right. The stakes are a little higher. After all, my life wasn't in danger with Fitzhugh. Whereas with the Russians…"

"I understand," Pierce said. "But I don't think they'll risk hurting you. After all, they don't want to start a war with the Villachis."

"You're assuming me being hurt would have that outcome. Frankly, I'm not so sure Big Tony wouldn't call it a favor." She frowned. "I know Lucinda would."

"That might be so, but the Russians don't know that, so for now you have the upper hand with them." He smiled at her. "Don't forget who you are now. What you're capable of. Plus, you'll have Temo and Neo there, a powerful backup team if ever there was one."

"True. Very true. I still forget sometimes that I have this whole new skill set. Thanks for the reminder."

"One more reminder. You need to feed. And by feeding me in return, I'll be a much more useful part of that team."

"You're right." She pushed up her sleeve. "Let's do this."

# CHAPTER 10

After picking Neo up, Temo parked in a twenty-four-hour garage a block away from Pravda. Valet parking would have been more convenient, but if something went wrong, none of them wanted to rely on someone to bring the car around.

This way, they also had a place to rendezvous if the meeting turned sour.

They all got out of the SUV and gathered beside it.

Temo tugged his suit coat into place. "How you want to do this, boss? Me and Neo in back, you and Pierce up front?"

Donna nodded. "I think that's good. But we need an escape plan too. If things go bad, Temo, you and Pierce get out and get the car. Neo and I will fight our way out and meet up with you somewhere."

"Boss," Temo started, "you realize that might cause some rumors. Two women taking down the Russian mob? They don't know you're both vampires."

She grinned. "I guess they'll get a fast lesson in woman power, then." She glanced around. "I don't know this area very well. Where can we meet up?"

"Rigby's Pub is about five blocks away," Neo said. "We could meet them there."

"Good. Temo, you got that? Rigby's."

"Got it." He nodded.

Donna rubbed her hands together. "Any other suggestions?"

Neo smiled at Temo. "Good with me." She held out her fist to him. "We got this."

He bumped his fist against hers. "Yeah, we do."

Donna didn't need any kind of supernatural power to see that Neo was crushing on Temo, who seemed to be crushing right back. It was pretty cute.

But Neo had brought her A game, fashion-wise. All in black, naturally. Skintight leather leggings tucked into combat boots, topped with a snug little jacket buttoned up to allow just a hint of lace bra to peek out. Her braids were pulled back into the fauxhawk style she favored, and the purple strands had been changed to deep burgundy.

Donna really liked that because it matched her own shoes and nails and made them look like a posse. Just thinking the word *posse* made her feel like a boss. And a posse wasn't something she'd even known she'd wanted, until now.

Pierce glanced at her. "Let me do the talking until we get into the meeting. They'll be watching us every step of the way, I'm sure. The more aloof and mysterious you seem, the more edge you'll have."

"You think?" Donna asked.

Neo nodded. "Def. Good idea, Pierce. You look

sharp tonight, by the way." She winked at Temo. "You too."

Pierce smiled. "Thank you. And thank you for accompanying us. You are the perfect addition to our party."

Donna snickered. "If the mutual admiration society is done meeting, maybe we could get going?"

They all laughed and started walking.

As they approached the club, Donna's smile faded. She was all business now. Serious and focused. A quick look around showed her the others had switched to that mood too. They looked like an intimidating group. She really hoped the Russians thought so, anyway.

They approached the line to get in. Pierce held out a hand, indicating they should wait. As they came to a stop, he broke away and went to speak directly to the doorman.

A few words and the man nodded.

Pierce waved them over.

The doorman unhooked the velvet rope and gestured to another doorman. In they went, following the first guy.

Pravda's interior seemed to be an homage to old-school Russia. The hammer and sickle were everywhere, as were pictures of Putin, Lenin, and Stalin. Bottles of what was probably very expensive vodka were prominently displayed. Red was the predominant color. The floor was concrete, but the seating was mostly velvet and leather.

Beams of light caught the manufactured fog

coming off the dance floor, turning the laser show into something vaguely sci-fi. The music was pure European house with the kind of pumping bass and reedy electronics that seemed to run on a loop. The people on the dance floor moved like a swarm of mindless insects.

The club looked about as she'd expected.

They passed through the main areas to an elevator guarded by a bouncer. Total lunk material in a suit. He reminded her of Yuri, the one she'd accidentally drained to death on her living room floor.

The doorman spoke to the bouncer. He nodded and ran a keycard through a reader. The elevator doors opened.

Pierce took a quick look inside, then nodded that it was all clear and let Donna go ahead of him. He started to walk in next.

The bouncer stuck his arm out. "Just her."

Donna stepped out of the car, pushing the man's arm out of the way as she did. She kept her sunglasses on. "They come with me, or I leave. Do you want to explain that to Mr. Reznikov?"

"Mr. Reznikov gave me those instructions."

Donna stared at him for a long time without saying a word. Did the glamour thing work through sunglasses? Probably not. She hadn't actually learned how to do that yet anyway. Plus Claudette had said it took practice.

The man wore an earpiece, which made her remember what Pierce had said about them being watched the whole time. This elevator would definitely be under surveillance.

She looked up, scanning the ceiling for the camera. She found it and stared right at it, then she drew her hand across her throat. She glanced back at the bouncer guarding the lift. "You can tell Reznikov those instructions just cost him five million dollars."

She walked away. Pierce fell into step next to her. "Nicely played. We won't get to the door."

"I don't think so either."

They were right. Not even ten yards away, a new man stepped into their path. He looked more like an executive than a lunk. He smiled at her as he smoothed his tie. "Mrs. Barrone, I am so sorry for the misunderstanding. I am Dimitri. Please, allow me to escort you upstairs."

"Did you miss the reason I'm leaving?"

He flattened his hand against his chest. "My apologies. I meant you and your party."

She tipped her head ever so slightly and narrowed her eyes. Not that he could see them. She waited to answer long enough that his smile wavered a bit. "Fine. Lead the way."

He ushered them to a different elevator, away from the crowds. He swiped his keycard through the reader, and the doors opened. He held out his hand. "After you, Mrs. Barrone."

She got on, then Pierce, then Dimitri, then Neo and Temo. There wasn't much personal space left in the car. She looked at the others to see how they were doing. Temo had his big-trouble face on, which almost made her laugh.

Thankfully, she held it together as they rode up. A moment later, the doors opened again.

The upstairs was much quieter, but the bass downstairs thumped like drums portending war. She touched her crucifix, hidden under her suit jacket, and prayed *war* wasn't what she was walking into.

Dimitri walked ahead. "Right this way."

They followed him to a set of double doors. He opened them to reveal a very large office filled with very large men.

One of them sat on a throne behind an ornate desk. Boris. Clearly.

Besides the desk and chair, a small bar was on one side, along with a pool table, two other smaller tables, and a scattering of chairs. On the wall opposite the bar were three flat-screens. One was showing a Russian station. Another was playing a James Bond movie. The third was tuned in to a telenovela. All three had the sound on softly so that they all kind of blended into white noise.

It was more of a seedy gentleman's club than an office.

Dimitri nodded at the man behind the desk. "Mrs. Barrone."

Boris waved his hand, the cigar stuck between his fingers dropping ash as he did. "Good." He nodded back, this time at Donna. "Welcome to Pravda."

Dimitri left, closing the doors. Neo and Temo

took up positions on either side. Donna and Pierce stayed where they were. Boris's men, six of them, were stationed all around the room. If she moved forward, she'd be in the middle of them.

Somehow, she wasn't afraid. She was a little angry. And a little wired from feeding recently and the meeting with Fitzhugh. But mostly, she was resolved to end her involvement with these men tonight. "Thank you."

"It's a bold move for you to request such a meeting." He smiled. "I like that very much. Too long the Italians have been timid. Let us drink to this monumental occasion."

The man behind the bar started lining up shot glasses and filling them with vodka.

Pierce looked like he was about to say something. She gave him a slight shake of her head. If Boris thought he was going to get the advantage by getting her intoxicated, he was so wrong it was comical.

She also thought it might be dangerous not to accept the drink. Or maybe she'd just watched too many spy movies. Whatever. She could do this. She smiled at Boris. "Fine. But I don't allow my team to drink on the job, so you'll have to settle with me."

Boris got up from his throne and walked to the bar. "I would not want your team to break your rules. I am happy to drink with you alone."

She joined him. The bartender had filled six shot glasses. Boris picked one up and saluted her with a Russian toast, then tossed it back.

With less fuss, she did the same with hers. The vodka burned a little going down, but she kept from grimacing.

He watched her for a second. Did he really think it was going to hit her that fast?

She tipped her head toward the remaining glasses. "Who are those for?"

"For us, of course."

"And after those are gone, we'll talk?"

"Sure, sure," he said. Amusement was thick in his voice.

This might be a joke to him, but it certainly wasn't to her. She was done playing. She picked up a second glass and tipped it back, then chased it with a third. She set the empty glass down, then repeated the action with his second and third shots.

When they were all gone and the glasses upside down on the bar, she looked at him expectantly. "Okay. Let's talk."

Soft murmurs filtered through the room from his men.

After a moment of stunned hesitation, Boris laughed. "That is a very nice trick, but you will regret that, girl."

Girl? What a chauvinistic pig. She held her tongue. For now. She needed this deal to happen.

She had yet to take off her sunglasses. Now felt like the right time. Just to show him how clear and bright her eyes still were. She removed them and held them out for Pierce. Or anyone, really. She just hoped someone took them.

Pierce did, understanding immediately what she wanted. He was great that way.

She held eye contact with Boris. "The only thing I regret is that we have not yet begun to talk. You're wasting my time and yours."

He threw his hand into the air. "Fine, fine, now we talk." He leaned on the bar. "What have you come to see me about?"

She straightened, just to make a point of how little the alcohol was affecting her. He knew very well what she was there for. But if he wanted to play it that way, so be it. This was his house, his game, his rules.

At least until those rules no longer suited her.

She kept her expression even and serene, like this was just a minor blip on the radar of her life. But he wasn't the only one who could play games. "You sent a messenger to my house. Yuri Lukin. He seemed to be concerned about an exchange of money between you, my husband, and my husband's sister, Lucinda Villachi. Why don't you tell me what that was about? Then we can talk about your money."

The subtle widening of his eyes told Donna that he knew what she was talking about. But then he laughed and shrugged like everything she'd said was completely new to him. "I sent Yuri to your house with a gift of condolence. Nothing more."

There was no polite way to call him a liar. "He did come with a basket. But that wasn't all he was there for. I guess I should assume, then, that the five million dollars he said you wanted back was some kind of scam Yuri was running?"

Boris swallowed. Five million was a lot to pretend not to know about. Especially when it was owed to you. "It must have been. I don't even know where Yuri is."

"How about that?" She saw a chance to sow a little discord and decided to take it. "I guess it hasn't occurred to you that I gave him the money, and he took off with it?"

"Yuri would not do that."

"And yet, you have no idea where he is." She knew. He was in cold storage at the FBI. "Well, if there was never any deal and never any money, I guess we're done here. We won't need to see each other again, will we? And by we, you understand I mean you or any of your men. Ever. Again."

Boris bristled with unsaid things.

"Anything else you want to talk about before I go?"

He glanced to the side at one of his men, the look so fast and sly she might not have noticed if she'd looked away for a split second.

She caught movement out of the corner of her eye. A movement that her years spent around the volatile Villachi crew had taught her to interpret instantly.

One of Boris's men was reaching for his gun.

# CHAPTER 11

Instinct and the driving need for self-preservation propelled Donna with a burst of speed unlike anything she'd experienced before. In the blink of an eye, she was in front of the man attempting to draw his weapon.

Her hand was around his throat, her newly manicured fingernails digging into his skin. She shoved him against the wall and up a few inches so that his toes scraped the floor as he danced for his footing. "Drop that gun, or I will tear your throat out."

Her eyes were probably glowing. Good.

The gun fell to the floor with a clatter. She dug her thumb hard into an artery, shutting down the blood flow. A few moments later, his eyes rolled back, and he passed out. She kicked his gun away, then released him.

He crumpled to the ground like a discarded grocery bag.

She turned to glare at Boris. "How dare you."

His eyes were round. He sputtered but said nothing intelligible. He muttered something in

Russian. A curse, maybe. Had the bar not been behind him, he probably would have backed up.

She wasn't done. She took a few steps toward him, her spike heels clicking against the ancient hardwood. "What did you signal him to do? Take me out? Make an example out of me?"

He cleared his throat. Then he seemed to get ahold of himself. His eyes narrowed and filled with darkness. "Your husband died owing me money."

"So now you own up to it?"

He rolled his shoulders. "I want it back. Or else." He waved his hand at the man on the floor. "You do not scare me."

Except she had. At least for a moment. Time to turn up the volume a little. With the same speed she'd used before, she closed the distance between them. Only an inch of air, maybe two, remained.

The height from her shoes made her slightly taller than him. "If I don't scare you, you're not paying close enough attention. You've never dealt with a woman like me before. I'm the kind of woman who will hide your body in my trunk while I help the police search for you. The kind of woman who knows you catch more flies with a corpse than a jar of honey. Do you understand?"

He nodded slowly.

"Good. If I see you or any of your men again, if they step foot on property I own, if they come within ten feet of my family, my friends, or my vehicle, I will destroy you and your entire organization. I'm talking burnt earth and salted ground."

He coughed like he'd just choked on his own saliva.

She smiled. "Now. The money you gave my husband. What was it for?"

Boris glanced around. Maybe he didn't want to talk in front of his men. Too bad.

"I'm waiting."

He exhaled in frustration. His breath reeked of cigar smoke and alcohol. "A deal."

"I get that. What kind?"

"He was going to start distributing for us."

"Drugs?"

Boris nodded.

Joe had been such a scum. That explained the drugs she'd found in the stash room. "And what's Lucinda's part in all this?"

Boris hesitated. Donna understood his reluctance. If one of his men were to reveal this kind of information, they'd end up in the river. Or wherever the Russians dumped their bodies. "For her cut, she would make sure Big Tony stayed out of it."

"How much did you give her?"

"The five million was for both of them."

No wonder Lucinda had wanted to get into that office so badly. That had to be the reason. She was there to get the money. And maybe even the drugs. That meant Joe must have told her about the stash room. At this point in her life, Donna shouldn't let something like that surprise her. But it did. "Good to know."

"I want my money back."

She bet he did. She also knew that she'd calmed down enough that her eyes were no longer glowing. That must have given him a new boost of confidence. "What do I get in return?"

"I will personally see that you are left alone."

"No. Not just me. My children, my sister, my friends."

He nodded. "*Da*. All."

She looked at Pierce. He gave a little nod like he thought that was a good deal. It was what they'd come for, after all. She returned her attention to Boris. "I'll give you four million, and we'll call it a deal. The outstanding million is the price you pay for bothering me with this."

He frowned.

To get her eyes to light up again, she thought about the drugs and guns and blood money she'd found in her house.

The anger worked.

He recoiled a little. "Fine. Deal."

She held the glow a little longer. "You break that deal in the smallest way possible, and I will return for you."

He snickered, but the sound seemed mostly for show. Bravado for the sake of keeping face in front of his men. Well, he could put on a show on his own time. She needed him to understand how serious this was. She called down her fangs. "I mean it. If I have to come back here, all that will be left of you is a bloodless corpse."

119

He snickered again. Louder this time.

She licked her top lip and, just for him, showed off her very pointy fangs. "You think I'm joking?"

Boris went pale. His head wobbled like a bobble-head. "I understand."

She smiled and put the fangs away. "Great. Pierce will take down the address where you want the money sent."

Pierce joined them, his iPhone at the ready. "I'll have the money messengered first thing tomorrow."

Boris spit out a location while he rapped his knuckles on the bar and glared at the bartender. The man hastily started pouring vodka again.

Pierce typed the address into his phone. "Nice doing business with you."

Temo already had the doors open. He held them and kept an eye on Boris and his men while Donna, Pierce, and Neo walked out. Then he shut the doors, and they all got on the elevator, which thankfully needed a keycard for access only on the main floor.

No one said a word until they were out of the club, back on the sidewalk, and headed toward the parking garage.

Then Temo exhaled loudly enough to be heard over the ambient sounds of the city. "We're clear. No one's following us."

Donna's own breathing came easier. "Good."

A soft curse slipped from Neo's lips. "Not much gets my heart pumping these days, but that did. Woo, that was like being in a movie."

Donna glanced at Pierce, then back at Temo and Neo. They were all smiling. But then, so was she. "We did it."

"Yes, we did," Pierce said. "But you carried the day."

"You were something else, boss," Temo said. "Something. Else."

"He's right," Neo said. "Girl, that was impressive. You are fearless."

Donna exhaled. She was shaking from the rush of adrenaline. "I don't feel fearless. But I'm glad that went as well as it did."

"Me too." Pierce reached out and squeezed her hand.

"I'm keyed up," Neo said. "Let's get a drink to celebrate. Let's do something."

Donna shrugged as they entered the parking garage. "We could go to Rigby's anyway."

"I'm game," Pierce said.

"Whatever you want to do, boss." Temo grinned. "But I'm game too."

"Just a round or two," Donna said. "I haven't unpacked a thing."

"You'll have time for that." Pierce reached out and touched her hand again. "You deserve a little celebration after what you pulled off back there."

"Yeah," Neo said. "Plus, you look too dope to just go home."

"Okay, but seriously, just a round or two." Donna laughed. "I do look pretty dope."

Temo hit the clicker and unlocked the SUV, then they all got in. Neo sat up front with him again, Pierce in the back with Donna.

They were just pulling out when Donna's phone chimed. She checked it and saw a text from Charlie.

*How long before you're home?*

*Couple hours. What's up?*

*We have a situation. Not sure it'll keep.*

*What kind of situation?*

A couple long seconds went by.

*A citizen requesting sanctuary.*

Donna looked up. "Charlie says there's a citizen requesting sanctuary. I don't even know what that means."

Temo glanced at her in the rearview mirror. "Basically, someone's in some kind of trouble and needs your help to stay safe. The governor's property is considered neutral ground. A safe place. Like a church."

"So should I grant it right now?" She looked at Pierce. "I know nothing about this person or their situation."

"They can stay twenty-four hours before you have to officially decide. If you haven't by then, they have to leave."

Donna rolled her eyes. "Why is there never a handbook?" She sent a text back to Charlie. *They have twenty-four hours, right? I'll assess when I get back.*

She didn't want to end the night early on account of something that could wait. Not after these people had helped her through a tough situation. They deserved a little fun. A few drinks weren't going to hurt anything.

Temo looked at her in the mirror again. "What do you want to do, boss?"

"Rigby's. I'll take care of this when we get back. It can wait." She couldn't imagine what kind of situation warranted sanctuary at the governor's penthouse, but if the person was there, then they were safe and that was all that mattered in the immediate moment.

Her mind shifted back to Boris. He'd confirmed Lucinda and Joe had been working the side deal together. That was valuable information. The kind Rico might be able to use. She'd talk to him in the morning. It was late, and even though he might be up, it was one more thing she didn't want to deal with at the moment.

Neo turned around so she could see Donna. "You know, anytime you need extra security, I'm down. This was crazy, but fun."

"I'll let you know. I could probably even put you on the governor's payroll as a part-time employee."

Neo made a surprised face. "Am I getting paid for tonight?"

"I don't see why you shouldn't. I'll talk to Charlie about it when I get back."

"That's what I'm talking about." She fist-bumped Donna. "Girl, I am so glad you showed up at group. Hey, speaking of, you looking forward to that party Francine is throwing for you at her place this weekend?"

Donna took a breath. "To be honest, I haven't really thought about it. There's been a lot going on. And I haven't gotten an official invite. You're sure she's still having it?"

"I'm sure," Neo said. "Francine loves to give parties. She'll get those invites out by email soon. Although she's got to be assuming you already know."

"I'll text her."

"I'll remind you," Pierce said softly.

"Thanks."

Temo found a parking spot near Rigby's, and they went in. The place was busy, but not uncomfortably so. Donna and Neo got their fair share of looks as they walked through to an available booth.

Donna smirked. "We might be overdressed for this place."

"Might? Please, this place hasn't seen women this good-looking since the Spice Girls tour bus broke down outside."

Donna chuckled as they slid into the booth. "You're funny."

Neo's brows arched in amusement. "Trust me, if we were alone, we'd drink for free all night."

"I'm sure you're right."

Temo sat next to Neo, Pierce next to Donna. A server came by, and they ordered, then sat back and rehashed the evening's events. Mostly, the conversation was about Boris. What he must be thinking, how Donna had handled him, and what was going to happen to the guy Donna had left unconscious on the floor.

Three rounds later, they were still at it, laughing and telling stories. Neo and Temo had inched closer together as the night wore on.

Donna's phone chimed. She thought about ignoring it, but she was the governor now. She really shouldn't do that. She pulled it out and checked the screen. "Hey, Temo, I got a notification from the camera app."

Her phone chimed again. Then again.

"More notifications." She looked up at him. "Someone must be at my house."

"Tap on the notification. It'll bring up the app and give you an option to view it."

She did as he said. The first screen that came up was the front door. She hit play, and the night vision picked up a figure dressed in dark colors, though a hoodie obscured most of his face.

"I think someone's trying to break into my house." She showed Pierce.

"Anyone you recognize?"

"No. Hang on. I'll play the next one." That one showed the man trying the door into the garage. But the angle was about the same, making it impossible to get a good look at the guy's face. If it was a guy. The body shape seemed to fit.

"Anything from the back porch?" Temo asked.

She nodded. "That's the last notification that came in. He must be trying all the doors." She tapped the button to play that one and watched.

She shook her head. "That hoodie is making it impossible to see what he—"

The figure looked up, enough that his face was plainly visible.

She gasped and almost dropped the phone. "No freakin' way. *No freakin' way.*"

"Who is it?" Neo asked.

Donna lifted her head to look at her, shocked to the core. "It's Joe. My dead husband."

# Chapter 12

Donna replayed the video two more times. Her hand shook with anger as she pressed play for a third viewing. "How is this possible?" She growled. "I know how. He faked his death. That freakin' piece of lying garbage faked his death."

Pierce had already called for the check and handed over his credit card. The server returned, and he quickly signed his name on the receipt and pocketed his copy. "All right," he said. "We can go."

They left Rigby's behind and went outside.

"I'm gonna walk," Neo said. "I'm not far from here, and you all need to get back. Donna, you let me know what I can do to help, and I'm there."

"Thanks, I will." She gave Neo a hug. "And thank you again for your help tonight. Talk to you soon."

"You know it." She gave Temo a little smile. "See you later."

He grinned. "Later."

But his smile vanished with Neo, and he was back to business as they headed for the car. "Where do you want to go, boss? Your old house or the penthouse?"

"The penthouse. There's nothing I can do at my old house. And Charlie's waiting on me to deal with this sanctuary issue." But her attention was solely focused on the appearance of Joe, not the situation waiting for her at the penthouse.

Pierce put his arm around her. "You okay? I know you're mad. How do you want to handle this?"

She couldn't do anything but stare straight ahead and fantasize about all the ways she wanted to do Joe in. "I want to kill him. He's supposed to be dead."

"I know."

She clenched her hands to stop the shaking. "Isn't there a statute of limitations on that? Couldn't I kill him and not get in trouble for it because he's already legally dead?"

"It doesn't work that way."

"Well, it should." She pressed her fists into her thighs. "He's not getting away with this."

"He won't. You going to talk to Rico?"

"I have to." She finally managed to break out of her rage-induced fixation to look at Pierce. "Who did I bury? Who was in that casket?"

"I have no idea. Not Joe, apparently."

"Yeah. Not Joe." She grimaced. "You don't think he became a vampire too?"

"Did he look like he'd benefitted from some kind of supernatural change like that?"

She thought about the image of him in that camera. "No. He looked the same."

"Then he's probably not a vampire."

"That's something, I guess."

They got in the car, and Temo leaned back to speak to her. "Boss? You can email those videos to Rico if you want to."

"I can? How?"

"See that little tab at the top of the—yeah, right there. Tap that and it opens up a menu. Tap share and select email."

"Perfect. Thank you. I'm sending these to Rico right now." While she typed in the message, Temo got them on the road toward home. She read over what she'd written, then hit send. Done, she turned to Pierce again. "I want to talk to him first."

Pierce frowned. "You want to talk to Joe?"

She nodded. "I do. I want to have it out with him, say everything to him I've ever wanted to say. Then the feds can have him. But I get my chance with him first."

"I'm sure Rico can arrange something."

"Maybe." She stared out the window. "Watch. The feds will arrest him, he'll decide to flip, and he'll be the one who ends up in WITSEC. Probably in Florida." She turned back toward Pierce, pointing her finger at her own chest. "I was supposed to be the one with a condo in the panhandle. Not that loser."

Pierce chuckled. "I think you're getting a little ahead of yourself."

She slumped back in the seat. "Yeah, maybe."

"Look, you have every right to be angry. But this

isn't going to end well for him. You have video evidence of him now. His get-out-of-jail-free card is gone."

"I hope so."

"The good news is, you don't live in that house anymore, so he can't bother you."

She straightened. Slouching was no good for the suit anyway. "That's true." She exhaled a long, exhausted breath. "I just thought I was done with him. That the Villachi chapter of my life was just about closed."

"It will be. Soon."

Temo grinned at her from the driver's seat, his smile visible in the rearview mirror. "Pretty sure the Russian chapter's closed, boss."

She smiled back. "I think so too. Just as soon as Pierce gets the money sent to them. Then that's that."

Temo nodded. "You really have four million dollars to send them?"

"Yes, but only because they gave it to my husband in the first place. I didn't know where it came from until they sent one of their lunks to try to intimidate me and get it back."

"That's the guy you…" Temo hesitated.

"Drained to death?" she finished for him. "Yep, that's the guy. Wasn't intentional. But yes, he's the one who led to everything that happened between me and Claudette. Ultimately, I guess I have the Russians to thank for my new position as vampire governor of New Jersey. How funny is that?"

"If only they knew." Temo chuckled. "You gonna

tell your not-so-dead husband what happened to you?"

"No. The less Joe knows about my new life, the better. Because trust me, if there's a way for him to use something to his advantage, he'll do it."

Her phone chimed. "Hang on." She looked at the screen. A text from Rico.

*Joe's alive??? You safe?*

*Yes. And yes. Moved to the governor's penthouse, remember?*

*Right. We'll talk in the morning. On stakeout. Need radio silence. Good?*

She typed back, *Good*. She wasn't in the mood to discuss the problem named Joe right now anyway.

She glanced at Pierce. "That reminds me. I absolutely have to talk to my kids. I'm not going to tell them about Joe just yet, but they definitely need to know what's going on in my life. I know I said I was going to do it in person, but I'm thinking a call might be the best I can do right now."

"They'll understand," Pierce said.

"I hope they do." She rested her elbow on the armrest and leaned her head into her hand. The adrenaline rush of dealing with the Russians and then seeing Joe had worn off, leaving her with an odd, melancholy feeling and a touch of fatigue.

She stayed that way until they reached the penthouse. Temo dropped them at the lobby, then went to park the car in the garage.

As she and Pierce rode the elevator up, Donna sent Charlie a text to let her know they'd arrived.

Charlie sent a quick note back. *In the conference room next to the office.*

Donna let Pierce know as they got off the elevator and went into the penthouse. "Charlie's in the conference room, so I'm headed there."

"Right behind you. Unless you need me to do something else."

"No, I'm good. Time to see what this sanctuary request is all about."

But Charlie met them in the hall. "How did everything go?"

Donna nodded. "Great. All things considered."

Pierce snorted. "She was a rock star. She handled the evening beautifully. I'll tell you the whole story when we're through here."

Charlie smiled, but there was tension in her expression, and it didn't reach her eyes. "Great."

"What's going on?" Donna asked. "You seem shaken, and that feels really unlike you."

Charlie sighed. "I've never had a situation like this before. Maybe best you just come in and hear her out yourself."

"Her? Okay." Donna immediately wondered if it was a woman trying to escape her husband, but she knew that was her own history coloring things. "Let's go."

Charlie took a breath, then opened the conference room doors. "Governor Barrone, this is Rixaline. She's half fae. And half vampire. She says that makes her a dhamfir. And she's come seeking sanctuary."

Donna's first thought was how young she looked.

And how scared. Rixaline wasn't sitting in the chair farthest away so much as she was perched on it. Her knees were drawn up to her chest, her hands clutching the ends of the armrests.

A glass of water on the table in front of her looked untouched.

The fae side of her was evident in the razor-blade cheekbones, pointed chin, and angular physique. Her skin wasn't as dusky as the one fae Donna had seen in person, but she had enough coloring to indicate she wasn't strictly human. "Hello, Rixaline. I'm Governor Barrone."

Rixaline nodded, eyes enormous and wide, mouth open as if she wasn't getting enough air.

"May I ask why you seek sanctuary?"

Her gaze went to Pierce.

Donna held her hand out toward him. "This is my assistant, Pierce. I promise you're safe here. But you need to talk to me, or I won't be able to keep you that way."

More silent seconds ticked by.

Donna tried a different tactic. "How is it that the iron protecting this building doesn't affect you?"

Rixaline glanced sideways at the walls. "I can feel it, but it's not painful."

"I guess that's your vampire side, hmm? But can you tell me why you seek sanctuary?"

The girl hesitated but finally answered. "They want to kill me."

Finally. "Who?"

"The fae. King Dredward."

Donna shook her head. She hadn't realized the fae had a king. Another subject she needed to educate herself in. "Why would he want to do that?"

"Because," Charlie said, "she's half vampire."

Rixaline nodded. "I am a dhamfir. An abomination."

"I'm sure you're not," Donna said.

"Because of my skills, they gave me a choice," Rixaline went on. "Help them. Or die."

Donna took a seat at the far end of the table. "Would you like something to eat? I don't know about you, but I've had a long day, and it's made me hungry."

Rixaline seemed to be struggling to answer.

Donna glanced up at Pierce. "How about two glasses of blood? And let's get a couple pizzas ordered." She looked at Rixaline. "What do you like on your pizza? I'm a meat-lover girl myself, but I'll pretty much eat anything covered in cheese."

Rixaline frowned. "You want to feed me before you know more?"

"You look like you've had a genuinely rough go of things. And I'm guessing we have a lot to talk about. So we might as well be comfortable doing it, right? Now, I assume being half vampire that you need blood, but maybe I'm wrong."

"No," she said softly. "I need blood. But I can survive longer without it than most."

"Okay, good to know. And for the pizza? You like pizza, right?"

Rixaline suddenly smiled. Just for a second, like a shooting star flashing through the night sky, then the smile was gone. "Yeah, I like pizza. Any kind."

"Wonderful," Pierce said. "I'll get to work on that."

Donna looked at Charlie. "Are you taking notes on all this?"

"I can."

"Join us, then."

Charlie took a spot on the opposite side of the table from Rixaline but close to Donna.

Donna put her hands on the table and smiled at the girl. "Now, back to you. What do they want you to help with?"

She stared at the glass in front of her. "Hunting down vampires. I refused."

Donna frowned. "How awful. Of course you refused." The girl looked young, but Donna wasn't sure if looks meant anything considering her bloodlines. But in the moment, all Donna could think about was her daughter, Christina, and how she hoped someone would help her if she was ever in a bad way.

Rixaline glanced at Donna. "That's why the king ordered my death."

"Well, that's not going to happen now."

Pierce came back in with two glasses of blood. He set one in front of Donna and the other in front of Rixaline. "Pizza's ordered. One meat lovers', one ham and pineapple with onions, and one with extra cheese."

Donna gave him a look. "Ham and pineapple?"

"That's for Temo. But he said he's happy to share."

"I'm good." Donna laughed. "You like pineapple on your pizza, Rixaline?"

"I don't know. I've never had it."

"Well, if you want to try it, you can." Donna sipped the blood Pierce had brought her in the hopes that Rixaline would feel comfortable enough to do the same. "I need to ask you some more questions, Rixaline. I hope you understand that."

She nodded, looking scared again.

"You said something about your skills. Because of them, you were given the choice to help or die. What kind of skills do you have?"

Rixaline carefully took a small taste of the blood in her glass, then swallowed a few big gulps. Almost immediately, some of the greenish-gray left her skin, and a more human tone appeared.

She wiped her hand across her mouth. "I really only have one skill."

"What is that?"

"I can find anything."

# Chapter 13

Donna shook her head. "Explain."

Rixaline shrugged. "It's really as simple as I said. I can find anything, whether it's lost or not. That's why they wanted me to help them hunt vampires. And other runaways."

Donna hadn't realized the fae had runaways. This conversation was getting pretty interesting. "So you find people, then?"

"Or things. Or animals. Anything."

Donna sat back. "That's an amazing skill."

"I don't know. Hasn't done me much good so far."

"Do they have anyone else with this skill?"

"No." Rixaline relaxed from her hunched posture and crossed her legs under her. "Probably why they've been keeping such a tight rein on me."

"I'm sure. How did you come to be half fae, half vampire? I've never heard of such a mix."

"Dhamfir. That's what it's called." Rixaline stared at the table again. "My mother, a vampire, was a fae prisoner. She managed to make her guard fall in love with her. It's said that her beauty was mesmerizing. Once he fell in love with her, he had to protect her. He knew there was no way she'd be set free, so they ended up running away together, but they were pursued, and the guards caught up with them."

She sniffed. "He sacrificed himself so she could escape. Nine months later, I came along, but the birth went badly, and she didn't survive longer than it took to get me to an orphanage and leave a note about my care. That's how I know I'm named after my father. He was Rix."

Donna nodded, fascinated, but her heart went out to the poor girl.

"The fae found me in the orphanage and took me in. More out of curiosity than anything else, I think. They made me do a lot of chores. Mostly cleaning."

Donna's heart clenched a little more. That didn't sound like much of a childhood.

"But when I came into my gift, they figured out I could be more useful. Then they gave me the ultimatum. And I ran. Just like my parents."

"Except," Charlie said, "you made it here."

Rixaline nodded. "I overheard some elders talking about what would happen if I ever escaped and asked for sanctuary with the vampires. After that, I could think of nothing else. I started planning my escape that very day."

"And you did it. You poor, brave girl. How old are you?" Donna asked.

"Seventeen. My gift arrived two years ago."

Younger than Christina. More vulnerable too.

Donna had to protect this child. "Do you have any other living relatives?"

"My father's people have disowned him. They want nothing to do with me. I wouldn't want to be with them anyway. And I don't think my mother had any relatives still alive."

Donna leaned in. "Those elders you overheard? What were they afraid would happen if you sought sanctuary with the vampires?"

"That the vampires would use me to hunt down King Dredward and eliminate the fae."

Charlie nodded. "He's notoriously hard to find."

"I see." Donna gave Rixaline a gentle smile. "I assure you we would never force you to do something you don't want to do."

"Oh," Rixaline said. "I think hunting down the fae king and killing him sounds like an awesome idea."

"Good to know," Donna answered. She held up a finger. "Excuse us for just a moment, won't you?" She turned to her admin. "A few minutes of your time outside, please?"

Charlie stood. "Certainly."

Donna got up. "We won't be long, Rixaline."

She and Charlie left, closing the doors behind them. They went into the kitchen, where Temo and Pierce were talking.

That conversation stopped when the women walked in.

Pierce looked at her. "Well? What's the verdict?"

"That's what I want to talk about." She leaned on

the counter. "Charlie, has a child like Rixaline ever existed before?"

"Not that I'm aware of, and there's no mention of a child being born of fae and vampire in any of the archives I've been able to access. I've come across the word 'dhamfir,' but it's always used in a hypothetical way. I'd say she's a very unique creature."

"And a very endangered one, if everything she says is true about the fae wanting her dead, which I don't doubt based on what I've heard so far." Donna looked at Pierce and Temo. "Rixaline says King Dredward has called for her death."

"Sounds about right," Pierce said. "He's not known for his peaceful disposition. And her refusing to do his bidding and subsequently running away would be considered high treason, I'm sure."

"Any way to verify her story and the king's feeling about her?"

Temo nodded. "I know some people who have fae connections. I can reach out to them."

Donna met his gaze. "Do it and tell me as soon as possible what you find out."

He pulled out his phone. "On it."

She turned to Charlie next. "What's the standard procedure for a sanctuary case like this?"

"There's never been a sanctuary case like this, but in a standard situation, we typically take a statement, and then the governor decides the outcome. In this case, we need to do a little more than that. The fae are the sworn enemy of the vampires. They'd like nothing better than to harvest every single vampire on the face of the earth. Granting Rixaline sanctuary would antagonize them even more."

"I expect it will," Donna said.

Charlie sighed. "Also, I hate to say it, but this could be a trap. The fae want to use her to find vampires, and she's found one. We have to be careful."

"I agree," Donna said. "But there's got to be a balance between caution and compassion. We can't turn her out. Not with a death sentence hanging over her head."

"Agreed," Pierce said.

Charlie glanced at him, then Donna. "And if Temo finds out there is no such death sentence? That she might be some kind of a Trojan horse?"

Donna took a moment. "Then we deal with her like we would a traitor."

"You know that will potentially involve the Immortus Concilio again."

Donna straightened and put on a smile. "They probably miss me anyway."

Pierce snorted softly. "You have an interesting way of looking at things. Does that mean you're giving her sanctuary?"

Donna didn't hesitate. "Yes. I'm not putting a seventeen-year-old child on the street. You saw her. Does she look like she's faring well? She needs a shower and food and some undisturbed sleep in a place she feels safe. We can give her that. And if something arises that indicates she's not what she seems…we'll deal with it."

"You want her in the other apartment, I assume?" Charlie's expression held too many emotions to process.

Donna understood anyway. Charlie was a little scared to host a girl who belonged, at least in part, to a species more bloodthirsty than any other on the planet. Sleeping a few rooms away from someone like that would give anyone second thoughts. But at the same time, Donna could see concern for the girl and worry in her admin's face.

Donna shook her head. "No, I'm the one making this decision, so she ought to sleep in one of the penthouse guest rooms. That's only fair."

Temo frowned. "No way, boss. She sleeps downstairs with us, and the door at the stairs will be locked. We could even lock down the penthouse elevator."

"I appreciate you looking out for me, but I can handle this. I don't think she's some infiltrator sent to kill us all in our sleep. I really don't. I have two kids of my own, and I understand them well enough to know that girl in there is hurting. That look in her eyes? That's honest pain." Donna took a moment, then motioned to Charlie. "Come on, let's go tell her."

"Yes, ma'am." Charlie followed her back to the conference room.

Donna opened the doors and strode in.

Rixaline was asleep with her head on the table. She woke with a start at the sound of the doors, jumping out of the chair to crouch against the wall.

Donna's heart nearly broke. Those weren't the actions of a killer. That was the response of someone who was used to being hunted. "It's okay, Rixaline. It's just Charlie and me."

Her wildly beating heart was almost visible under the thin T-shirt stretched over her birdlike frame. Slowly, she rose to her feet. "Sorry. Habit."

"I'm sure. Would you like to get a shower and get cleaned up before the pizza gets here?"

Rixaline stared at her, blinking a few times. "Are you…letting me stay?"

Donna nodded. "Until I have a reason not to, I am granting you sanctuary. But if you break this trust that I've extended, you will stand before the council. Vampires aren't any kinder to traitors than the fae are."

Charlie cleared her throat. "Actually, they are."

"Point taken," Donna said. She looked at the girl again. "Do you understand?"

Rixaline nodded. "Yes." A tentative smile bent her mouth. "I won't break your trust, I promise. Thank you."

"You're welcome. Now come on, I'll show you to your room."

By the time the pizza came, Rixaline had showered and dressed in a pair of Donna's leggings and one of her oversize sweatshirts.

She looked remarkably different. Not just because she was no longer dirty, but because she wasn't a tightly wound spring ready to uncoil at the next sign of trouble.

Donna had changed, too, leaving her suit and heels behind for yoga pants, a T-shirt, and a big cardigan. Temo, Charlie, and Pierce had all changed into lounge clothes as well and now gathered in the big lounge, aka living room, to watch a movie and eat pizza.

The family vibe of the little gathering, however odd an assortment of folks it was, warmed Donna's heart. She realized how much she missed her children and how absolutely necessary it was for her to talk to them and tell them the incredible details of her new life.

The worry was there, of course. Finding out your mother was a vampire wasn't covered in any life skills class either of them had ever taken.

But they were good kids who knew a lot about the world, thanks to their criminal father. Donna had high hopes that the changes in her life wouldn't throw them for long.

And so, as she settled in to eat and be entertained, she held on to that thought.

On one side of her was Pierce, then Charlie. On the other, Rixaline, then Temo. The movie was a fast-paced comedy, but Rixaline lasted for only ten minutes after she'd finished her fourth slice of pizza. Then her head slumped to one side, and she fell asleep.

They let her. It was clear that she was a child in great need. Donna knew, as a rational human being and a woman who'd spent twenty-seven years living with the mob, how terrible and conniving people could be. But her heart as a sister and a mother demanded she care for this child until given a solid reason not to.

She wondered what Cammie, also known as Sister Mary Lazarus Immaculata, would have to say about the orphan she'd just taken in.

Donna wanted to think Cammie would be pleased. Maybe she'd call her tomorrow and see.

After she called her children and told them the news she'd been dreading. But waiting wasn't going to make that news easier to bear.

Twenty minutes later, something buzzed, and Temo pulled out his phone. He spent a few minutes staring at the screen, then grabbed the remote and hit pause. He looked over at Donna, holding his screen toward her. "I have confirmation, boss. Not only has the king called for her death, he's put up half a million as a reward. A full million if she's brought back alive."

Donna glanced at Pierce and Charlie, then back at Temo. "We need to make sure our security is strong. Whatever that means. I'm sure what's here is very good, but I don't want to take any chances."

He nodded. "On it first thing."

"Thank you. Thanks for getting that information too. I think we can all rest a little easier now."

They went back to watching the movie then, and when the credits rolled, Rixaline was still asleep.

Temo got up. "I'll carry her in."

"Thanks," Donna said. She walked with him and helped tucked the girl in. Then she closed the door, and they went back to the kitchen together. Pierce and Charlie were in there. She looked at them. "You two still aren't convinced, are you?"

Pierce glanced at Charlie before answering. "I wouldn't say we're unconvinced. Just cautious."

"I understand that. I am, too, honestly." She smiled at Charlie. "Lock the door between the apartments when you turn in." Then she turned to Pierce. "You can sleep downstairs if you like. It won't hurt my feelings."

"Not a chance I'm leaving you up here alone."

Temo shrugged. "Maybe we should all sleep up here."

Donna hesitated. "Look, there's a small window when we're all asleep. The three of you will be up before me since I go to bed later and sleep longer. I don't think there's anything to worry about."

Charlie smiled, but Donna could tell the expression hadn't come easily. "How about this? We can turn on the monitoring system. If her bedroom door opens, we'll know about it. Everyone keep their phones on, and I'll make sure the notifications are set to go out wide. Then, for that few hours we're all sleeping, we won't have to keep one eye open."

Donna hadn't been planning on it anyway, but she nodded. "Good with me. Pierce? Temo?"

They both nodded.

"Make it so, Charlie. Now, I'm getting a glass of wine and going to read. Sun will be up in a couple hours, and tomorrow's going to be an incredibly busy day. And not just because of our houseguest. I'll see you all when I get up. Good night."

"Good night, Governor." Charlie brought her laptop to life and started working on the monitoring system.

"Night, boss." Temo hooked his thumb toward the living room. "I'm going to grab the last of that pineapple pizza."

Donna laughed as she walked toward her room. "All yours."

Pierce fell into step alongside her. "She makes you think about Christina, doesn't she?"

Donna nodded. "She does. How can I turn that child away?"

"You can't."

"But you still think I'm making a mistake."

"No, I don't. But to think this situation isn't going to cause problems at some point is foolish."

"I agree. We just need to anticipate those problems. And be proactive about them."

"Good. That's smart. But then, so are you." He laughed. "And thank you for not telling me I'm overstepping."

She snorted softly. "You probably are, but I value your opinion, so I don't mind. Anything else you want to tell me before I turn in?"

They stopped at her bedroom door.

"Just that I think your heart is uncommonly large, and while I don't want to dissuade you from being the kind, generous person you naturally are, you're the governor now. Puts a new wrinkle in things."

"I know. Trust me."

"I do."

She leaned against the jamb and crossed her arms. "Any suggestions?"

"No. And I feel like I should be offering you something. But this is new ground for me too." He smiled sweetly. "I don't want this job to change you, Belladonna. Not for the worse. You're wonderful the way you are."

"Thanks." She leaned up and kissed his cheek. "I promise to call you if I need you."

"Okay. Maybe I'll come up with some suggestions overnight. Sleep well."

"You too." She went into her room and closed the door. Pierce was right that taking Rixaline in was going to cause problems, but Donna knew all about those. She'd been dealing with them her entire adult life.

Thing about problems was they always had solutions. Sometimes those solutions were hard. Sometimes they were easy. Neither were they guaranteed to make everyone happy. Sometimes, in the Villachi family, solutions were permanent.

Donna's real hope was not to avoid problems, but to find solutions that didn't result in anyone dying.

If she could manage that, she'd call it a win.

If she couldn't manage it, then maybe this wasn't the job for her.

# CHAPTER 14

Donna woke up to her phone pinging, screen flashing. She rubbed at the sleep in her eyes before checking the screen. Sunrise was still forty-five minutes away.

More important, Rixaline's door had opened.

Phone in hand, Donna grabbed her robe and threw it on as she bolted for the guest room.

But a cold light in the kitchen stopped her. The refrigerator was open, silhouetting the slender frame of one half-fae girl.

Donna sent a quick text to everyone. *I'm handling it. She's just hungry.* Then she dropped her phone into her robe pocket.

"Hey," she said softly.

Rixaline jumped away from the fridge, leaving the door open. "You scared me."

"Sorry. I tried not to."

Rixaline swallowed. "I, uh, I'm pretty easy to startle."

"After what you've been through? I'm sure." Donna tipped her head toward the fridge. "Hungry?"

Rixaline shut the refrigerator. "Nah, I'm okay. Sorry, I'll go back to my room."

Donna doubted Rixaline's claim very much. In fact, she was willing to bet hunger was what had woken the girl. "You know what I always used to crave in the middle of the night when I was human?"

"What?"

"One of two things. Cake. Or a peanut butter and jelly sandwich on white bread. Both with a big glass of cold milk. Of course, I never ate either of them because, as a human woman, I was more concerned with my weight than my stomach growling. Being able to eat what I like has been one of the best perks of becoming a vampire."

Rixaline smiled. "I like cake. I stole a piece once. But I've never had peanut butter and jelly."

Donna's brows rose. "Never? What did the fae feed you?"

"A lot of porridge. A lot of watered-down soup. Rice with gravy and sometimes scraps of meat." She stuck her tongue out. "Nothing good, but then, I was treated like a servant."

"How they expected you to help them under those circumstances—"

"They said if I helped, I'd get better food. A nice room. Time outside." She shook her head. "I never believed them."

"Good for you. And now, you need to taste a PB&J." Donna flipped on the under-cabinet lights so they weren't completely in the dark. "Sit down and get comfy."

Rixaline did as Donna told her to. Donna got to work, pulling out ingredients, some of which took some searching because she wasn't used to this kitchen yet. But at last she had everything assembled. She laid out the bread on paper plates before slathering the slices with creamy peanut butter and strawberry jam, then slapped the sides together and poured two big glasses of ice-cold milk.

She slid a plate to Rixaline, then put the second plate in front of the empty spot next to her. Donna carried the glasses of milk to her seat. She put one in front of the girl and one at her own place. As she settled in to eat, she took a good look at the sandwiches she'd made. "Rats."

"What's wrong?" Rixaline asked.

"I should have cut them in half."

"Won't taste any different."

Donna snorted. "No, I suppose they won't. All right. Have a taste and see what you think."

Rixaline took a big bite. She either wasn't afraid to try new things or was still so hungry she didn't care. But her eyes lit up as she chewed. Then she smiled. "Dith ith good."

"Peanut butter really makes your tongue stick to the roof of your mouth, doesn't it?" Laughing, Donna took a bite of her own sandwich.

The two were silent while they ate. Rixaline finished her sandwich and her milk before Donna got halfway through hers.

She glanced over at the girl. "You want another one? Or would you like to go for the cake now?"

Rixaline stared at her in disbelief. "I can have cake too?"

"Honey, you can have whatever you'd like. I don't want you to be hungry." Donna got up and retrieved the large cake box she'd seen in the pantry when she'd been looking for peanut butter. She lifted the lid enough to check that the top of the cake didn't say *Happy Birthday, Temo* or *Welcome, Governor* or something else that would mark it as off-limits. Although, technically, if it had said *Welcome, Governor*, she'd be perfectly within her rights to eat it.

Regardless, no such writing. Good enough for her. As far as she was concerned, the cake was fair game. And if it *was* supposed to be for something special, they could just get another one.

It was cake, not a donated organ.

She put the box on the counter, opened it up, and lifted out the confection inside. Seeing it in all its glory made her sugar-loving heart skip a beat. "Hello there, gorgeous."

White buttercream frosting was decorated with swirls of chocolate ganache. More chocolate dripped down the sides. Half of a peanut butter cup stuck out of each chocolate swirl, and the scent of peanut butter and sugar was nearly overpowering in the best possible way.

"It's so pretty," Rixaline said. "Are you sure we're allowed to eat it?"

Donna looked at her. "You know I'm the governor, right?"

Rixaline laughed, a soft, sweet sound that made Donna's heart lighter for hearing it. "Yes, ma'am."

"I say we can eat it, so that's that."

"What kind is it?"

"My guess, judging by the decorations, is probably peanut butter and chocolate. You good with more peanut butter?"

"Definitely."

"Great. Why don't you refill our glasses while I cut two slices? We're going to want milk with this too."

"Okay."

With Rixaline doing that, Donna grabbed their plates and a big knife from the block. She sliced two generous pieces and served them up.

Rixaline took her seat in time for the cake.

"Hang on," Donna said. "We need forks." She set the knife beside the cake box, then grabbed forks and went back to her place. "Here. Let's see if this thing tastes as good as it looks."

They dug in.

It did. Actually, it tasted better than it looked.

Donna let out a little moan of happiness. "Oh wow. That is *good.*" She looked over. "You like it? Never mind, half of yours is gone. I'd say that's a yes."

Rixaline paused. "I eat too fast."

"You do eat fast. I'm sure that will change with time. I promise no one's going to take your food away from you here, okay? And there will always be more."

She nodded. "Okay."

Donna pointed at the cake with her fork. "I don't know where this came from, but we should order another from this bakery. We should try at least three or four of their cakes, just to see if they're as good. For purely scientific purposes."

Rixaline nodded. "No argument from me."

She was nearly done with her cake. Donna leaned over. "You want another piece?"

The girl's gaze darted toward the confection still sitting nearby, but then she shook her head. "Nah. I'm good."

"Really? Because you look like you want a second piece. If you do, just say so. It's absolutely okay."

Rixaline glanced at Donna. "I don't want to be…needy. Taking without giving seems wrong. And I've already taken a lot."

"Sometimes we have moments in our life when we need to allow ourselves to be helped. When we're not able to give as much as we'd like because of circumstances beyond our control. That's where you're at. And you know what? It's okay. You know what else? It's very often a blessing to the people who get to help you. I'm very happy to do the giving right now. I really am."

Rixaline stared at her hands. "You're helping me because it makes you happy?"

"Yes, but also because, as the vampire governor of New Jersey, I'm supposed to take care of people like you. And I want to. Not only are you in a terrible situation through no fault of your own, but you don't have family to help you. To me, that means the rest of the vampire community must become that family."

Rixaline shook her head, still not looking up. "That's very kind, but it doesn't feel fair that it's so one-sided."

Donna thought for a moment. "There is something you could help me with."

Her head came up. "There is?"

Donna nodded. "Do you like animals?"

Rixaline smiled. "You mean like Lucky?"

She'd met him briefly yesterday when he'd shown up to check out the pizza situation.

"Yep. See, here's the thing. He's getting a little chunky. He needs more playtime, but we're all pretty busy. If you could play with him for about ten minutes two or three times a day, that would be a big help. Maybe you could even brush him once in a while."

Rixaline grinned. "I can do that. If he'll let me."

The black-and-white beast strode into the kitchen, probably having heard his name. He sat by his food dish and meowed.

"Good morning to you," Donna said. "Did you hear us talking about you?"

Lucky just squinted.

"He wants his breakfast," Donna said. The sun was starting to brighten the horizon.

Rixaline jumped off her chair. "I can get it." Then she hesitated. "You have to tell me what to do, though. Taking care of a pet is new to me."

"No problem. He needs a clean dish, which are those little white ones in the cabinet next to the fridge. Then he gets half a can of food, clean water, and a scoop of his dry food. There are little plastic lids that fit the food can so you can put the remaining half in the fridge for his dinner."

"Okay, I can do that." She got to work fixing Lucky's breakfast, and when she happily set the dish on his food mat, she glanced back at Donna. "Can I pet him while he's eating?"

"Sure, he won't mind that."

Rixaline cautiously stroked Lucky's head. "Wow," she whispered. "He's so soft."

Donna smiled. "He is. You should try brushing him later."

"I would love to do that. He likes that?"

"He loves it. Just avoid the belly. He may roll over and show it to you, but trust me, it's a trap. Other than that, you'll pretty much become his new best friend."

"Who's becoming whose best friend?" Pierce wandered in wearing a robe over pajamas.

Donna wondered if he'd slept in the pajamas because of Rixaline, or if he always wore them. Not that his sleepwear was any of her business, but he looked so dapper in them.

"Rixaline is going to help me take care of Lucky. He needs more playtime than he's getting, and she's now in charge of that."

"That's great," Pierce said. His gaze shifted. "Cake for breakfast?"

Donna grinned. "You want some?"

"Not without coffee."

"Oh, coffee, yes," she answered. "I need that too. Especially if I'm going to stay up. Which maybe I should with all the work in front of me."

"I'm on it." Pierce headed to the Keurig.

"No, you get yours first. But grab yourself a fork," Donna said. Rixaline was still crouched beside Lucky. "Rixaline?"

She jerked her hand back. "Too much petting?"

"No, not at all. You can pet him all you want until he gives you a sign he's done. Which will usually be him walking away or switching his tail. I was just going to say that we need to get you some clothes." Donna got another paper plate, then cut a slice of cake for Pierce.

"I have a few things in my bag." Rixaline bit at her lip. "They're a little beat, but they'll do. They just need a washing."

Pierce brought Donna a cup of coffee despite her telling him to fix his own first. She smiled up at him. "Will you sit with Rixaline and order her some things today?"

"Be happy to. Are you thinking just the basics, like jeans, T-shirts, shoes? Anything more specific?"

"Whatever she wants is cool. I'll ask Charlie if she'll help later with underwear and such."

"Thanks, that's not really my department," he said with a smile as he went back to the Keurig for his cup. "What's your style, Rixaline?"

She stood, leaving Lucky to finish his breakfast without pets. "I don't know, really." She glanced down at what she had on. "I like this. It's warm and comfortable."

He brought his cup over to the seat beside Donna, where his slice of cake was waiting. "I'm guessing you haven't really had a chance to figure out what your style is. We can work on that."

Donna winked at the girl. "Pierce is really good at clothes. That outfit you first saw me in yesterday?"

"That was crazy-cool."

"He helped me with that. Styled it."

"Really?" Rixaline grinned at Pierce. "Can you make me look like that?"

Pierce forked up a mouthful of cake. "I don't think the governor's budget will cover designer suits and heels for sanctuary guests, but we can definitely shoot for a look that's right for you. For the record, however, the governor already had that suit. I just helped with the shoes, hair, and accessories."

Donna grinned. "All of which I would have done differently, so stop trying to not take credit."

He laughed. "As you wish." Then he looked at Rixaline. "Give me three words that describe how you'd like to appear."

Donna sipped her coffee while Rixaline and Pierce talked fashion. She liked this very much, this happy, helpful, family vibe that was going on. It reminded her of the times when Joe had been away and it had just been her and the kids in the house. No pressure that he might do something or say something to ruin the mood. When he'd been away, there had been peace in the house.

Not just in the house, but in her. At least for those fleeting moments.

This had none of that impermanence about it. Mostly because there was no reason for it to change. No Joe to come rushing back and ruin it all, even if he was still alive. He couldn't affect her now.

She was the boss here. This was her domain. She made the rules. Being in charge was potent stuff. She could see how this kind of power could go to your head and make you forget what mattered if you didn't hold fast to the good things in your life. The things that were right and true and solid.

That one thought was enough to make her realize she had something that needed doing immediately. She slid out of her chair and picked up her coffee cup.

"Leaving us?" Pierce asked.

"Headed to my bedroom for just for a little bit," she answered. "I need to call my kids."

# CHAPTER 15

Donna knew her kids' schedules pretty well. Joe was an early riser, thanks to the Air Force's insistence on his 0700 arrival at work. Christina's first class wasn't until ten, so she'd be asleep for another hour yet, at least. Maybe longer.

Donna tapped the contact for her son and listened to it ring.

"Hey, Mom. How are you?"

"I'm really good. How are you?"

"Outstanding. You're up early. Is everything okay?"

"Everything's fine. I wanted to talk to you. Do you have a minute?"

"Sure. I'm just ironing my pants. Let me put you on speaker so I don't burn myself." She heard the sound click over. "All right, go ahead."

"You're going to make some woman a fantastic husband one day, you know that?"

He laughed. "Is that your way of asking me if I'm seeing anybody? Because I'm not. Although there is a woman in supply who's pretty cute."

"Are you going to ask her out?"

"Maybe." A small burst of steam from the iron punctuated his pause. "I'm not sure I'm her type."

"Honey, you're a very handsome man with great manners and a terrific sense of humor. You're every woman's type. She'd be crazy not to say yes."

He laughed. "You're obligated by law to say all that."

"Doesn't mean it's not true. Just ask her. You have nothing to lose."

"Except my pride."

"You'll heal."

He snorted. "Spoken like my mother. How are you doing with…everything?"

She took a breath and sat on her bed. Then stood up again. "That's kind of why I called. There have been a lot of changes in my life, and I need to tell you about them. Big changes. The kind I probably should be telling you in person, but I don't want to put this off any longer than I already have."

"Okay, now you're freaking me out. What's going on? Please tell me you haven't met someone and you're getting remarried."

"What? No. What on earth would make you think that?"

"It's the only thing I could think of."

"It's not that. I promise."

He exhaled. "Good. Whatever you have to say can't be that bad, then."

She hoped he still thought that in a few minutes. "Honey, do you believe in the supernatural?"

161

He was silent for a few seconds. "Yeah, I guess so. I mean, anything's possible, right? There are pilots who claim to have seen UFOs, so why not? And Aunt Cammie's dedicated her life to the service of a higher power." Suddenly, he groaned. "Do not tell me Dad came back as a ghost."

"No! Mary and Joseph, the places your mind goes." His guess was scarily close, but that was a conversation for another day.

He laughed. "Then tell me what's going on already."

"I'm trying. It's hard."

"Just say it."

That was the easiest way. And the only way. "Something happened to me right after your father's funeral. I became a vampire."

Dead silence. Then laughter. "Aw, come on, Mom, tell me what's really going on."

"I'm not kidding. I swear on the Holy Rosary. I went to the cemetery the night after the funeral to yell at your father, and I was attacked and bitten. Another vampire saved me by turning me into one."

More silence. "Are you kidding me?"

"I wouldn't kid about this."

"How is this, I don't... Mom, are you for real? A vampire?"

"Yes. A hundred percent real. Can you handle a little more?"

"There's more?"

"Some."

He took a long breath. "Go ahead."

"Due to circumstances, which I am happy to explain in detail when and if you want to hear them, I am now the vampire governor of New Jersey."

"I...I don't even know what that means."

"It basically means I'm the head vampire in charge of our state."

"Do you get paid for that?"

That was Joe Jr. Very much like his father in some ways, always wanting to know what the bottom line was. "Yes, actually. Very well too. I get a salary, plus staff and an amazing penthouse on the river with a view of the city you wouldn't believe. You're welcome to come visit anytime you want. I'll buy you a ticket."

"I think I should probably do that. And soon. Because this all sounds like stuff I need to see in person. Have you told Christina?"

"Not yet. Pretty sure she's still asleep at this hour."

"Yeah, I suppose so."

"You seem remarkably calm."

"I'm processing, that's all. Not sure how to respond."

She understood. It was a lot to take in. "I'm sure you have questions. It's okay. You can ask me anything."

"Are you okay? You said you were attacked. Were you hurt?"

"I'm better than I've ever been, actually. I was hurt a little, but it was nothing serious, and now I heal very quickly."

"Do you have to drink blood?"

"I do. Sounds gross, I know, but it's really not."

"Yeah, going to have to agree to disagree on that one. Can you go out during the daytime?"

She didn't want to lie to him, but she wasn't going to confess this secret over the phone. She tried to answer in a way that wasn't completely untrue. "It's not a good idea, no."

"You're really a vampire, Mom? With fangs and everything?"

"Yep. Fangs and everything. Just when I need them, though. Not all the time."

"Man."

"I know, Joe. Trust me."

"A penthouse, huh?"

"And a driver and an administrative assistant. I also have another assistant." Explaining that Pierce provided her with blood seemed like too much information at the moment.

"I should come visit. Maybe in a couple weeks. You going to tell Christina today?"

"That's my plan. I'll call her in a couple hours, when I know she'll be awake."

"She might freak out. I'd be surprised if she didn't, really."

Donna laughed. "I was worried you might, too, but you've handled it pretty well."

"I think I'm still in shock. Are you immortal?"

"Mostly, yes."

"Wow. Can I text you later if I think of other questions?"

"Honey, you can text me, call me, email me, whatever you like any time of day or night, okay?"

"Okay." A smile was in his voice. "Thanks. I should probably get going. The gate gets busy."

She relaxed a little upon hearing the lightness come into his tone. "You know what hasn't changed?"

"What?"

"How much I love you."

"I love you too. Talk to you later, okay?"

"Okay." They hung up, and she sat on the bed, a huge weight leaving her. Joe Jr. had handled it incredibly well. And he wanted to come visit, which she took as a really good sign. Now she just had to talk to Christina.

That would happen a couple of hours from now, but talking to Joe Jr. gave her hope that things with Christina would go well too. She twisted to look out at the sunrise. Streaks of pale pink and peach lit the sky. Today would be a good day. Even if her rat of a husband had faked his death.

She groaned softly at that thought. What was that man up to? Nothing good, that was for sure.

He'd be dealt with. She wouldn't let him get away with this.

But first, she'd have a quick shower.

That quick shower turned into a long one. The hot water felt too good to rinse and run. She lingered and tried to spend a few moments without dwelling on everything she had to do, but that was easier said than done.

Was there a woman alive who didn't sometimes feel the weight of the world on her shoulders? Probably not. But then, women were incredibly strong and immensely capable. Herself included. The thought gave Donna a little comfort and a boost of confidence.

Whatever the day held, she'd handle it.

Refreshed, she got out of the shower and dressed. Jeans and a sweater, nothing fancy. As far as she knew, there was no one to meet with, and she certainly couldn't leave the house while the sun was up, so putting on anything dressier wasn't necessary.

She stuck her phone in her back pocket, then went out to the kitchen to see if Charlie was in there yet, since that seemed to be the gathering place for everyone. No sign of her. Donna put in a K-Cup and got a fresh mug of coffee going.

Pierce and Rixaline were sitting side by side on the big sofa in the living room with his laptop open. They were shopping.

Donna walked over while her coffee brewed. "How's it going?"

Rixaline's face was bright with happiness, and Donna suddenly noticed how pretty the young girl was. "Really well. I'm getting basics."

Pierce nodded, his expression buoyant. "Jeans, some good T-shirts, leggings, two sweaters, boots, ballet flats, a cardigan, and a sturdy coat."

Donna patted his shoulder. "Thank you. Maybe get a dress or a skirt too." She looked at Rixaline. "If you'd like."

"Sure. Thank you."

"No problem. Pierce, when are you taking care of that other matter for the Russians?"

He looked up at her. "Boris is getting his package shortly. Temo and I are meeting the messenger at nine at a coffee shop several blocks away. I thought that was smarter than sending it from here."

"That's excellent thinking. Well done."

He winked at her. "Just earning my keep."

With a laugh, she gave his arm a little squeeze, then walked back through the kitchen to get her coffee. She added cream and sugar before going down the hall to the office.

Charlie was at the smaller desk. Her laptop was open, but she also had a headset on and seemed to be listening to something.

"Morning, Charlie."

She put her hand over the microphone. "Good morning, Governor. I'm on with the governor of Pennsylvania's office. They'd like to set up a meeting in the next few weeks."

"Okay, sounds good."

Charlie moved her hand away. "Yes, that sounds fine. Governor Barrone is looking forward to it. We'll confirm by email. Have a great day." She typed something on the laptop before looking at Donna again. "Sorry about that."

"Don't apologize for work."

A little smile curved Charlie's mouth. "You're in early. I expected you to go back to sleep after dealing with Rixaline."

"I probably should have, but I had some things to take care of. I'll settle into a more normal routine soon, I'm sure. Might need to nap later, though. But I figured since I was up, I might as well stay up and get some things done."

"How did it go with Rixaline? You said she was hungry?"

"It went fine. And yes, I found her in the kitchen with the refrigerator open. I don't think that pizza went very far, considering how little she'd had to eat lately. We fixed that with peanut butter and jelly sandwiches and cake."

Charlie smiled. "Good. I'm glad that's all it was. I saw Pierce earlier. He told me they had shopping to do."

"The girl needs some clothes that don't have holes or look like prison hand-me-downs."

"She does. That's very nice of you, ma'am."

Donna leaned against the door, her coffee cup in both hands, the warmth seeping into her in the most pleasant way. "Seems like if you grant someone sanctuary, you're also agreeing to take care of them for as long as they're under your protection."

Charlie nodded. "I agree with you."

Donna was glad for that. So far, Charlie and Temo had seemed pretty amenable to the decisions she'd made as governor. "I think Rixaline could be a very valuable asset. Not that that's the reason I offered her sanctuary. Clearly, she was in desperate need. But if she wants to be part of the team, I'm not opposed to giving her a chance."

"Maybe like an internship?"

"Sure. That sounds good." Donna sipped her coffee. "Did Claudette ever have any sanctuary cases?"

"No. It doesn't happen all that often. Maybe one every few years. Sometimes once a decade."

"Do we need to notify anyone about it?"

"Like Artemis?" Charlie answered. "Completely up to your discretion."

"Okay, I'll mull that over. Anything else on my schedule I should know about?"

"Not yet."

"Good. I have some personal business to take care of. Like calling my daughter. And talking to my contact at the FBI."

"Oh?"

Donna went to her desk and sat, putting her coffee down. "In the interest of keeping you in the loop, you should know that last night my supposedly dead husband appeared on the surveillance cameras Temo installed for me. Pretty sure he was trying to get into the house. Of course, I'd already changed the locks and the alarm codes, so he was out of luck."

Charlie's mouth dropped open. "He doesn't sound very dead to me."

"Not even slightly dead. Sadly." Which freakin' meant she was still married to him. Crap.

"You're sure it was him? Never mind. Of course you're sure. But that's just…crazy."

"Yeah," Donna said. "It really is."

"What are you going to do?"

169

Donna took a sip of her coffee. "Nothing until I talk to Rico. He's my FBI contact. He was on a stakeout last night, so we couldn't really talk, but I sent him the videos so he'd know what's going on. I'm sure he'll have a plan." She hoped. "Whatever happens, regardless of my feelings, I want Joe to end up in custody." Dead was okay too. She wasn't going to quibble.

"No kidding." Charlie shook her head. "What are you going to do about the fact that you're still legally married?"

Donna rubbed her left temple as the reality of those terrible words set in. "I don't know. That just hit me a second ago."

Pierce appeared in the doorway, laptop in hand. Rixaline hung behind him in the hall. "We want your opinion on this dress, but I overheard what you're talking about, and I know what you should do."

"About me still being married?" Donna said. "What?"

He nodded. "File for divorce. Immediately."

# CHAPTER 16

Pierce seemed to think for a moment. "You should contact your insurance company too. You do not want to get wrapped up in a fraud dispute. If they find out he's alive before you tell them, and that check is on its way..." He made a face. "Call them and tell them you have reason to believe he's faked his death. Trust me, you want to be on the good end of this."

Donna pressed a hand to her forehead. "That's for sure. I have enough going on." She picked up her cup, in desperate need of more coffee. "Can you handle the divorce? I know it's not your area of legal expertise."

"I'll do as much as I can. At this stage, we really just need to get the paperwork ready so that the moment he's officially not dead, you can file and get things underway." He paused like another thought had just come to him. "Any chance you can prove adultery?"

"I can, actually. I have a file of stuff. Receipts, mostly, that I found in his pants pockets when I was doing laundry or getting dry cleaning ready."

"For what kinds of things?"

"Motels I never stayed at, meals I never ate, gifts I never received. All the usual. Is that enough?"

"Would be better if you had photos or could get the woman, or women, involved to testify, but I think I can work with that. Regardless, let me look at them and see."

She sighed. "They're at the old house. You still have the key I gave you?"

"And the alarm code. We'll get them. Temo and I can go by after we take care of our business at the coffee shop. You'll just have to tell me where they are."

She nodded. "Okay." Then she smiled, ready for a distraction. "Show me and Charlie the dress in question."

He turned the laptop around and brought it closer. The dress was burgundy with a tiny flower print and flouncy skater skirt. It wasn't anything Donna would have guessed that Rixaline would choose.

"I like it," Donna said. "I think it's super cute." It was also very feminine, and she wondered if that's what the girl liked about it.

Charlie nodded. "That would be great with boots and a little leather jacket. I love that whole edgy-but-girly vibe."

"Me too," Donna agreed. She looked up at Rixaline. "Maybe edgy-but-girly is your thing, huh?"

"Maybe." Rixaline smiled a little. "Mr. Pierce ordered me some boots, but…"

Donna looked at Pierce and gave him a little nod. "Get a leather jacket too."

"On it," he said. "And I'll dig into the divorce stuff." He turned the laptop around. "C'mon, Rixaline, we have more shopping to do before I have to leave."

As they went back to the living room, Donna's phone chirped. She pulled it from her pocket and checked the screen. Instantly, she answered the incoming call. "Hi, Rico."

"Hey, sorry we couldn't talk last night, but wow, how are you doing?"

"You mean now that I know Joe's alive?" She laughed. "Surprisingly well. Sure, I'm having a lot of fantasies that, if acted upon, would land me in jail, but otherwise, I'm just peachy."

"You know, we suspected him of this, but the dental records matched." He blew out a breath. "He is not getting away with it."

"Good. And I guess this is a great reminder of why you should never underestimate the mob."

"You got that right. Listen, do you have any idea where he might be holed up? I'm thinking it can't be too far away."

"Not a clue, but if anyone knows, it's his shady sister."

"We're thinking that too. We've been keeping a close eye on Lucinda, but so far, she hasn't done anything outside of her normal routine."

"Which is what?"

"Basically, coffee with the rest of the wives, the nail salon, the grocery store, and the bakery."

"When did coffee with the rest of the wives start?"

"A couple days after Joe's funeral."

Donna snorted. "Didn't take long for her to find a way to make sure they all reported in to her. She's so afraid of losing control. What about Big Tony?"

"He's not leaving the house much. He's had some visits, though. Some interesting faces, but nothing we can act on. Yet. Which reminds me, those ledgers you gave me are getting more interesting the longer we work on them. My boss wants things airtight, so we're still deciphering them and building up the streams of evidence, but there's a lot there. *A lot.*"

"You said before that the ledgers don't include any names."

"The more we dig, the more that's changing. And since Joe was meticulous about recording everything the crew did, we'll have a ton of stuff to seek indictments for. When we start putting this gang away, they're going for a long time."

She let out a happy sigh. "I'm so glad to hear you say that. What about Joe? What will happen to him?"

"We have to find him and get him in custody first, but if we can do that…the truth is, I don't know. He was smart enough to write those ledgers in such a way that they don't actually incriminate him. Not in any kind of major way. So far, he's made himself look like an errand boy."

"He was a lot more than that."

"I know, I know. We just don't have him on anything concrete."

"Then we need to get him on something concrete."

"I'm not arguing with that at all. We just have to figure out what that is." Rico hesitated. "What do you think he wanted from your house? The money? Or the gun?"

"I'm sure he wanted to get in that stash room. So maybe the gun? Do you have anything off that yet?"

"Not yet, but I should have the report by the end of the day, tomorrow morning at the latest." Rico took a breath. "Do you think Joe knew you weren't home?"

"The only way he would have known whether or not I was home was if he was watching the place. Which I suppose is possible. In fact, I saw a Chevy Tahoe there that could have been him. But if he'd been watching, wouldn't he have known about the new cameras?"

"Only if he was watching when they were installed. And he didn't act like he knew about the cameras."

"He didn't. I'm guessing he thought I was in the house and just figured he'd be quiet enough not to wake me. After all, his office is on the first floor, and our—*my* bedroom is upstairs. Plus, I've been known to fall asleep with the television on."

"Or..." Rico started, his tone darker, "he had other plans for you."

Donna's blood chilled. "You think he was going to kill me?"

Charlie whipped around in her chair, eyes wide with concern.

"We don't know," Rico said. "But we're not leaving out any possibility."

"He can't hurt me." Donna waved at Charlie. This was nothing for her to be concerned about. "He doesn't even know where I am. Or what I've become."

"All true." But there was something else in Rico's voice.

"What?" Donna asked.

"We think the only way to draw him out is for you to be at the house."

"No. I'm not moving back there. I'm the governor now. I have responsibilities."

"I realize that," Rico said. "But I'm not asking you to make it permanent. Just for a few nights, until he tries again."

"He'll try again tonight. This time, he'll come with the proper tools to break in. You don't need me."

"Is he still on the deed?"

"I guess. But isn't that a technicality?"

"You can't be arrested for breaking into your own home. But if you were there, and you got him talking, you might be able to get him to say something we could use."

"Or even better, maybe he'll attempt to kill me?" Donna laughed, but the sound was humorless and bitter. "You realize that the way I feel about him right now, if he came after me, I'd probably tear his throat out." She knew she shouldn't say things like that over the phone, but her irritation at Joe's reappearance in her life was back.

"I understand. Just think about it, okay? We'd wire the house and have agents in place ready to go. I'd be there with you too. All you'd have to do is get him to admit a few things out loud, and you'd be done. Then he'd be done. For good."

"I'll mull it over."

"We want to do it tonight."

"I have group tonight."

"That's fine. He didn't come by until after 1:00 a.m. last night. We're pretty sure he'll stick to that schedule."

She closed her eyes and ground her teeth together while she reached for her crucifix and prayed for strength. And patience. "I promise I'll think it over. I'm barely awake. Give me a few hours."

"Okay. We need time on our side to get things set up too."

"I understand. I'll be in touch."

"Thanks."

She hung up and tossed the phone onto her desk.

"You okay, ma'am?"

Donna picked up her coffee, but she could tell by the cream congealing on the surface that it had gone cold. "The FBI wants me to help with a sting to catch Joe. They want me to stay at the house tonight so that when he shows up again, I'll be there to talk to him and get him to confess enough stuff that they can put him away for a long time."

"Seems...reasonable. It's a solid plan, right?"

"It is." Donna couldn't argue with that.

"And getting your husband dealt with would be a good thing."

"It would be." She couldn't argue about that either.

"But you really don't want to deal with him, do you?"

She looked at Charlie. "Not in the slightest. I'm so tired of dealing with that whole corrupt family, and now to find out that Joe's still alive? How much more could he lie to me about?"

Charlie's look held all kinds of sympathy.

Donna growled softly. "Everything he does complicates my life. Alive, dead, or otherwise. Now I have to deal with the insurance and getting a divorce. If not for my kids, I'd wish I'd never married him at all."

"You know we'll help you with whatever we can. But this with the FBI seems like something you should do."

"I know." She took a deep, cleansing breath. Then she flicked her eyes up at Charlie. "So you're my admin and my conscience now?"

"I didn't mean—"

Donna's gentle laugh interrupted her. "No, you're right. I didn't mean that to sound harsh. I know I need to do this. Not wanting to because Joe gives me murderous thoughts isn't really reason enough not to. If anything, it's probably another check in the For column rather than Against."

Charlie smiled. "It still wasn't my place."

"Listen, don't think that way. We all need a little kick in the keister sometimes, right? I'm a big girl. I can take it."

"If it makes you feel any better, you have that party at Francine's tomorrow night."

"Ugh. I keep forgetting that's tomorrow. I feel so scattered. I still haven't gotten an invite."

"You did, actually. It came to the governor's email. I left you a note about checking it."

"Oh." She looked at the laptop on her desk. Charlie's note was right beside it. "I suppose I should turn this on and do that, hmm?"

"I have access to the governor's email as well, so I check it constantly, but I guess I should have reminded you. If you don't want me to have access, feel free to change the password. Claudette always liked me to keep on top of it."

Donna pushed the power button. "No, I'm with Claudette on this one. You stay on top of it. I'm perfectly happy with that."

"Very good. There are a few emails you should probably read. Some upcoming events, a couple petitions for help, things like that. Nothing too pressing."

As the laptop came to life, Donna pondered Francine's party. "Do you remember what the invite said about attire?"

"Dress to impress," Charlie answered.

"My wardrobe's a little weak on formal wear. I suppose I could wear that black dress I wore to dinner with Pierce."

Charlie grinned. "I have some things being sent over from Neiman's. I hope that's okay. We keep an account there. I checked your closet yesterday for your sizes."

Donna wanted to kiss her. "Thank you!"

Charlie's grin widened. "Dresses, shoes, and evening bags."

"Fantastic. I need to remind Pierce to get his tux in order. I'm pretty sure he has a tux."

"He does. It's being pressed. Should be back this afternoon."

The computer screen lit up with a picture of a deep-green forest. "You really make this job a piece of cake, you know that?" Donna chuckled. "Too bad taking care of Joe isn't as easy."

# CHAPTER 17

Before Charlie could respond, Pierce stuck his head in. "Temo and I are headed out. He wants you to know that there are two new security people joining the team today, but they're not really that new. One has been used before for special events, and one is Temo's cousin, who he personally vouches for. Obviously."

Donna nodded, about to tap the touchpad of the laptop. "Those both sound good. Tell him I said thanks. Where's Rixaline?"

"She's in the living room playing with Lucky." He smiled. "They both seem pretty happy too. Where are those receipts I need at the house?"

Donna's fingers paused over the keyboard. "They're in a manila envelope stuffed between the mattress and the box spring in my bedroom. My side of the bed."

He nodded. "We'll get them and bring them back. Anything else?"

"Yes. Take a walk around the house and check that Joe hasn't tried to get in again through a window. The three doors are the only spots that have cameras on them. I know the alarm's on, but still. Will you look?"

"Absolutely."

He left, and she went back to the laptop, but couldn't get further than the log-on screen. She looked at Charlie. "It wants a password."

"Governor." Charlie rolled her eyes. "I know, too easy. But there's not much chance of that laptop falling into the wrong hands. Although…" She pursed her lips but said nothing more.

"You're thinking about our guest?"

She smiled apologetically. "I'm not saying she would do anything. But it's my job to think about things like that."

"It's okay." Donna understood. Rixaline was still very much an unknown, despite Temo's confirmation that the king had put a price on her head. "I can change the password. But now that I'm logged on, I'm actually thinking I might deal with this later. My lack of sleep is catching up with me, and I still need to call my daughter."

Charlie scribbled a note on the scratch pad beside her computer. "I didn't expect you up this early anyway. Would you like me to RSVP to the party for you?"

"Yes, thank you." Donna stood. "I'm going to make that call, then get a few more hours of rest. Unless there's something pressing you need me to deal with?"

"Everything's good. Take all the time you want. Except..."

"Yes?"

"Do you need to give the FBI an answer about tonight?"

Donna tipped her head back and sighed. "Yes. Ugh." Then she smiled at Charlie. "But thanks for the reminder. I'll take care of that too."

"Are you doing it, then? The sting?"

"I pretty much have to, don't I?" She rubbed the back of her neck. "I know it's the right thing. Even if it's not the thing I want to do."

"I can call him for you, if that helps." Charlie picked up a pen like she was ready to take down his number.

"Thanks, but I'll text him and tell him I'm in, but then I'm going to give him the governor's contact information so he can send all the important stuff there. And I'll let him know you're available if he needs to talk to someone. Is that cool?"

"Perfect. Sleep well."

"Thanks." Donna started out. "Oh, don't forget. Rixaline needs underwear."

"Right." Charlie nodded. "I'll do that now while I'm thinking about it. Budget limit?"

"Not really. Whatever she needs. Socks, bras, tights, underwear, you know. Enough to get her through two weeks without doing laundry."

"Okay."

Donna stood there for a moment longer. "She probably needs toiletries too. Plus a toothbrush, hairbrush, that kind of stuff. Will you see to all that?"

"I will take care of it."

"Thanks, I'll tell her to come see you." With a smile, Donna headed for her room. She stopped to watch Rixaline sitting on the floor in the living room brushing Lucky. The fluffy beast looked like he was in a bliss coma. The only sign of life was the occasional air biscuit. "You have a new best friend, I see."

"I didn't know cats were so cool. He's such a handsome boy, aren't you, Lucky?"

Lucky couldn't be bothered to emerge from his cocoon of happiness to respond.

Donna smiled. "Charlie's ready to order the rest of the stuff you need. She's in the office. Think you can take a break for a minute?"

"Sure." Rixaline got up. "I'll go see her now."

"Anything else you need, you let her know, and she'll order it."

"Thank you."

"You're very welcome." Donna went into her room and shut the door. The little nervous tingles started up again at the thought of calling Christina, but it had to be done. And it would be so nice to hear her daughter's voice.

Funny that after all she'd been through, the thought of talking to her daughter was what made her nervous. But then, she'd never had to tell Christina something like this. Both she and Joe Jr. had figured out the truth about their father on their own, despite Donna trying to shield them from it.

She tapped the button to call Christina, then sat on the bed and kicked her feet up as she listened to it ring.

When Christina answered, a lot of other sounds filtered in. Cars in the distance, youthful voices, birds, wind, the bell of a bike, and the soft scuffing of her daughter's footsteps. Christina was clearly outside. "Hi, Mom! How are you?"

"I'm really good. How are you, honey?"

"Swamped with classwork, but what else is new?" She laughed.

Donna closed her eyes and let the sweet sound wash over her for a second. "You're always so busy."

"That's college. What's up with you?"

"You sound like you're walking somewhere. Can you talk?"

"Sure. I'm headed to the library. I don't have class for another hour and a half."

This wasn't exactly how Donna wanted to tell her daughter. "I have something pretty big I'd like to talk to you about. Maybe another time would be better?"

"Big? Like what? Did something happen between you and Aunt Lucinda? Ohhh, did you finally pop her in the mouth? What did she say? What did Uncle Tony do?"

"Nothing happened between us. Settle down. You sound almost gleeful about it." Donna nearly snorted. Leave it to Christina to think that was what was going on.

"Well, if you were ever going to pop anyone in the mouth, it would be Aunt Lucinda."

"No argument there."

"Ugh, that woman. I am so glad we're done with them."

"I know." Except they weren't. Not with Joe still alive. But Christina didn't need to know about that. Donna smiled. She couldn't love this child more if she tried. "But the Villachis are not what I need to talk to you about. Why don't you call me back when you get somewhere private?"

"Seriously, I'm good to talk. There's no one around other than someone walking by once in a while. The quad is pretty quiet."

Donna took a breath. "You may freak out a little."

"Okay, now you *have* to tell me, or I will freak out from not knowing. Mom. Come on. What is going on?"

"Well, there's been a big change in my life."

Christina suddenly squealed. "Are you dating someone?"

Donna pressed her fingers to the small space between her eyebrows. "No, sweetheart. I am not dating anyone. But good to know where you stand on that."

"Then what is it?"

Donna inhaled. "I've been turned into a vampire."

A moment of silence passed, then her daughter laughed. "My connection went funny. It totally sounded like you just said you've been turned into a vampire."

"No weird connection. That's what I said."

"I don't get it. What do you mean 'turned into a vampire'? Do you mean you're becoming a night owl? Is this some slang you picked up from Vinnie, because, Mom, he just makes that stuff up trying to sound cool."

"For one thing, I haven't seen any of Big Tony's lunks in a while. For another, it's not slang for anything. I have literally become a vampire. An actual sun-avoiding, blood-drinking, super-fast, really strong, immortal vampire."

The silence lasted longer this time. A lot longer.

Donna worried her bottom lip with her teeth. Christina had been a huge fan of the *Twilight* books. Was that what was going through her head right now?

Just to be safe, Donna added, "I do not sparkle. In case you're wondering."

The footsteps stopped. "That's not funny, Mom. None of this is funny."

"Sweetheart, I'm not trying to be funny. I'm trying to tell you about something that's just happened to me. The big change I've been going through. I didn't intend for this to happen. I didn't choose it. I was attacked by a rogue vampire, then another vampire saved my life, and the result is that now I'm one too."

When Christina spoke again, her voice was thin and a little wobbly with impending tears. "How is that possible, Mom? Vampires aren't real."

"I don't know, honey, but I promise you, they are.

I wouldn't have believed it either a couple weeks ago, but here I am, living proof that the supernatural exists around us. And they're doing really well, by the way."

"This is…real."

"Yes. A hundred percent."

"Are you still…living?"

"Absolutely, I am. But I'm also pretty much immortal."

"I'm not sure I can deal with this. This is, like, *a lot*."

"I know. And I wish I could have told you in person, but I didn't think something this major should wait."

"You're a hundred percent being for real?"

"I am…" Donna wanted to tell Christina more, but wasn't sure she could handle it.

"What? You sounded like you were going to say something else. Is there more?"

"Yes, but we don't have to go into all of that now."

"Tell me." Her tone changed, going very sharp and snappy. "Might as well. We've come this far. Are you also a werewolf?"

"Okay, you're clearly upset. We can talk again later."

"My mother just told me she's a vampire. How do you think I should be?"

"What about this news upsets you the most? Because I promise you, I am still very much your mom. And I still love you very much. None of that has changed. I know this is a lot to process. I understand that. But this isn't a stranger talking to you on the other end of the phone. It's your mother. Who just happens to be a vampire. I'm the same woman who changed your dirty diapers and bandaged your scraped knees and helped you move into your dorm room. None of which your father did, I might add."

A little sniff answered her.

Donna kept talking. "You need to come for a visit and see for yourself that, while I've changed a lot, I haven't really changed at all. You should also see the new penthouse. And meet my staff."

"I guess that would be—hang on. What penthouse? And why do you have staff?"

"Because the rest of what I was going to tell you is that I have also become the vampire governor of New Jersey. It's a long, complicated story that I'd rather tell you in person, but the upshot is I now live in the governor's penthouse, which is the top floor of the Wellman Towers on the river."

"Are you kidding me? The penthouse at the Wellman Towers. And you're the governor. Of the whole state."

"Yep. That's how it works. I have an admin, a driver, and an assistant. Lucky I moved in yesterday. Would you like to come up next weekend?"

"You're still really my mom?"

"I am. Which means I'm still going to embarrass you in public, ask you about your love life, and wonder out loud why you can get straight A's but not put your laundry in the hamper or put the cap back on the orange juice."

She laugh-snorted. "Yeah, you're still my mom. I'd be happy to come. I can't promise I won't still freak out a little about the vampire stuff until I get used to it. *If* I get used to it."

"I understand it might take some time. I can't wait to see you. Charlie, my admin, can take care of flights and all that. My driver can pick you up too."

"A driver and an admin. So fancy," Christina teased. "Really, though, it sounds pretty amazing. I can't wait to hear how it all happened. Are you happy?"

"I wasn't initially. But I am now. It was a process."

"I bet it was."

"Listen, this has to be a family secret. Same as it was with Dad's stuff. Okay?"

"Trust me. Not about to blast this on social media."

"Thank you. I love you, sweetheart."

"I love you, too, Mom."

"Now go study and keep up those grades."

"I will. Give Lucky a kiss for me."

"Will do. Bye now." Donna hung up and put her hand to her chest. Christina's reaction was pretty much what she'd expected from her daughter. A little panic, a little freak-out, then reserved acceptance. Donna would take it. Both her kids knew she was a vampire and were still talking to her. Better yet, they were coming to see her.

If that wasn't a win, she didn't know what a win was.

Her eyes were heavy, but she couldn't sleep yet. With her phone still in her hands, she started texting Rico.

*I'll help you tonight on two conditions. The sting starts after my group. And Joe better end up in handcuffs. Send the details to my email. Contact my admin if you need anything else. I have to sleep for a few hours.* Then she sent a second text with her email and Charlie's contact info.

With that, she pulled the drapes, put her phone on silent and her head on the pillow. Sleep came fast, and when she opened her eyes again, the light seeping through the curtains had gone weak and watery. It was definitely later in the day.

She wasn't sure how long she'd slept until she looked at her phone. Five hours. Wow. She'd made up for not sleeping last night, but then, with what lay ahead of her, that was probably a good thing.

Wouldn't do to pass out in the midst of Rico's sting.

Her screen had more than the time on it, though. Messages from Rico and her kids.

She looked at the one from Joe Jr. first. As soon as she opened it, she laughed. He'd sent a GIF of *Sesame Street*'s Count saying, "One!" and his message said, *ONE mother who's a vampire!*

That kid.

Christina's was simply, *Love you. Sorry for freaking out.*

191

Donna smiled. That was nice.

Rico's wasn't as long as she'd expected. *Sleep well. I'll send details as soon as they're finalized.*

Guess she'd better go see if Charlie had gotten that information yet. It wasn't quite three o'clock, but tonight was going to be busy since she'd have to go straight from group to her old house. Plus, she was hungry, and what she needed to get her through the rest of the afternoon and evening wasn't cake.

She checked herself in the bathroom mirror and ran a brush through her hair before heading out to the kitchen. The place seemed empty. No sign of Rixaline, Lucky, or Pierce. There was a covered rack of clothing in the living room, though. Next to it were several Neiman Marcus shopping bags. Those would be fun to look through.

She went into the kitchen, warmed up a glass of blood, then took it down to the office.

Charlie was at her desk. She glanced at Donna when she came in. "Feel better?"

"Much."

"Good. Rixaline's in her room watching a movie. Or possibly napping. I think Lucky's in there with her. Pierce and Temo are playing racquetball."

Donna smiled. "That's nice. I didn't even know there were courts. Did the information come from Agent Medina?"

"It did."

Donna sat at her desk and logged in to the laptop. "I'm going to read it, but anything that stood out?"

Charlie turned a little to see her better. "I've never read the breakdown on an FBI sting operation before, so to be honest, it all stood out. At least they're not going to wire you up. That seems smart considering how close you'll be to him and the chance that he might want to check."

"Just the house, right?" Rico had mentioned that. "I think that's safer too. I hope so, anyway."

"Me too. But he won't be able to hurt you. He's human, right?"

Donna took a moment to drink a few sips. Instantly, her energy picked up. "He is. But he shouldn't be underestimated either. He's a coldhearted criminal. He's spent his entire adult life working on how to get away with things and how to intimidate people into doing what he wanted. He can go from smiling to beatdown faster than you can blink."

Charlie cringed.

"I know. You're thinking why did I marry him, right? It's okay. Everyone does." Donna shrugged. "I honestly didn't know that side of him until it was too late. And leaving without a foolproof plan to keep my kids safe wasn't an option."

Charlie nodded. "You had to protect your kids."

"I did. So I stayed while I worked on a way to get us safely away from that monster." She made a noise of disgust. "And now he's back." She clicked on the email from Rico. "But not for long."

# CHAPTER 18

Donna read through what Rico had sent. "They're going to have two agents outside and two inside. Rico will be one of the two inside. It's going to be fine."

"What about having Temo and me there?" Charlie asked. "Just in case. We have skills the FBI can't hope to duplicate."

Donna smiled at her. "Thanks, but Rico's a werewolf, so he's pretty capable."

Charlie grinned. "Oh, is that right? Well, now. What does this Rico look like?"

Donna laughed. "What is it with everyone and the werewolves?"

With a little shrug, Charlie sighed. "They're just hot. From what I hear, anyway. Never had any personal experience with one. Although I'm open. Is Agent Medina single?"

Donna shook her head. "He is. Would you like to meet him?"

"Heck yes." Suddenly, Charlie stopped. "Wait, you two aren't…"

"Nope. He is very handsome. All around easy to look at. But we have a working relationship. For a while, he was going to be my ticket out of the Mafia. Then Joe died, and my level of involvement changed."

"What about now that Joe's not dead?"

"Well, I'm about to do this sting so that hopefully Joe becomes a nonproblem again. All I have to do is get him to talk about something incriminating, and the FBI will do the rest." She drained the rest of her glass in one long swallow.

"I hope it goes really well for you this evening."

"Thanks." Donna realized she'd left her coffee cup on the desk from this morning. "I'm going to take this mug and this glass back to the kitchen, then I'm going to have a look at those dresses. Care to weigh in with an opinion?"

Charlie nodded. "I bet Rixaline would too."

"Speaking of, did you get the rest of her stuff ordered?"

"We did. In a day or two, she's going to be the best-dressed half-fae, half-vampire teenager this side of the Hudson."

A few minutes later, all the deliveries from Neiman Marcus, including the bags of shoes and purses, had been moved into Donna's room. Rixaline, Lucky, and Charlie were waiting in the living room for her to try on the first dress.

Donna didn't expect much input from Lucky.

She started at the front of the rack with a simple, basic black dress with an off-the-shoulder sweetheart neckline. Not all that exciting on the hanger, but really lovely on the body with the way it hugged Donna's curves. This wasn't the dress for Francine's party, she knew that. It was too safe. And the party was in her honor.

A guest-of-honor dress should make more of a statement. And a much bigger entrance.

Regardless, she put on a pair of black stilettos and walked out to see what the girls thought.

They made all the appropriate noises of appreciation, but Donna wasn't convinced. "It's pretty, but it's not a wow. I need a wow."

"Agreed," Charlie said.

"Lucky and I say, 'Next!'" Rixaline had Lucky on her lap. He didn't seem nearly as interested in Donna's outfits as he did in the chin scratches he was getting.

"Back in a minute." Donna went to change. The next dress was blush pink and a little glittery. The shape was fine, but overall it wasn't her style or color. She tried it on anyway, because sometimes you just never knew.

Although, sometimes you did.

This wasn't her dress. She went out to show Charlie and Rixaline anyway, announcing, "Nope," as she walked into the living room.

Charlie's brows went skyward. "That is way too Disney princess."

Rixaline snorted and shook her head. "You look like Vampire Barbie."

Donna made a U-turn and went back to the

bedroom. She chose an emerald-green lace number next. It had a few crystals for some added sparkle, and the lining beneath the lace went into a deep vee at the neck. There was skin, but lace-covered skin.

Sexy, but classy, and the color was stunning.

She showed the girls that one next.

Rixaline clapped. "I love it."

Charlie nodded. "This is a contender."

Donna did a slow twirl. "I think so too. But there are a lot of dresses left on that rack."

"Yay!" Rixaline grinned. "I like fancy clothes."

"They can be fun," Donna said. "But I wouldn't want to wear them every day." She put her hands on her hips. "All right, this one is going in the maybe pile. Back with a new one shortly."

She continued through the rack. There was a beaded ivory number that, while stunning, seemed more wedding than black tie event. A scalloped-edged navy dress was pretty but felt too matronly.

Three more black gowns, one with subtle feather trim, a bold flowered one, and a shimmery purple made it into the maybe pile. There were a few she didn't try on because they just seemed wrong. She picked shoes and purses to go with the maybes, then decided to wait until Pierce and Temo returned so she could get a male perspective on the looks as well.

She didn't have long to wait. Pierce came back while she was making herself a cup of coffee and chatting with Rixaline and Charlie in the kitchen about the merits of each possible option.

He was sweaty and smiling. "What's all this?"

"Trying to pick out a dress for Francine's party tomorrow. I was hoping to have you and Temo weigh in with the male point of view." She wiggled her finger at him. "After you're showered, though. Did you have fun?"

He nodded. "Temo's a good player. And there was no one else on the courts. We had the whole place to ourselves." He grabbed a Gatorade out of the fridge. "I'll go shower, and then you can show me the dresses."

Charlie got her phone out. "And now that I know Temo's back, I'll tell him to come up when he's showered too."

About twenty minutes later, the fashion show entered round two. She tried on all the dresses, listened to all the comments, and narrowed it down to three. Then she changed back into her regular clothes and rejoined the others.

"So?" Rixaline asked. "Which one are you going to wear?"

"I'm still not sure. I'm going to wait until tomorrow night and see what kind of mood I'm in." She took a seat on the big sectional with the four of them and looked at Pierce. "Did you get the receipts?"

"I did. And it's all I need to prove adultery, which means you don't have to go through the separation period. I've already pulled the necessary forms and will have them ready to go in a day or two. You'll be ready to file that soon."

"And how long before I'm officially divorced?"

He pulled an unhappy face. "Six to eight weeks."

She exhaled. "I thought you were going to say months. That's fine. With him behind bars, it won't matter."

Temo leaned forward. "You sure that's where he's going to end up, boss?"

"He has to," Donna said. "It's the only way I can move forward. Which means I absolutely have to get him to incriminate himself."

Charlie nodded. "I'm sure you'll pull it off. But how do you know he's going to show up?"

Donna tucked her bare feet under her. "I don't. That's what makes this whole thing a crapshoot."

Pierce's eyes narrowed a little. "And if he doesn't show up tonight, how many more nights is Rico going to expect you to hang out there?"

"Good question." She thought about that. She wanted that life behind her. And Joe in jail. "I'm going to call him. I need to know what the big picture looks like." She pulled her phone out but hesitated before she got up to go into the bedroom. "What are you guys going to do while I'm at the sting?"

Temo and Pierce gave her odd looks. Temo spoke first. "Aren't I driving you?"

"Only if you drop me off," Donna said. "Which I guess you could. I can't have a strange car there."

He didn't seem to like that answer. "I can do that. If that's what you want."

"Don't you think I could be there?" Pierce asked. "I could hang out upstairs. I hate the idea of leaving you alone."

She laughed softly. "Thank you, but I won't be alone. Rico and three other agents will be there. He said for me to come alone so nothing throws Joe off. He's got to think I'm in the house by myself so that it's safe for him to come in."

Pierce crossed his arms. "I don't like that. I know you can take care of yourself and that Rico has his own wolfy skill set, but it doesn't sit well."

"I know. And I appreciate that. But this isn't my deal, and these aren't my rules. I'm just a bit player."

"I'd say you're more than that," Charlie chimed in. "Without you, all they get is Joe breaking into his own house. Not the kind of crime that'll put him away."

Rixaline sat quietly, obviously listening but saying nothing.

"Well," Donna said, "he did fake his death. But then again, how much is that worth? I know. I'm an important part of this scheme. But, guys, we're talking FBI here. I might have some pull as the vampire governor of New Jersey, but that means squat to them. They don't even know I'm a vampire. Except for Rico. It's going to be fine. I promise."

Three skeptical faces and Rixaline's slightly confused one looked back at her. It was pretty sweet how they all cared.

Then Rixaline leaned forward, her hand out. "Please, take this with you."

On her palm lay a well-polished wooden heart slightly larger than a nickel. Donna picked it up.

Rixaline smiled. "It's the only thing I have left of

my mother's, and it's kept me safe. I know you're going to be in danger. I want you to take it."

Donna shook her head, touched by Rixaline's kindness. "I can't take this. It's too important to you."

"You can take it," Rixaline said. "And then you can give it back to me when you return."

Donna understood what a big gesture this was for a girl who had so little. She didn't want to diminish the offering by refusing it a second time. She closed her hand around the heart. "Thank you. This is very kind of you."

Rixaline sat back, giving Donna a happy little nod.

Donna smiled at the group. "So what are you guys going to do?"

"Pizza and movies?" Rixaline said hopefully. "I kind of fell asleep during the last one."

"Up to Mr. Temo, Ms. Charlie, and Mr. Pierce," Donna said. She got up. "I'm going to call Rico. Then I should feed. You, too, Rixaline."

Pierce caught her eye. "With you going into that potentially dangerous situation, you'd better do more than just drink a glass."

She nodded. He wanted her to feed directly. She did too. With the possibility of seeing Joe on the horizon, she needed to be at her strongest and sharpest. "I will. Right before I leave for group."

"Okay," he answered.

Temo's brows lifted. "Am I driving you into the city?"

Donna wasn't going to come between him and a chance to see Neo. "Yes, please."

He smiled. "You got it, boss."

Charlie pushed to her feet. "I'll warm up a bag for you and Rixaline to share."

"Thanks." Donna went into her bedroom and called Rico.

He answered right away. "Hello, Sleeping Beauty."

She smirked. "Hi. I got your email, but I have some questions."

"Shoot. I'm already here at the house setting up."

"You are? How did you get in? What about the alarm? And my security cameras?"

"We…took care of all that. We are the FBI. Plus, we have a warrant."

"Well, then, that makes it all okay." She sighed. He was in her house. Her old house. It was an odd feeling, but she didn't have time to sort that out. It needed to be done. And she didn't live there anymore, so what did it matter? "Getting the recording stuff in place?"

"Yes. I'm sorry this upset you, but you know it's our best shot at catching Joe."

"I know, and it's fine. Where are you putting it all?" She turned Rixaline's little wooden heart in her fingers. It was smooth and warm. Comforting.

"We're not going to tell you. We don't want you to be self-conscious about it. But trust me that there will be plenty of it to catch whatever goes on. Although we're limiting it to Joe's office, the living room, the kitchen, and the master bedroom. If you can, try to keep Joe to those spaces."

"Will do. Where are you going to be? I at least need to know that."

"I'll be in the pantry. It's a good spot for quick access to the living room, office, and kitchen. The other benefit is that, with careful listening, you'll be able to hear me. That way, if I need to communicate with you, I can."

Of course. Her vampire hearing would allow her to pick up his voice even through walls. "Okay, I like that."

"And if you head upstairs for any reason, I'll follow. Agent Kowalski will be in Christina's room. Her walk-in closet and bathroom give him more hiding spaces if necessary. And there will be two agents outside as well."

"That all sounds good, but what about the elephant in the room here? What if Joe doesn't show up?"

"We've taken some steps to ensure he shows."

"You've taken steps? Like what?" She genuinely couldn't imagine what they'd done to get Joe there. Especially when they'd only just found out he was alive.

"We have ways of leaking information on purpose. And we've let it be known that the FBI is obtaining a warrant and plans to do a raid on your house tomorrow night. Granted, we don't know how connected Joe is at this point, but we're banking on him still being in touch with his sister, and we made sure Lucinda got the word."

How about that. "All right, that could work. But if it doesn't?"

"Then we try this again until it does."

She hadn't signed up for that. And she didn't want to. She had a life to live. And a state to govern. "I can't tomorrow night. Big party in my honor. Already committed."

"Donna—"

"Nope. Don't waste your breath. I'm not canceling. This has to be wrapped up very soon. Christina is coming to visit next weekend."

A few seconds of silence filled the airway before he spoke again. "Did you tell your kids?"

"That their father is still alive? Or that I'm a vampire?"

"About Joe. But also the second one."

"No and yes. I don't want to tell them about Joe until he's locked up and no longer a problem. They don't need to worry about him for a second longer than necessary."

"Understandable. How'd they take the other bit of news?"

"Joe Jr. was as cool about it as I suspected he'd be. Christina had a little freak-out, but she's going to be fine. It's a big adjustment to find out that not only are the things that go bump in the night real, but your mother is now one of them."

He laughed. "Yeah, I suppose that's true. Hopefully, it goes well when they visit."

"It will. Christina will be overcome by all this luxury. She's not a shallow child, but she does like nice things. Joe Jr. just wants to know that I'm okay, and if I'm happy, he's happy."

"They're good kids."

"Yes, they are. The best. They deserve a life free from looking over their shoulder."

"We're going to make that happen. Hopefully tonight."

"Rico…" She felt she had to tell him the truth burning in her heart.

"Yes?"

"If things don't go the way we all hope they do this evening, you have to know I'm not going to let him terrorize me or my kids. And to be honest, I don't trust him just to disappear into the ether. He's not the kind of guy who can do that, which he's proved by showing up again. Power is his drug, and I can guarantee you he's in desperate need of a fix."

Rico's sigh held a weight she could feel. "This conversation can't go any further. But I understand."

"Good. I'll see you tonight."

# CHAPTER 19

Temo let Donna out in front of the New Manhattan Health and Wellness Center a little before ten. She went straight in and up to suite C on the twelfth floor. She rode the elevator alone, which made her wonder who would be here this evening.

Dr. Goldberg, obviously. She was the facilitator and the therapist who ran the group. She was also Donna's personal therapist, although meeting with her one-on-one wasn't going to be possible anymore now that Donna couldn't be seen out during daylight hours.

Surely La would understand. Donna was going to mention that before she left.

Bunni was away, and Francine might be too busy with her party planning. Neo would probably show. If she wasn't already downstairs talking to Temo.

There were two other members Donna had yet to meet. LaToya and Meghan. Maybe she'd meet them tonight. She was a little nervous about Meghan. Claudette was her sire, too, which according to Francine made Donna and Meghan blood sisters.

Which was all well and good, but how was

Meghan going to react to Donna's part in Claudette's losing the governorship?

Donna walked into suite C to find Francine, Neo, and Dr. Goldberg already there.

Francine gave her a big smile. "Hi there, Madam Governor. I got your RSVP today."

Donna smiled back. "It's so kind of you to throw a party for me."

"I'm looking forward to it. And to introducing you to Lionel, my sire. I'm so glad you're bringing Pierce. I can't wait to see him in a tux."

Donna laughed. "Me either, really."

The door opened behind her, and two women walked in. One was gorgeous and curvy, with Diana Ross hair, and the other was a tall, willowy redhead whom Donna instantly recognized.

Her jaw fell open. "You're Meghan Murphy."

The woman tipped her head. "I am. And you must be Belladonna Barrone."

"That's me." Donna had never imagined that the Meghan Claudette had sired was *the* Meghan Murphy. The same woman who had just graced the cover of *Sports Illustrated*'s first swimsuit edition shot entirely at night. Meghan was a supermodel famous for her pale, translucent skin, but most recently she'd caused a stir by announcing she'd work only at night in order to preserve her pristine Irish skin.

Now Donna knew the real reason. Working in the sun would turn her to ash.

Donna swallowed down her surprise and smiled at the second woman. "You must be LaToya."

The woman nodded. "That's me, baby. How you doing?"

"I'm doing good, thanks."

LaToya grinned. "Word has it you're the one who took Claudette's place. I heard about you, baby."

"I hope only good things." Donna glanced at Meghan. "Taking over for Claudette wasn't intentional, I assure you."

Meghan smiled, which only made her more beautiful. Donna thought it was entirely possible that being turned into a vampire hadn't changed a thing about her. How did you make perfect more perfect? Weren't models already some kind of supernatural? "You have nothing to worry about from me. Claudette was rather underwhelming as a sire. Congratulations on your new position as governor. I hope you do well."

"Thank you." Donna's shoulders suddenly relaxed, and she realized how much she'd tensed up when she'd realized Meghan was one of Claudette's children too. It was good to know Meghan's experience with Claudette hadn't been much different than Donna's.

Dr. Goldberg clapped her hands. "Ladies, if we could all sit and get started?"

They took their seats in the small grouping of chairs.

Dr. Goldberg smiled at them. "Welcome to the First Fangs Club. LaToya and Meghan, nice to have you back this week. Why don't you introduce yourselves, and then Donna can do the same?"

LaToya started. "I'm LaToya Shay Jones. I was turned four months ago. I'm a stay-at-home mom to a six-month-old, and I do medical transcription." Her smile turned sly. "And my boyfriend is a werewolf."

"Show-off," Neo said with a laugh.

"You know that's right, baby." LaToya winked at Neo.

Meghan followed. "I'm Meghan Murphy. I was turned two months ago. Being a vampire has made working as a model tricky. I'm studying photography in the hopes of finding a new way to support myself." She twisted her hands together. "A lot of people think I'm just being a diva by refusing to work during the day."

Donna felt for her. That had to be hard. "Couldn't you say you've developed some kind of allergic reaction to the sun? Maybe get a doctor friend to back you up?" She looked around the group. "That has to be a thing, right?"

"Severe sun allergies are a thing," Dr. Goldberg answered. She gestured with her pen. "That's not a bad idea, Meghan. What do you think?"

Neo nodded. "It might make people sympathetic."

Francine sat up a little straighter, which caused her feet to no longer touch the floor. "You could start a foundation and throw a benefit. You could be the face of severe sun allergies. You wouldn't be considered a diva that way."

Meghan blinked a few times like she was taking it all in. "Do you really think I could do that? I don't know what doctor I'd talk to. I know my own wouldn't do it. He's not the flexible type."

Dr. Goldberg scribbled something down. "Here, I have someone for you." She handed the paper over.

Meghan accepted it but looked at Donna. "Thanks."

Donna shrugged. "That's what blood sisters do, right?"

She nodded. "I guess so." She tucked the paper into her Valentino bag. "I'll let you know how it goes."

Neo laughed. "Like we won't read about it on TMZ first."

"Donna," Dr. Goldberg said, "why don't you introduce yourself for LaToya and Meghan's sake?"

"Sure," Donna said. "I'm Belladonna Barrone, but you can call me Donna. I was turned about two weeks ago. Due to some very interesting circumstances, I am also the new vampire governor of New Jersey."

"Which we're celebrating at my house tomorrow," Francine added, eyes sparkling with excitement.

"Baby," LaToya started, "are you really that mobster's widow?"

Donna took a breath. "I am that Belladonna Barrone, yes."

LaToya tsked. "You poor thing. I'm glad that all worked out for you and you were able to get rid of that man."

"Thanks." Donna's gaze narrowed. "Most people assume I was involved in the family business. Why didn't you?"

She got a funny look on her face. "Baby, those wolves don't keep secrets from each other. And Isaiah talks in his sleep."

"You mean…"

"Uh-huh. Your boy Rico is in the same pack with my man. Don't worry, he's not telling tales. But he's said a few things, and everyone knows he's FBI." She shrugged. "How come you're not hitting that?"

Donna swallowed to hide her shock at the question. "We have a strictly working relationship. Anything else would be awkward."

"Yeah, I guess so. Too bad." LaToya laughed.

With a sigh, Dr. Goldberg raised her hand. "Ladies, I feel like I have to say this at every meeting, but we should refrain from questions that are overly personal. Thankfully, as you all know but I will remind you anyway, what is discussed in group stays in group."

Meghan crossed her long, slender legs. "Yes, agreed."

"Why don't we discuss our highs and lows for the week?" Dr. Goldberg looked at Francine. "Would you like to start?"

"No lows," Francine said. "Lots of highs. I love planning parties."

"Neo?" Dr. Goldberg asked.

"No lows either." She grinned. "Got to help Donna with a little project. And met a fine new man."

Donna laughed. "He likes you too. I'm pretty sure of it."

Neo's grin got bigger.

Dr. Goldberg looked at Donna. "How was your week?"

"Crazy. As you can imagine. Just getting settled in as governor, which has been mostly a high. Finally told my kids I'd been turned, and they took it well, so also a high. No real low, I guess."

Neo snorted. "Really?" Then she put a hand to her head. "Sorry, never mind what I said. You probably don't want to share that."

Donna knew she was talking about Joe. "I suppose it would be okay. It'll be news soon enough. And like Dr. Goldberg said, everything discussed here stays here." She took a breath. "I found out last night that my dead husband isn't so dead. He faked his death."

The group, minus Neo, let out a collective gasp that was instantly followed by questions and condolences and expressions of outrage on her behalf.

Donna was glad she'd shared. These were definitely her people. "It's okay. I mean, it's not okay. But it's being dealt with. Trust me. I can't say more than that. But I appreciate the concern." She looked at the time. "Speaking of Joe, I really need to get going. I'm sorry to leave early, but I don't have a choice."

"Baby, you do what you gotta do. We'll all see you at Francine's."

Donna grinned. "That's wonderful. I'm happy about that. It was lovely to meet you and Meghan."

"You too," Meghan said.

Donna stood. "See you all tomorrow, then!"

Neo gave her a nod. "Tell Temo I said hey."

"Will do," Donna answered with a smile. Young love was so cute. Then she remembered she had one more thing to do. "Dr. Goldberg, I think it goes without saying I won't be able to make our Tuesday sessions anymore."

She nodded. "Of course. If you ever need me, I'm just a phone call away."

"I appreciate that." With a little wave, she left. She texted Temo that she was on her way down.

A few minutes after she stepped out onto the sidewalk, he pulled up. She didn't wait for him to get out and open the door, just hopped into the front seat next to him.

"Boss. You're supposed to be in the back."

"Yeah, I know, but this way we can talk better."

He laughed. "You are not Claudette, that's for sure."

"No, I'm not. And by the way, Neo says hi."

His grin went from ear to ear. "Back to the penthouse? Or straight to your house?"

"The penthouse." She'd dressed up for group. "This outfit is far too nice for Joe."

A little over an hour later, Temo dropped Donna off at her old house. He wanted to stay, but she told him just to go back to the penthouse and wait. Everything had to go off without a hitch this evening. With a promise to call him when she was ready to be picked up, she said goodbye.

When the car disappeared around the turn, she

went up the drive and into the house through the front door, leaving the alarm off.

She stood in the foyer for a moment. The house seemed like a foreign place. After the sleek, modern sophistication and expansive views of the penthouse, this McMansion had become a dreary, Tuscan-inspired cave filled with memories better forgotten. Sure, there had been some good times here. Mostly those moments that involved pivotal points in her children's lives, but that didn't change how grateful she was for the recent supernatural twists and turns that had taken her away from here. Away from this life.

Funny that when it had first happened, becoming a vampire had seemed like the end of her freedom. Now it felt like the opening of a door onto an amazing world she'd never imagined existed. A world that offered her a chance to do some good. To balance out some of the terrible things the Villachis did.

She closed the door behind her. "Hello?"

Rico answered, "In the kitchen."

She headed that way. The lights were off. She could see him well enough, but instinct made her start to turn them on. She hesitated, her hand on the switch. "Lights?"

"Sure," he said. "Just act normal."

She flipped the switch. He was leaning against the island, looking very good. He had a couple of days' worth of stubble covering his jaw. She liked it. And for a moment, she wondered what he looked like in his wolf form. Would she ever see him that way? She couldn't imagine why, but then, stranger things had happened. Enough fantasizing. She was here for a very different purpose. "How are you?"

"Good. Are you ready for this?"

"I guess so. I know you need me to get him talking, right? Get him to incriminate himself?"

Rico nodded. "We need something actionable. Like where a body's buried, a bank account we don't know about, something like that. But if you can get him to confess to a crime, that's even better."

"I'll do what I can." Talking to Joe had never gone that well historically. She turned away from Rico to put her hands on the counter. She took a big breath. Her nerves were kicking in.

"You sure you're okay?"

"I'm about to see Joe after thinking he's been dead all this time. The same man I've lived in fear of for decades. The man I really and truly want nothing to do with. I don't know if I'm okay or not."

# CHAPTER 20

"Understandable," Rico said. "What are you feeling most? Afraid?"

She looked over her shoulder at him. "Mad. Murderous. Stabby. I just really want to hurt him, basically."

"Also understandable. You know you can't...*do* what you're capable of doing." He wasn't going to mention she was a vampire. Not with the FBI listening in. "This whole place is wired. Everything you do is being recorded and videoed."

She nodded as she faced him again. "I know. But you can't expect me to be the old Donna either. I'm not going to be the good little wife here. I'm not going to welcome him back with open arms and a plate of pasta. Those days are over."

"We don't expect that. I'm sure he doesn't either."

She snorted. "You'd be surprised what he might expect. After all, I played that role for nearly twenty-seven years. Why wouldn't he expect me to fall back into it upon his return?"

"Well, we don't think he intends to interact with

you at all. Just break in, get what he wants, and get out. Your interaction is all our doing. In the hopes of incriminating him, obviously."

"I get that. But I'm telling you, once he's aware that I know he's alive, he's going to think he can tell me what to do again. And that's not going to happen."

Rico's smirk said it all. "I'm here for that, trust me. You've put up with enough. Just…play the game as best you can so that we get what we need, all right? Then you're done with him. I promise."

She nodded. "I'll play along. But only because I want him locked up more than you do."

He laughed softly. "We're banking on that."

She pointed up. "Kowalski's in Christina's room?"

"He is. Cheng and Franklin are outside."

"Okay, everyone's in place. What now?"

"Sit and wait. We don't expect him until he thinks you're asleep. So just do whatever you'd normally do if you were home alone."

"I guess I'll…go upstairs and watch a movie or something."

"Are you going to change into pajamas?"

She cocked one eyebrow. "So I look like I'm living here?" She crossed her arms. She was in skinny black jeans, a white T-shirt, a deep-red leather jacket, and black ankle boots. She had Rixaline's wooden heart tucked into her bra and her crucifix around her neck. The outfit made her feel tough and confident.

"Well…" Rico started.

"No. I don't care what Joe thinks about why it's late and I'm still in street clothes. Besides, I'm going straight back to the penthouse after this."

"Okay. Just checking."

She looked around the kitchen. "I am going to have a snack, though. That's what I'd usually do while watching a movie. Or at least a glass of vino. Sadly, I took all the wine to the penthouse. There's got to be *something* here. We didn't clean everything out yet."

"Good hunting. I'll be in the pantry." He started toward it.

She followed.

He gave her a funny look.

"What? The pantry is snack central."

"Oh. Right." He stepped aside as he gestured toward the door. "Have at it."

"Thanks." With a little rummaging and careful avoidance of the surveillance equipment, she found a bag of M&M trail mix, a tub of gummy cola bottles, which were one of Christina's favorites, and some white cheddar popcorn. She took them all, plus a large bottle of Pellegrino from the fridge.

Rico's brows went up, and he laughed. "Are you taking snacks to Kowalski too?"

"Nope." She smiled and showed a little fang. "You know that crazy metabolism of mine."

"Right. I do. Well, enjoy."

"Thanks. Should I introduce myself to Kowalski?"

"No, I can do it. Come on. I'll go up with you. Then I'll turn off all the lights down here."

They went upstairs together. Rico made the introductions, during which she kept her fangs in check, then Rico left, and she went to her bedroom. She clicked around the channels but ended up looking through the on-demand selections. She happily settled in to watch one of her favorite movies from high school, *Better Off Dead*. There was something oddly fitting about the title and the whole situation with Joe, but she didn't think too long or too hard about it.

She was halfway through the gummy cola bottles and just at the start of her second movie, *Say Anything...*, when Kowalski stuck his head in. "Ma'am, we have a person walking up the driveway."

She tensed. "Is it Joe?"

He put his hand to his ear, listening. "Appears to be."

Anticipation pinged through her, little zaps of nervous energy lighting her up inside. "I should go downstairs. Be waiting for him when he tries the front door."

Kowalski nodded. "Yes, ma'am."

She left the snacks and stood, brushing off a few stray popcorn husks. "Okay. I can do this." She'd rehearsed seeing him again in her head, but there were so many possibilities for how it might go, she wasn't sure what was actually going to come out of her mouth.

Kowalski gave her a thumbs-up, then returned to Christina's room.

Donna headed for the front stairs. "Can you hear me, Rico? I'm coming down."

"I can hear you," came his muted reply from the pantry. It sounded like he was much farther away, but at least she could understand him. She wasn't sure how he was going to explain this supernatural-enhanced communication to the FBI, but that was his hill to climb, not hers.

"Good." She swallowed down the fear threatening to close her throat. What was she afraid of? She was stronger than Joe. Faster than Joe. And hopefully, she'd be smarter than him too.

She stood at the bottom of the stairs for a moment, then took a few steps toward the foyer. She could see a shadowy figure through the sidelights of the front door. Metal scraped against metal. He was trying to pick the lock.

Was that really Joe out there? The man who'd made her life such misery? The man she'd feared would try to take her kids from her? The man who was still causing her problems?

Anger welled up and over her anxiety. Enough that she moved forward with purpose. She reached the door just as the knob jiggled.

He was trying to get in.

With her incredible speed, she rushed forward, unlocked the door, and opened it, leaving nothing but air between her and her previously "dead" husband.

He was crouched down, lock-picking tools in hand. For a long moment, he didn't seem to realize the door was no longer there or that she was standing in front of him.

Silly human.

She flicked on the foyer light to give him a small advantage.

He looked up. And smiled tentatively. It was definitely Joe. "Hey, baby."

She ought to act surprised, but she couldn't manage that level of pretend with this idiot. She scowled down at him. "I am not your baby. What are you doing here?"

He stood, shrugging like he couldn't figure out why she wasn't grateful for his miraculous return. Something about him was different, but she couldn't quite put her finger on it. "Ay, is that all you have to say to your husband? I'm back from the dead, baby. Hey, you look good. All that grieving took some pounds off you."

Her right eyelid twitched, and for a moment, she could see colors. Mary and Joseph, he was a freakin' piece of work.

Deep within her, a force gathered. It happened quickly, a storm surge. She was powerless to stop her body's response. The way her fingers curled tight against her palm. The rising of her elbow. The cocking of her arm. The path of her fist as it flew through the air.

Her knuckles collided with his face.

It wasn't the hard impact she'd expected. More like punching a gravel-filled marshmallow than a brick wall.

A full set of dentures went flying out of his mouth and clattered to the floor of the front porch. *That's* what was different. His teeth! That must be how he'd fooled the dental forensics.

He tilted hard, going down to his hands and knees next to the false teeth.

A muffled snort sounded from the pantry.

Joe shook his head and blinked hard, then seemed to regain enough of his senses to scoop his dentures back into his mouth. "What the hell, Donna?"

"Sorry. Hot flash." She crossed her arms to keep from hitting him again. "Is that how you fooled the forensics into thinking it was you all burned up in the accident? You had your teeth pulled and put them in the car?"

"No." He frowned and looked almost... embarrassed. "That doesn't work. Apparently. I had to have the dental records swapped."

She read between the lines enough to realize he'd had his teeth removed before learning that trick wasn't feasible. What an idiot.

He stood, wobbling enough to give her the satisfaction of knowing she'd rung his bell. How many times had she wanted to do that in the last twenty-seven years?

Hitting him had been *very* satisfactory. Maybe she could work in another punch before the evening was over. "You still haven't answered my question. Why are you here?"

He was mad. She knew it by the crinkle between his brows and the way his jaw set. She didn't care.

"Because I ain't dead, and I need something outa my office."

She didn't move. "Why aren't you dead?"

"Because I ain't. Why aren't you happy about it?"

So. Many. Reasons. "Because I've moved on. And away from the Villachi stain."

He snorted. "Yeah? Then let me in, and I'll get out of your hair. I won't even make a stink that I'm alive so you can still collect that fat insurance check I know you got coming."

She had to let him in. The FBI needed him in. She needed him in. She stepped aside, wishing she could tell him she'd already canceled that insurance check.

He walked into the house, preening like a peacock. He smelled like perfume she didn't recognize. Lucinda's?

She closed the door behind him. "Why did you do it?"

He went down the hall toward his office. "Do what?"

"Fake your death." Moron. She followed him, not about to let him go in there alone.

"Because I had no choice." He flipped on the light in his office. "Why didn't you let Lucinda in?"

Donna stood in the doorway. "How do you know I didn't let Lucinda in?" Except she had let Lucinda in, so not only was Lucinda still in contact with Joe, she was lying to him. For what end?

He gave her an ugly look. "You think I'm not gonna stay in touch with my sister? Family means something to me."

Not the family he'd made with her, obviously, but she was thankful for that. Hopefully, that meant the kids would be safe. "Then Big Tony knows you're not really dead?"

He lunged at her, his speed impressive, considering. Only her own swiftness kept her throat out of his hands. Still, she'd allowed herself to move only a few inches out of his grasp so as not to arouse suspicion in him.

"Don't you breathe a word to him, or I'll kill you, you understand?"

"I want nothing to do with Big Tony, so don't worry yourself."

Threatening to kill her had to be something the FBI could use, but it wasn't enough. Not to put him away for the length of time she wanted. She knew that. She wondered if Rico would confirm, but she didn't hear anything from him.

Joe started to walk behind his desk. "Get out of here."

She stayed put. "No. This is my house now. You're the one who should leave. Get what you're getting and get out."

He glared at her. "You dumb piece of—"

"You're wasting time. The longer you're here, the longer you argue with me, the greater chance there is something will go wrong."

If looks could kill vampires, she'd be dead. Then he turned his back on her and reached for a book on the shelf. *The Godfather.*

He was going for his secret stash room. This was going to be interesting.

But she had to work fast to get more out of him before he saw his stash room was empty. So she pressed, "What kind of game are you and Lucinda running, anyway?"

He hesitated, his hand on the book. "I don't know what you're talking about."

"So the name Boris Reznikov means nothing to you?"

He pulled the book down and finally looked at her. "How do you know that name?"

"Because one of his lunks showed up here. Looking for you. And five million dollars."

Joe grinned. "Those dumb Cossacks can look all they want. They ain't getting it back."

"So the money exists?"

"Don't worry about it," he snarled.

"What was your deal with them?"

"Why do you care?"

She needed him to share, and he was being his usual cagey self. Time to insult him. "So you had no deal. That makes more sense. I knew you couldn't pull off something with the Russians unless Big Tony was in the mix. It was his doing, wasn't it?"

"Oh, there was a deal all right, and it was all me." His eyes narrowed. "Why are you so interested? You wired? You working for Tony?"

She pulled her T-shirt up to show him her wireless torso. She realized a second later that meant Rico had probably just seen her in her bra. Whatever.

She was glad she'd worn the nude lace. At least it was pretty. She pulled her T-shirt back down. "Not wired, not working for Tony. I just want to know, for once in my life, what's going on."

He stared at her, his gaze stuck on her chest for the moment. Finally, he made eye contact again. "You want to know what's going on? Lucinda and I were going into business together because Tony is a cheap bastard, and it was time for the Barrones to get some. We made a deal with the Russians to distribute their drugs into our territories for a cut."

"So what's the five million for?"

A very familiar cockiness lifted his brows and the right corner of his mouth. He was pleased with the deal he'd made, that was for sure. He rolled his shoulders with a proud swagger. "Part of it is money I laundered for them. Part of it is payment for the first shipment. And part of it is for taking out one of the Ukrainians trying to cross into Russian territory."

She almost smiled at his confession.

He shrugged. "Boris figured if I did that for him, it would seal the deal. So I did."

Rico's distant voice filled her ears. "That's perfect. See if you can get him to tell you where the body is buried."

She swallowed. She'd always suspected Joe of being capable of murder. But to actually hear him admit to it with such...pride. It was chilling. She tamped down her disgust. "You killed someone? I don't believe you."

"So what? It's no skin off my nose."

She had a sudden thought. "Was that the man who was in your car when it burned up?"

He grinned. "You're not as dumb as you look."

She hoped that was enough for Rico, because she was done talking about it. "You make me sick."

"Like I care." Joe reached into the open space where the book had been and pressed the button.

The bookshelf released with a hiss and began to swing open. She did her best to watch with feigned interest and surprise. After all, she wasn't supposed to know this mystery room existed.

The light inside flickered on.

Joe snickered like he was so proud of himself for having this hidden room. For having kept one more secret from her.

Then he turned. And all laughing stopped.

# CHAPTER 21

Donna inched toward the door, which put her at an angle to Joe and allowed her to glimpse his gaping mouth and rounded eyes.

She knew what he'd expected to see in that space. His drugs, his guns, his ledgers, but most important, his five million dollars. What he was actually looking at was an empty room.

"Any time, Rico," she whispered.

"What the hell?" Joe turned toward her. He was livid. "Did you know about this? Did you do this?"

"Do what? This is your office. Look around you. I haven't even started to clean it out."

That seemed to calm him. Marginally. "Then who's been here?"

Donna was almost at the door. She shrugged as she shook her head and put on her best oblivious face. "The only people who've been in here since you supposedly died are Big Tony and some of the boys. Vinnie. Franco. Nick."

He came around the desk, leaving no obstacles between them. He stabbed a finger at the empty space. "You swear you had nothing to do with this?"

She put one hand in the air and grasped her crucifix with the other, holding it so he could see it. That was as far as she could go. "This is your office, Joe. You know I never came in here."

She prayed that worked, because she couldn't swear she had nothing to do with it when she'd had everything to do with it. Not with her hand on her crucifix, anyway. Not when there was any possibility that such a blatant lie might erase all its protective powers.

"Then where is my money?"

"Talk to Big Tony. Or Lucinda. The day of your funeral, I found her hovering around outside this door." Not a lie. She wasn't going to mention Lucinda looking for the photo. That seemed like something that might annoy him, and he was already irritated enough.

His mouth twisted. "Don't bring my sister into this. I know she doesn't have the money."

Donna held up both her hands in surrender. "You asked who's been around your office. I figured I should tell you—"

"*You* did this." He stalked toward her.

She heard Rico's voice again. "We've got all we're going to get. Let's take him in."

Relief filled her, until Joe pulled out his phone and spoke into it. "Time to leave."

Kowalski's voice came through the walls next, fainter than Rico's, but still understandable. "Hold up. He might not alone. An SUV just pulled up."

229

Joe pointed at her. "You think this is over? You're wrong. You're gonna pay for this. Whatever your part. You're gonna pay."

The next thirty seconds blurred into the kind of slow-motion, fast-forward chaos that made reaction times meaningless no matter if you were vampire, werewolf, or human.

Footsteps sounded on the stairs. Joe glanced up and shoved past her, still talking into his phone. "It's a setup, Carmella."

Carmella? Who was that?

A woman's voice came through the phone. "I got this."

Two loud pops followed. Donna froze. Those were gunshots.

Kowalski's voice was rough-edged with alarm. "Agent down. We have an agent down."

Spurred into action by the terrible announcement, Donna went after Joe, determined not to let him get away.

She caught up with him as he was headed out the front door. An SUV rumbled in the driveway, a woman at the wheel. Carmella. Even at this distance, Donna picked up on her scent. The same perfume that clung to Joe. Had to be his new girlfriend. What a scumbag. "*Joseph!*"

At the sound of Donna calling his name, he stopped in the front yard and glanced back, eyes wild with desperation. Something dull and black glinted in his hand, caught in the faint moonlight. A gun. "You're gonna pay, Donna. Snitches end up in ditches."

She started down the steps after him. "And you're going to get caught, Joe." By her.

He backed toward the SUV, and a blinding flash of light erupted from his side.

He'd shot at her.

Searing pain followed as the bullet went through her.

The impact sent her sprawling onto the porch, gasping. Fire exploded across her side. She clutched at her belly.

Rico and Kowalski flew past, but Rico hesitated, looking back at her.

"Go," she wheezed. "I'm okay."

She wasn't okay exactly, but she wasn't going to die either. She hoped.

With a nod, he fled down the steps.

She crab-crawled back into the house and collapsed, head down on the carpet. Joe had actually shot her. He hadn't been kidding. He really intended to make her pay.

The pain lessened a little. Or she was going into shock. Okay, that really needed not to happen. She tried to assess how bad things were. Her hand was on her stomach. And it was wet. She gingerly lifted it for a look, cringing as she saw what she'd expected. Blood.

The squeal of tires was followed by more pops of gunfire.

Her anger came back as she stared at the ceiling. Joe had freakin' shot her. Just when she'd thought it wasn't possible for him to be any worse of a husband than he already was. Her anger turned to protective rage. It spun up and spooled out into something larger than herself. Joe might come after her, but what if he went after the kids? She no longer cared what Rico or the FBI wanted.

Joe had used up all the patience she'd had left. It was time for her to take matters into her own hands.

Just as soon as she was no longer leaking blood from the holes in her back and belly.

Rico ran back in. "Donna, you still conscious?"

"Yes."

He knelt next to her. "How bad is it?"

"Pretty sure the carpet's ruined."

He frowned at her. "I need to look."

"Help yourself."

He lifted her T-shirt. "Wound already looks smaller. Still bleeding, though. Did it go through?"

"No idea."

"I'm going to check." Carefully, he tilted her toward him and ran his hand over her back on the other side. He nodded. "Yep. Through and through, although that side is closing up too. You sure you're okay?"

She did a quick head-to-toe assessment. The pain was there, but manageable. She no longer felt like she was going into shock. With some effort, she sat up. "I'm fine. Or soon will be. But I've never been angrier in my life. He freakin' shot me."

"I know. But the good news is we got enough to put him away for a long time."

She narrowed her eyes and not just because of the pain in her side. "What's the bad news?"

"Cheng got shot too."

"Is he going to be okay?"

"His shoulder will probably need surgery, but he should be."

"Then that's not so bad. It's one more thing to use against him."

"Joe didn't shoot Cheng. The woman with him did."

"Semantics." But Rico wasn't done. She could tell by the hesitation in his voice. "What else haven't you told me?"

"Joe got away. We didn't have vehicles close enough. And we didn't anticipate that he'd have help."

New, hot anger spilled through her like fresh lava. She stared at Rico. "How could you let that happen?"

Outside, the whine of an ambulance approached.

"Donna, your eyes are glowing. You can't let the EMTs—"

"Bite me, Rico." She got to her feet, causing new blood to trickle from the remaining wound and fresh pain to wash over her. That didn't mean it wasn't healing, but nothing happened instantly. She put a hand on the wall, glancing down. Her clothes were ruined. She couldn't let Pierce see her like this. He was already going to lose it when she told him she'd been shot. Thankfully, she still had some clothes upstairs.

Rico stood, putting his hands on his hips. "Donna, we'll get him."

She straightened and turned toward the steps. "You're officially off this case."

"It doesn't work that way."

She started up. "It does when one of us is a vampire."

"Donna."

She kept going. She no longer cared what Rico thought or what his fellow agents wondered about how she'd been shot but wasn't dead or in need of medical assistance. She had to look after her own now. She took her phone out and called Temo.

"Yes, boss?"

"I'm ready." The ambulance's wail came through loud and clear. Must be close now. "How soon can you be here?"

"Ten minutes or so. Everything okay there? I hear sirens."

"It's fine enough. I'll explain when I see you." She paused. Ten minutes was a lot faster than she'd expected. "Where are you?"

His tone was a mix of amusement and apology. "At a place called Blue Bell's Diner. Great pie."

He hadn't gone back to the penthouse like she'd told him to. She smiled as she walked into her bedroom. He was a good man. "They do have great pie. Get a bourbon-pecan and a chocolate silk to take back to the penthouse. I need sweets."

"You got it. Be there as soon as they're boxed up and the bill is paid."

"If Nell's your server, leave her an extra-good tip. I'll cover it."

"She is. Will do."

"Bye." Donna hung up and tossed her phone on the bed, then went into her closet to see what clothing was left. She found some well-worn pieces of her old uniform—a big sweatshirt and leggings. The sweatshirt had a small hole near the ribbing on the neck, and the leggings had a couple of bleach spots, but they weren't soaked with blood, so they'd do.

She took them and her phone into the bathroom, locked the door, then stripped down and got in the shower.

The hot water stung the healing wound, so she soaped up fast. Once the blood was gone, she dried off and found some bandages under the sink. She fixed one on each side of the wound so that she wouldn't get blood on her clean clothes. Hopefully, the bandages would last until she got home. Or maybe she'd be all healed by then.

Satisfied she'd done what she could, she got dressed, making sure to tuck Rixaline's little wooden heart back into her bra for safekeeping. She dug around for a pair of old sneakers to wear. They had splatters of paint on them, which was why they hadn't made it to the penthouse.

Finally, she bagged up the bloody clothes and took them downstairs via the front steps to stick in the trash.

Rico was in the kitchen talking to Kowalski. Another agent was in there with them. Franklin, she guessed. The conversation was deep and serious and a sufficient distraction for them not to see her.

She didn't stop. She detoured to the garage to ditch the bag of clothes in the bin, then walked past the bloodstain on the carpet and out the door. More agents were outside, just arrived by the look of them. Some EMTs tended to the agent who'd been shot.

The house and the surrounding woods were lit up in blues and reds.

She walked past all of them. None of them paid much attention to her. Not enough to make them try to stop her.

Her breath steamed out in puffs of vapor on the chilly night air. It was cold out, but her anger kept her plenty warm. She walked until she reached the end of the driveway. She turned to look at the house and the chaos surrounding it. She wanted nothing to do with any of that right now. Not Rico, not the FBI, not the house, not the memories, nothing.

Rico might think he was in charge of this, but that time was over. She was in charge now. Joe was her mess to clean up. And she would. Her own way. Her own permanent way. Because the world didn't need a man in it who was craven enough to shoot the woman who'd been at his side for twenty-seven years, that much she knew.

Not to mention the guy he'd killed and used as his body double in the car accident.

The whirr of an insect made her swat at the pest even though she didn't see it. What kind of bug would be out in these temperatures? She stared at the house. Did Rico even know she was gone? The lights were blazing, and movement was visible inside and out.

Joe wouldn't come back here. Not now that he knew the feds were involved. She had no doubt he'd do everything in his power to find her, though. Especially if he thought she'd taken the money.

That absolutely meant he could go after the kids. He knew how easy it would be to use them against her.

The cold hit her suddenly. She wrapped her arms around her torso. She had to deal with him now. Immediately.

The insect buzzed closer, and again she swatted at it without seeing it.

Then a third time, closer still. Enough that she ducked and swung around toward it. The twisting caused a sharp pain to pierce her side. Had she reopened the wounds?

Her eyes found the insect, which wasn't an insect at all. She shivered.

A fae drifted in the air above her. Close. Too close.

Two thoughts crowded her mind. *Hurry up, Temo. I really need some iron jewelry.*

The fae smiled at her, its skin stretching hideously over its angular features. "Hello, wounded vampire. I smell your blood. Your delicious blood." It closed its eyes and inhaled. More smiling. Then the smiling stopped. "I smell fae on you. The girl. You have been with the dhamfir."

Rixaline's wooden heart. Did that carry the girl's scent?

The fae spread its wings. "You are quite the prize, aren't you? Too bad I have to take you alive."

Donna had no weapon, only her heightened abilities, and in her wounded state, she wasn't sure how far those would get her.

Time to find out.

# CHAPTER 22

Fangs out, Donna brought her hands up to fend off her attacker. The growl of a car engine caught her attention, but the fae seemed oblivious. Its wings spread wider as it prepared to strike.

She couldn't take her eyes off the fae to see if the car was driven by friend or foe, but she prayed it was Temo.

It was. The SUV screeched to a stop beside her, and he jumped out, engine still running. Temo threw himself between her and the fae, then stomped his foot and gave a fierce cry. "*Tofa!*"

The ground rumbled, tilting and lifting, and shockwaves radiated from the spot where Temo's foot had struck the ground.

The fae was thrown back like it had been punched in the stomach. It screeched as it disappeared into the night sky.

Donna fell to the ground. She winced as she landed, letting out a little gasp of pain.

Temo turned, his expression full of apology. He

reached for her and helped her up. "Boss, I'm so sorry. Are you okay?"

"I'm fine. Thank you." She brushed her backside off, moving gingerly to keep the wounds from opening up any more than they just had. "Pretty sure you just saved my life. That was impressive. What was that you did?"

"Mini quake. Basically. C'mon, get in. Before it comes back." Temo suddenly grimaced. "Sorry. Please."

"You don't have to tell me twice. And you don't need to apologize in times of war." She went around to the passenger's side and climbed in.

He got behind the wheel, hitting the button to lock the vehicle as soon as her door was shut. "War?"

"What else would you call a fae trying to capture me?"

"Good point." He glanced at her. "You sure you're okay?"

"I am." She looked in the rearview mirror. "What about the pies, though? That was a hard stop."

"Nell gave me a bigger box to put the smaller boxes in, so I think they're fine." He put the SUV in drive and circled around to head back to the penthouse. "You, I'm not so sure about. What's going on? First the fae, then I saw the ambulance. What happened?"

She put her seat belt on. Carefully. "The fae was unrelated. It just showed up as I walked to the end of the drive. I wasn't thinking, frankly. My mind was on what had just happened."

"Which was?"

"In a nutshell, it didn't go as planned. Joe confessed to some things that will put him away for a long time, but he didn't come alone, and his partner, some woman named Carmella, helped him escape. She shot one of the FBI agents."

Temo glanced at her before looking back at the road. "That doesn't explain why you're not wearing the clothes I dropped you off in."

This wasn't going to go over well. "Joe shot me."

He muttered something she didn't understand, presumably in Samoan, then spoke to his phone, which was clipped into a dashboard mount. "Dial Charlie."

Ringing filled the car, then Charlie answered. "Hi, Temo. What's up?"

"I have the boss with me. She's been shot. Better call Dr. Fox."

"Shot?" Charlie's calm disappeared.

Donna leaned toward the phone. "I'm fine."

"Was the bullet wood?" Charlie asked.

"I'm pretty sure it was a standard bullet. Whatever metal they're made out of."

"Is it still in you?"

"No, through and through."

Charlie's questions kept coming. "Are you still bleeding?"

"A little, maybe. I don't think it's completely closed up. Still hurts when I move. I put some bandages on it."

"Good. Did you die?"

Donna hesitated. "Say that again?"

"Did you physically die? Are you breathing out of necessity or habit? If you blacked out, you may have died."

"I don't remember blacking out."

"Hold your breath. If you don't feel the urge to take a breath pretty quickly, you died. It's nothing terrible," Charlie said. "Most vampires are dead."

Donna took a breath and held it. A couple seconds later, she exhaled. "I still want to breathe."

"Okay, that's good to know." Some of Charlie's calm had returned. "I'll get Dr. Fox here."

"I don't think I really need—"

"Ma'am, with all due respect, you're the governor. We're not taking any chances. Especially when you've been shot. This is standard operating procedure."

Temo looked at her and nodded.

Donna gave in. It was easier. And they meant well. Plus, she'd taken the job, so she needed to follow procedures. "Okay, whatever you need to do. Thanks."

"Great. See you when you get here." Charlie hung up.

Temo hit the end call button. "Better safe than sorry."

She nodded. "I understand."

"How'd it happen?"

"He was trying to get away, and I went after him, and he shot me. Then he jumped into the car with his girlfriend—"

"Ouch."

Donna laughed, although it came out a little bitter. "It's nothing new. He's had several over the years. It's kind of expected with these Mafia guys. But apparently, this new one, Carmella, she's in on the whole faked-death deal. She'd have to be, I think."

Donna looked over at Temo. "I did slug him when he first came to the door. That was nice. Knocked his false teeth right out of his mouth, which was how he was going to pull off the body in the car being his until he learned that wouldn't work."

"So how did he do it?"

"He got his dental records switched. Can't imagine what that cost." She sighed. "Joe always was a schemer."

"That's pretty hard-core, though. Being willing to get your teeth pulled to make it look like your body is the one that got burned up. Although putting someone else's body in a car and setting it on fire to fake your own death is pretty next-level too."

"I agree. But that's how these guys are. Ruthless. Willing to do whatever it takes to get what they want. And what Joe wanted was to take the Russians' five million and disappear. I guess with his new chickie."

"And leave you and the kids behind?"

She looked out the window. "Apparently. I can understand him leaving me. We haven't had much of a marriage in a long time. But our kids? If I'd known he had so little love for them, I would have left with them years ago. I just always assumed he'd come after me because of them. Maybe he would have. Who knows? He probably would have done me in then. With a man like Joe, anything is possible. That body in the car? That was a Ukrainian mobster he killed for the Russians."

Temo grimaced.

She sighed, setting off a little twinge in her side. "What's done is done, right? No point bemoaning the past. Can't change it."

"Nope." He grinned. "Glad you got to slug him. Wish I could have seen that."

"You probably can. I'm sure the camera by the door caught it. Rico might give me the footage." Although they hadn't exactly parted on great terms.

"Looking forward to that." He went silent a moment, his smile fading away. "You think he'll leave you alone? Now that you know he's alive?"

"Absolutely not, but not for that reason. He thinks I had something to do with his money being gone, which I did, obviously. Of course, I didn't tell him that."

"Pierce made sure it's back where it belongs."

"All but the one million I donated to the church. But Joe said he intends to make me pay. Although...I wonder."

"What about?"

"If he thinks I'm dead. For all I know, he thinks that bullet killed me."

"You think he really intended to kill you?"

"Definitely." She leaned her elbow on the console between them. "It's more than that, though. He

244

knows I was complicit with the feds on this. That I was part of the setup to catch him." She frowned. "He won't let that go. Rats don't get forgiven in the Mafia. It's part of the code."

"Does he know you're a vampire?"

"Nope. Not a clue. Not sure he'd believe it even if he somehow found out."

Temo shrugged. "That gives you an advantage."

"It does."

"So what are you going to do?"

She stared at her hands. "I pretty much told Rico that I'm going to handle this myself, and at the time, I meant it. I was overcome by rage."

"But?"

"But I don't know if I can. Killing accidentally and killing on purpose are very different things. And I'm not a killer."

"Do you know where Joe is? We could just go get him and subdue him and then turn him in to the FBI."

She thought about that. "That would be the right way to do it. At least then he'd stand trial and face all the terrible things he's done. Plus that would prevent him from going after the kids to punish me. But no, I don't know where he is. Probably in some cheap motel. Or at that floozy's house."

"So? How many Carmellas can there be?"

Donna laughed. "In Jersey? A lot. I'm sure the FBI is on it, though."

"Yeah, but are you sure they'll be able to get him tonight?"

"No, I'm not." She took a deep breath, and the little wooden heart tucked into her bra shifted. An idea began to form. She leaned toward Temo slightly. "But we have something the FBI doesn't have."

"We do?"

She nodded. "We have Rixaline."

Temo grinned. "The finder of things."

"The finder of things." Donna shook her head. "Part of me hates to ask her to use that skill for me. After all, that's exactly what the fae wanted of her, but this is a different situation."

"Very different," Temo said. "We're talking about your life and the lives of your kids. And they don't have your skills to protect themselves. Boss, I think she'd love to help you. I think she wishes she could do more now. Although she loves taking care of Lucky."

"I hope you're right, because the last thing I want her to do is think I'm taking advantage of her. Or only helping her because of her skills."

"I don't think that's how she'll feel at all. You've been very kind to her. The way you've taken care of that girl makes me proud to know you." He shook his head. "Claudette wouldn't have done that."

"You don't think so?"

He shot Donna a look that was followed by a gruff laugh. "I know so."

"Well, then, I'll ask her. And we'll be very careful that finding him doesn't turn into a dangerous situation. We'll track him down and handle it very swiftly."

"Right."

"We have to take him and the girlfriend, because she shot one of the agents. They're going to want her too. So we grab them, then dump them in front of the FBI headquarters and call it in."

"I like that. It's a good plan." He got a dreamy look on his face. Like he was thinking about something that made him happy. "We could get Neo to help."

Scratch that. *Someone* who made him happy. Donna smiled. "Call her. I want to do this tonight."

"I don't think Dr. Fox is going to clear you for that."

"I don't care. I want this handled. It needs to be handled. The longer Joe's free, the more damage he can do. What if he decides to call Joe Jr. or Christina and tell them he's not really dead? Or worse, tries to lure them home and into his grasp? I don't need them dealing with that. No, this happens tonight. We have a little over five hours before sunup. Plenty of time. Especially because I'm sure he's not far away."

"You're the boss, boss."

"That's right. And in this case, what I say goes. Call Neo."

She was on his speed dial, no surprise there. Donna was going to do her best to make sure they had more time together. Like by giving Temo a night off as soon as it was possible.

Neo answered quickly. "Hello there." Her voice was a smooth, low purr. Not the Neo Donna was used to.

Temo cleared his throat. "Hi. You're, uh, on speaker with me and Donna."

"Oh." She giggled. *Giggled.* "Hey, Donna."

"Hi, Neo. I feel like I'm always calling you for help, but how'd you like to help me out again?"

"More muscle?"

"Something like that. Probably a little more hands-on this time."

"Gimme some deets."

Temo tilted toward the phone. "Joe shot her."

"What?" Neo's screech nearly cracked the windshield. "No he *didn't.* You okay?"

"Yep, he sure did. But I'm fine," Donna stressed. "It was a flesh wound that's almost healed."

"What happened?"

"I helped the FBI run a little sting operation this evening, and things didn't go quite as planned. That's why I had to leave group early. Anyway, Joe and his new girlfriend evaded arrest, and with the way he threatened me, I can't let him run free."

"Also, girl, *he shot you.*"

"That too. So you in?"

"Hells *yes.* When?"

"Tonight. I need to see the doctor about this gunshot wound, then we're out the door. Plan is to track down Joe and his girlfriend, truss him and the sidepiece up, and dump them at FBI headquarters."

"I'm down. I can head to your place in about ten minutes."

"You know I'm at the penthouse now, right?"

"Oh yeah." Donna could practically hear the smile in her voice. "Even better. See you soon. Bye, Temo."

He got all moony again. "Bye, Neo."

"That's the plan, then," Donna said. "Tonight is Joe's last night as a free man."

"You got that right." He pulled into the parking garage of the Wellman Towers. "You going to tell your FBI buddy?"

"No. Not until we have Joe and Carmella in the back of this SUV and we're about to leave them on his doorstep. I think Rico would try to stop me. And I'd rather ask forgiveness than permission."

"What if he just wanted to come along? Help?"

"He'd still want to do things by the book. And this is not going to be that kind of operation."

Temo nodded. "Roger that."

This was going to be down and dirty. Tonight she wasn't so much a vampire as a mama bear protecting her cubs.

Joe wasn't going to know what hit him.

# CHAPTER 23

Temo carried the pies as he and Donna went up to the penthouse, then he put them in the kitchen and went back down to gas up the SUV. And possibly wait on Neo, but that was just Donna's hunch. She kind of hoped that was exactly what he was doing.

Charlie and Pierce greeted her at the door, with Rixaline not far behind them. All three looked exceedingly worried.

She held her hands up. "I'm fine. I feel better now than I did thirty minutes ago. I'm sure it's healing."

Charlie frowned. "On the outside, maybe, but the inside takes longer."

"Oh?" Donna hadn't realized that. One more thing that ought to go in the vampire handbook that desperately needed to be written.

"Yes. But Dr. Fox is here, and he's set up in the salon. If you'd like, I'll introduce you."

"I would like, but first…" She reached through the neck of her big sweatshirt and retrieved the little wooden heart. She held it out to Rixaline. "Thank you. I think this came in very handy tonight."

Rixaline didn't need to know about the fae Donna had run into.

The girl took the heart, smiling. "I'm very glad."

"Do you think you could do something else for me?"

Rixaline nodded eagerly. "Of course."

"This is a big thing to ask you. And I don't feel like I have any right to do this, but the man who shot me, Joe, my former husband, got away with his girlfriend, who also shot one of the agents working the case. And the thing is, no one knows where Joe is."

Rixaline's eyes lit up. "Yes. I will find him for you."

Donna exhaled. "You will? You don't mind? I don't want you to think I'm taking advantage of you."

"I'm happy to do it. And I don't think that at all. Not after everything you've done for me. Is he a supernatural?"

"Nope. A regular human."

"Then I just need a seed. That's what I call the little trigger that helps me locate something."

"Like what?"

"Something of his. Or a picture of him. Or his scent. Even something he's touched can be enough, but I have to have that seed."

"I can provide you with that. Right after I'm done with Dr. Fox." She looked at Pierce and Charlie. "Neo's coming over, then we're all going hunting. I'll fill you in as soon as Dr. Fox checks me out. But

I'll tell you this about our expedition. It's going to be very fast and very safe where Rixaline is concerned. And you're not going to talk me out of it."

"Right," Pierce said. "Wouldn't try."

"Good." She smiled at Charlie. "Let's go meet Dr. Fox. Is he a vampire too?"

"No, he's a gnome. They're inherently protectors, and he's an excellent doctor on top of that. Been the official governor's physician since before I was here. Good man. Very skilled."

"Glad to hear that."

They walked into the salon.

He was a blocky, balding man with a muscular build, glasses, and tufts of gray hair sticking off his ears. He looked like the kind of guy who might have played football or wrestled in high school. He had a crinkly smile and bright eyes that gleamed like he had a joke to share. Donna liked him immediately.

Charlie gestured toward him. "Dr. Ezrun Fox, please met our new governor, Belladonna Barrone."

He gave her a little bow, holding on to the stethoscope around his neck. "Hello there, Governor Barrone. Sorry to meet under such unfortunate circumstances, but I understand someone's done you a great indignity."

She laughed. "Well, my former husband did shoot me, so you're not far off." She stuck her hand out. "Nice to meet you, Dr. Fox."

He shook her hand. "The pleasure is all mine, Governor. You seem to be doing well. I'm happy to see that."

Charlie smiled. "If you'll excuse me, I'll let you get on with it."

She left, and Dr. Fox patted the massage table. Behind him, on one of the rolling beauty carts, he'd set out a few things. Bandages, some implements, gauze pads, a small bottle of liquid. His doctor's bag was on the counter behind that. "Why don't you have a seat and tell me what happened?"

Donna eased up onto the table, careful of her side. Her feet dangled just above the floor. "I was chasing my former husband, who was supposed to be dead, by the way, and he shot me. As best I can tell, the bullet went clean through my side. The impact of it knocked me down. Hurt like a son of a gun too."

"I imagine it did." He'd been nodding the whole time she was talking. "Mind if I take a look?"

"Please do. That's what you're here for." She lifted up the sweatshirt. Bunched up, it was too bulky for her to see the area in question. "I took a shower and cleaned myself up at the house, then put these bandages over the entry and exit wounds to deal with the bleeding. Wasn't much, but I figured it was better to have the wounds covered."

"Smart thinking." He rubbed his hands together slightly. Maybe to warm them up. "I need to take them off to see how it's healing."

"Of course. Go right ahead."

He had a gentle touch, peeling each one back slowly. "There's some dried blood on your skin and the bandages, but looks like the flesh has closed completely."

"That's good, right?"

"It is." He didn't make it seem like it was anything to get too excited about. She supposed a vampire's ability to heal fast was just expected.

He wet a gauze pad with sterile solution, then cleaned her skin. When he was done with that, he palpated the area. "Any pain?"

He asked just as she winced, making it impossible to say no. "It's not pain, exactly, but it is tender."

Nodding, he prodded the area a few more times. Higher up and closer toward her belly button. "I don't feel anything that alarms me, but the internal structures heal more slowly, so the tenderness is to be expected. It's good that the bullet went through cleanly. If it was still inside you, you'd need surgery."

"I'm glad to hear I don't. What do I need? Anything?"

"Yes. Forty-eight hours of bed rest."

She sighed. "And if my obligations make that impossible?"

He peered over the rims of his glasses at her. "If you're asking for permission, you're not going to get it." He shook his head, like a parent disappointed in a child. "But I understand that you're the governor, and there are certain things you need to do."

"So you *are* giving me permission?"

"No. But I'm not going to give you grief over it either." He sighed. "You can drop the sweatshirt."

"I appreciate you not making me feel bad about what I need to do." She let the sweatshirt fall back into place. "What's the worst that could happen to me?"

"If you don't rest?"

She nodded. "Or if I'm, say…more active than I should be. A lot more."

He took his glasses off and cleaned the lenses with a cloth from his pocket. "The supernatural physique is an amazing thing. Strong, resilient, self-healing. But the speed at which that healing comes creates its own issues." He put the glasses back on. "When you were human and you had an injury, how did you deal with it?"

"Rest and time."

He nodded. "And you were careful with the injury. If you had a sprained ankle, would you walk on it?"

"No."

"But now that you're a vampire, and your body repairs itself so quickly, you no longer see an injury the same way. You think if it looks healed, you are. And in some ways, that's true. But there's no strength there yet." He pushed his glasses up a little higher. "If I put some effort into it, I could push my finger through the skin where that bullet entered. It's still very thin there. Internally, it's the same. The tissues that are in the process of rebuilding are weak. They need time. Not as much as if you were human, but some."

"Interesting. I didn't know that. I'm pretty new to being a vampire. And there's no manual, you know."

He smiled. "There should be."

She laughed. "I keep saying that." Then she got serious again. "So basically, I run the risk of re-injuring myself."

"Yes. And if you do that…" He shrugged.

"What?"

"Your body could decide to make rest mandatory. It could shut down and put you into a state of involuntary hibernation until you're completely healed."

She frowned. That was kind of an important thing to just be finding out. "How long would that last?"

"As long as necessary."

"That would put a crimp in my schedule."

"It would. There's no telling when it could happen either, but fortunately for you, as governor, you aren't alone much. Very little danger of you collapsing into a coma where you might be caught by the sun."

She grimaced. "Yikes. That would be really bad."

"Indeed." He rocked back on his heels. "So do I need to be on call?"

She smiled tentatively. "It's probably not a bad idea. Sorry. I have work to do this evening that involves hunting down and capturing the man who shot me. And his equally awful girlfriend. Then I have a party to go to tomorrow night, which should be no work at all, unless you consider chitchat and cocktails work. Still, I'll be on my feet a bit. And in heels. Is there anything you can give me to help me heal faster?"

"Rest and blood. That's the only prescription there is. Standard human meds would do you no good. The vampire physiology metabolizes them too fast for them to be effective."

"Right. Well, not much else I can do but be careful and hope for the best."

His bushy brows rose. "You could delegate."

"I could. But this isn't just any man who shot me, Dr. Fox. As I mentioned, he's my former husband, who was already supposed to be dead. This man is a killer, a mob boss, and a ruthless criminal out for his own best interests and little else. But besides all that, he's a very real danger to our children. I can't delegate his capture with my kids at stake."

She eased off the table to stand on her own two feet. "I need him to know that I'm the reason he's losing his freedom tonight. That the woman he thinks he killed has come for him. Because I don't ever want him to imagine he can come against me again. I need him to know I am a force of nature. That there is no winning for him in this or any situation that involves me or my kids. Can you understand that?"

Dr. Fox nodded. "I have three sons and two daughters. All grown, all living their own lives, but if anyone were to threaten them…" He straightened slightly, pulling himself an inch or two taller. "I'll be on call if you need me. Be safe out there. And good hunting."

"Thank you."

She left him to gather up his things and went back out to the living room. Temo and Neo had joined the group. They all looked at her expectantly.

Pierce stood. "What did the doctor say?"

"That I need to rest and heal but also that he understands why I'm not doing that until I've dealt with Joe."

Temo got to his feet as well. "Should I bring the car around? I got everything else ready that I thought we might need. Zip ties, duct tape, tarps, bungee cords, ropes, shovels—"

"Wow, hang on there. That is everything we might need. Although not the tarps and shovels. We're bringing them in alive."

Temo squinted. "You sure?"

"Yes. And you have a few minutes before we leave. I need to change and get Rixaline something of Joe's so she can find him. Also, I want to take two cars. I want Charlie, Pierce, and Rixaline in one, leading the way. Then you, me, and Neo in the other SUV. That way, as soon as Rixaline locates Joe, she, Pierce, and Charlie can come straight back here. Then the three of us will handle capturing Joe and Carmella and taking them to the FBI."

They all gave her nods of agreement.

She looked at Neo. "Depending on the hour when we get back, you may need to sleep here."

She shrugged. "I'm cool with that."

Temo made a very innocent face. "We have a guest room downstairs too."

Donna fought hard not to smile. "Okay, then. We have our plan. Everyone ready to go?"

They all nodded again.

"All right, good. I'll get changed." She looked at Pierce. "I also need to feed. Doctor's orders."

He came around to her side of the couch.

"We'll be back shortly." She and Pierce went to her bedroom.

He rolled up his shirt sleeve. "I'm not going to feed from you this time."

"But it's part of the deal."

He shook his head. "You need to heal more. Plus, you just fed me. I'm fine."

She cupped his face. "You take such good care of me. Tomorrow, before the party. I should be good by then."

He gave her a skeptical look. "Pretty sure that's *not* what Dr. Fox told you."

"Hush." She took his arm, dropped her fangs, and bit into his wrist. Energy filled her immediately, making her suddenly aware of how depleted she'd been. Healing took more energy than she'd realized. With some effort, she made herself disengage. She ran her tongue across the punctures, then let go of him.

He fixed his sleeve. "You weren't done, were you?"

"You're too perceptive for your own good."

He winked at her. "That's what makes me a great assistant. I'll prep a thermos for you to take along. I know very well how much blood a healing vampire needs, and it's more than what you just had."

She smiled at him. "Thank you. I'll be out shortly."

"Take your time." He left.

With the boost of fresh power flowing through her, she went into her closet and picked out an outfit.

All black seemed appropriate. Jeans, T-shirt, leather jacket, and new flat-soled boots. No jewelry, save her crucifix, which was safely tucked beneath her shirt.

She started to walk out of the closet, then had a second thought and went back for one more thing. Her handgun. She wasn't taking any chances with Joe or his trigger-happy girlfriend. Donna put the magazine in, fully loaded, then secured the gun in the back of her waistband before heading into the bathroom.

She pulled her hair back into a ponytail, then tried to figure out what seed item to give to Rixaline. She'd kept nothing of Joe's.

Except the picture of him and Lucinda.

She grabbed it off the shelf in her closet where she'd left it in a box with the rest of the things from her safe.

There was a real sense of justice in using that photo to hunt him down. She went back out and held the little frame so Rixaline could see it. "Will this do?"

Rixaline reached for the photo. "May I?"

"Sure." Donna handed it over. "It's probably been a while since he touched that, so I don't know if—"

Clouds of gray and black covered Rixaline's eyes, and she seemed to stare at something no one else could see. After a moment, her lips parted, and she shook herself. Her eyes went back to normal.

"Are you okay?" Donna asked.

Rixaline nodded and handed the photo back. "I know where he is. And the woman in the photo. And the accounts."

Donna took the frame. "I don't need to know where Lucinda is. But what accounts are you talking about?"

"The ones that match the numbers on the back of the picture. They're in Grand Cayman."

Frowning, Donna opened up the frame and this time pulled the photo out. A piece of paper covered the back of the photo. That paper was what had the L and J printed on it. Underneath that was the actual picture.

And on the back of that were two strings of numbers.

"Oh," Donna said. "This just got interesting." She snapped a pic of the numbers with her phone and texted it to Rico with a note. *Grand Cayman accounts, Joe & Lucinda.*

Then, with a smile on her face, she was ready to hunt.

# CHAPTER 24

The two SUVs drove out of the parking garage and onto the street. Charlie was behind the wheel in the lead vehicle, since she knew the area better than Pierce. He was in the passenger's seat, and Rixaline was in the second row behind them. Donna wanted it that way. The tinted windows made the dhamfir much harder to see, and that seemed smart, considering that taking her out of the penthouse probably wasn't the wisest move.

Necessary to accomplish Joe's capture. But not wise. Not for Rixaline's sake.

Especially after Donna's encounter with the fae, something she hadn't told anyone about. Of course, Temo knew, but he'd kept it to himself, as far as she knew.

He was driving their vehicle with Neo in the passenger's seat. No real reason for that arrangement other than Donna liked whatever budding romance was happening and wanted to encourage it.

Worried about Rixaline being threatened, she'd given Pierce her gun for protection. She wasn't sure what good it would do against the fae, but she wasn't taking any chances that her new ward would come to harm. Not while Rixaline was under Donna's grant of sanctuary and certainly not while Rixaline was helping her.

Donna's phone buzzed. She checked it and saw Rico's response to her text. *Excellent. Looking into it. Thanks. And I'm sorry tonight didn't go better.*

*Me, too.* But that was about to change. She was also hopeful those account numbers would turn into solid evidence. She called Pierce next.

He answered right away. "Hey."

"Put me on speaker?"

"Sure." A small beep came through. "Okay, you're live."

"Thanks. Rixaline, how far do you think?"

"I don't know the area, but there's still some road left to go. The signal in my head gets stronger as we get closer, and by that I can tell we have time left. Just not how much."

"No rush. Just curious. Do your thing. And thank you!"

"You're welcome," Rixaline said.

"Pierce?"

Pierce came back on. "You're off speaker now. How are you feeling? Nervous?"

"Not nervous, just charged up and ready. Thank you for taking care of Rixaline. That's really important to me. I don't want her, Charlie, or you getting hurt."

"We won't, I promise. Plus, we have Charlie to look after us. Don't forget she's got some skills too."

"I'm counting on that. See you back at the penthouse."

"You got it."

She hung up and tucked her phone into the back pocket of the passenger's seat before putting her thin black gloves on. She wasn't going to risk taking the phone with her and getting it smashed up. Not that she couldn't afford a new one, but that would be such a hassle.

"Everyone have their gloves on?" Donna could see that they did, but she wanted the reassurance.

Neo raised her hands to show Donna, and Temo said, "Yep."

Donna leaned forward a little. "I was thinking when we get there, what if you do one of those mini quakes again, Temo?"

That got Neo's attention. She looked at him with great curiosity. "A mini quake? What's that all about?"

Donna answered for him, knowing how modest Temo was likely to be. "Temo is a descendant of Mafui'e, the Samoan god of earthquakes."

By the arch of her perfect brows, Neo was clearly impressed. "You're descended from a god?"

He got a sly little smile. "Way back, yes."

"How about that." Neo made a little noise with her tongue. "We're going to talk about this some more, I can guarantee you that. Now, go on with the plan, Donna."

"Well, I was thinking Temo's quake would disorient them. Then the three of us can rush in, subdue them, and truss them up. We'll have them in the back of this SUV before you can say FBI."

Neo nodded. "I'm cool with that. We just may not have the element of surprise if we don't do a little recon first."

"Meaning?" Donna asked.

"If they're in a cheap motel, rushing in is no problem. They have nowhere to go and nowhere else to be but in the room. But if they're holed up in a house somewhere, there's all kinds of rooms they could be in. Better to know before we go, you see what I'm saying?"

"Yes, totally. We definitely need to adjust based on where they are."

Twenty minutes later, that question was answered as Charlie's SUV turned into a retirement community called Holiday City, and both vehicles slowed to a crawl.

Donna looked at the houses. Very few had been updated since they'd been built, most likely in the eighties. Very few of them looked well maintained. This place was one step up from assisted living. And not the really nice assisted living either.

"This must be it," Neo said.

"Must be." Then a new thought came to Donna. An unfortunate thought. She pressed her fingers to her temples. "This isn't good."

Temo glanced at her in the rearview mirror. "Why not?"

"This is a fifty-five-and-over community. Joe's not fifty-five, and Carmella didn't look remotely fifty-five. At best, she's a well-worn thirty-six."

"So?" Neo said.

"So I didn't take into consideration that they might not be alone. What if this is where Carmella's parents live, and she and Joe are in the house with two senior citizens? Temo can't do his quake here. It might cause pacemakers to go haywire. People could stroke out. Oxygen tanks could explode."

"Boss," Temo started, "I don't think my quake could do *that*."

"I'm just saying, this changes our approach big-time. We have innocents to protect. We can't let people get hurt." She shook her head. "Joe and Carmella? They can get as bruised up as necessary, but I don't want anyone else becoming collateral damage."

Neo turned a little to see Donna better. "We can handle that. But it might not be a bad idea to have Charlie and Pierce help us. Maybe they could get the old people out."

"No, I need Rixaline safe and back at the penthouse as soon as possible." Donna frowned. "The fae know I have her."

Neo's eyes rounded a little. "They do? How?"

Donna snuck a look at Temo before answering. "I ran into one at the house as I was leaving. I was furious and not thinking, and I walked to the end of the driveway—"

"That's a long way from the house."

"I know. And just outside the property line and the protection of iron. Like I said, I wasn't thinking. Anyway, Temo got there in time to help me out, but the fae smelled Rixaline on me. It knew right away that I'd been in contact with her. I'm sure it figured out she came to me for sanctuary."

Neo was silent for a moment. "What's the worst they can do? Your building is completely protected."

"But," Temo said, "she's not in the building right now."

"Exactly." Donna looked at the car ahead of them. "That's what I'm worried about. And why I want her back at the penthouse as quickly as possible."

"Point taken," Neo said. "It's just the three of us, then." She looked at Temo. "This quake of yours. Can you control it? Direct it?"

"I can control the strength of it, and I can direct where it goes, but the effects are still very broad. When I knocked the fae away, the governor fell down."

Donna nodded. "Not a big deal, though. I could tell the shockwaves that went out in front of you were much greater than what I felt standing behind you."

Neo gave that some thought. "So how about this? Temo doesn't set this quake off until we know if there are seniors in the house and where they are so they can be shielded a little. Does that work?"

Donna sat back. "Yes. So long as they aren't frail to begin with. If we're talking walkers and oxygen, then no quake. I don't want us to be responsible for hurting them."

"Cool," Temo said. "Me either."

The car ahead slowed to a stop, and Donna's phone vibrated with an incoming call from Pierce. She answered. "Which house?"

"The blue one just ahead on the left. Number 1320."

"Okay. We'll take it from here. Get Rixaline back to the penthouse."

"You sure you don't want help?"

"You're helping by keeping her safe. We're good. Thank you. See you as soon as possible."

"You all be safe too. Bye." Pierce hung up.

The SUV Charlie was driving made the next right turn to head for home.

Temo looked up. "We can't park in front. Too obvious and too great a chance of being seen. But the way these streets are laid out, we could come in from the back."

"Sounds good," Donna said.

"Wait." Neo put her hand on the door. "Let me out here. I'll do a little recon around the front and meet you in the backyard."

"Be safe," Temo said.

"Yes," Donna agreed. "No risks. Just recon."

"Got it." Neo hopped out, letting in a burst of cold air before she shut the door.

It felt good. The chill was just the thing Donna needed to bring her into the moment.

With a burst of speed, Neo disappeared into the darkness, and Temo rolled slowly forward. He and Donna both took long, hard looks at the house as they went by.

Temo ran down the details. "Single-story ranch, two-car garage. No ramp, so whoever lives there is able-bodied enough to use the steps. Probably three bedrooms, two baths. Maybe a half bath in the basement, which might only be partially finished. That could be where Joe is."

"Agreed. Especially because the basement probably has access to the garage, which would give him an easy way out. Although I'm guessing they ditched the SUV they had at my house."

"The basement is pretty easy to defend too. One set of steps going down. Maybe a walk-out access. Maybe not." He turned the corner and went around the block. "Anyway, if that's where he and Carmella are, I can easily use my skills to give them a good jolt and leave anyone on the main level mostly untouched. Maybe a little rumble. Not much more."

"Perfect. We'll know more when we hit the backyard."

"Neo might have it figured out too." He parked in front of a house with no lights on and no cars in the drive. "This okay?"

They were three houses away. Seconds in vampire time. "Perfect."

"All right." He turned the motor off. "Ready to go when you are."

"You have zip ties?"

He patted the pockets of his cargo pants. "And duct tape."

"Even better."

They got out and made their way forward, then along the side yard of the house behind Carmella's parents' house. If this *was* where her parents lived and not some weird setup she'd scammed her way into because she thought a retirement community was a good place to hide with her scummy boyfriend.

Although Joe was fifty-three. And had a full set of dentures.

Neo met them at the property line between the two homes. "We have a problem."

Of course they did. "It's not her parents' house, is it?" Donna asked.

Neo shook her head. "I don't think so. The woman inside looks more like a grandmother, an elderly aunt, or some poor random woman she's manipulated. Whichever it is, there's a little old lady in the living room asleep in a recliner. TV's still on."

"Any sign of Joe or Carmella?"

"No, but there are enough dishes in the kitchen sink to tell me that there's definitely more than one person in this house."

Donna grinned. "You do a pretty thorough recon."

Neo smiled. "Yeah, well, take a deep inhale. What do you smell?"

Temo answered before Donna. "Cigar smoke."

Neo nodded. "Does Joe smoke cigars?"

"Yes. And it's unlikely that's a habit of Grandma's. Joe's in there. He has to be." Donna stared at the house. "Is there basement access from outside?"

"Not that I found."

"Good," Donna said. "Makes it easier for us. Temo thinks that's where Joe and Carmella are."

Neo smiled at him. "I know they are. The side of the house has two basement windows. They have sheers over them, but there was enough light from the TV for me to make out two shapes. They're definitely down there. Besides that, I counted four heartbeats in the house."

"Four?" Donna asked.

"Grandma has a dog that looks as old as she is. Pooch is sleeping in a bed near the recliner. Pretty sure it's not a guard-dog situation. The thing looks more fluff than fierce."

Temo grinned. "Good recon."

"Thanks." Neo fluttered her lashes at him.

Donna almost rolled her eyes at the pair. "Okay, so once Temo does his quake, how are we going to get Joe and Carmella out but still protect the old lady and Fido?"

"I have an idea," Neo said. "One that would give us an advantage."

"Oh?" Donna was all about advantages.

She nodded. "I can cut power to the house. That'd put them in the dark, but it wouldn't affect us, and if we're quiet, Grandma might not even wake up."

Donna considered that. "We might be quiet, but what about Joe and Carmella?"

Temo tapped his fist against his open palm. "We gotta strike hard and fast. Don't let them get noisy before we slap that duct tape over their mouths."

"I'm all for that," Donna said.

"Good." Neo turned toward the house. "There's a side door into the garage. I want to cut the power from the breaker box so I can turn it back on when we're done. Don't want to leave Grandma without heat or lights."

"That wouldn't be good," Donna said. "They've been talking about snow. Last thing we want is an old woman and her dog freezing to death. Did you bring anything to pick a lock with?"

She shook her head. "But I won't need it. A good twist of the knob, and we're in. Grandma will just have to lock the door into the house since the outside door's knob will have to be replaced."

"All right," Donna said. "Let's get this done. Remember, quick in and out. And protect the old lady. Temo, make sure Neo and I are behind you when you do your thing."

"You got it, boss."

The three headed for the door at the side of the garage, keeping to the shadows as much as possible.

Neo put her hand on the doorknob and wrenched it until it popped open with a tinny, metallic squeak. She leaned in, listening for a moment, then shook her head. "No movement."

Donna nodded.

In they went. There were two cars in the garage. A gold late-model Honda Accord that looked well kept and a flashy red Miata that had a dent in the door panel and a long, unmistakable key scratch down the same side. That had to be Carmella's.

Donna almost laughed imagining Joe in that car.

Neo went to the breaker box, opened it, and threw the main switch.

The garage had already been dark, but the soft sounds of the two televisions that had been coming through the walls disappeared.

A muted male voice cursed.

"Joe?" Temo asked.

Donna nodded. "Let's go grab us a gangster."

# CHAPTER 25

Joe kept making noise, oblivious to the beatdown that was coming. He was clomping around in the dark, running into things, and complaining about Carmella not paying the bill.

It was pretty funny, at least to Donna.

Temo led the way, since he was their first line of attack. They went into the house, found the door to the basement steps, and went down. A small hall split to the finished side and the unfinished side. Easy to tell where Joe was. And not just because of the stench of cigars, Carmella's perfume, and the cheap floral air freshener losing the battle with both.

Donna felt bad for the old woman upstairs. No one should have to put up with Joe and his disgusting ways.

Temo gave her and Neo a hand signal to wait, then went down the hall to the end where it opened up. He repeated the same thing he'd done with the fae, stomping his foot and saying, "*Tofa*." He spoke the word a little differently this time, with more restraint and focused power.

The ground under Donna and Neo trembled, but they stayed standing.

In the other room, two cries were followed by the thumps of two bodies hitting the floor.

Neo and Donna raced forward.

Temo was already beside Joe, holding him down. Both he and Carmella looked like they'd been knocked out, but Donna knew that was too good to last.

"Temo," she hissed. "Zip ties?"

He dug into his pocket. "Here." He tossed some to Donna.

"Thanks." She grabbed them, then she and Neo went to work securing Carmella's hands and feet.

Temo did the same to Joe, who was already coming around.

He tried to sit up. "What the he—"

Temo tore off a strip of duct tape and slapped it over his mouth.

Joe did his best to curse and scream anyway, but it just came out a ragey mumble.

"Neo?" Temo held up the tape.

She nodded and raised her hand. He threw the roll to her. She caught it, then ripped a piece off and covered Carmella's mouth before standing up. "Hey, you think one of us should go check on the old lady?"

Donna got to her feet as well, brushing her hands off. "I don't hear any sounds of distress. I'm sure she's okay. But we can have a look when we go back up."

At the sound of Donna's voice, Joe's head whipped around.

His eyes went wide, and he said her name, although through the duct tape it sounded like, "Nohna?"

She went over and leaned down. "That's right. It's me. Not dead like you thought, huh? How's that for a shocker?"

He just stared, eyes round and wide. Maybe a little fearful. Good. He should be afraid. He was about to get what had been coming to him for a long time.

She straightened. "Temo, why don't you take Joe, and I'll take Carmella. That way, Neo's free to get the power back on."

"You got it, boss." He squatted, then hoisted Joe over his shoulder. Joe's nose whistled as the air came out of him.

Neo pulled Carmella to her feet, who was only now coming around. She squirmed, but Neo snarled at her. "Move again, and I will bite you."

A little mew of acquiescence was all that answered Neo. She glanced at Donna. "You grab her, and I'll zip upstairs."

Donna came over and put Carmella over her shoulder. The woman didn't weigh a whole lot and seemed rather timid, then Donna remembered this was the same woman who'd shot an FBI agent.

However she was acting, there was a good chance she was putting on a ruse in hopes of getting one over on them.

Neo started for the hall, then stopped and held up her hand. "You hear that?" she whispered. Then she pointed upstairs.

Donna listened. Some small, shuffling noises. "The dog?"

Neo nodded. "Yep. Okay, getting the lights."

She disappeared down the hall. Donna and Temo followed after her with their human cargo. They were almost to the steps when Neo called out to them.

"You guys? We have a problem."

They rounded the stairwell and looked up, seeing exactly what she was talking about.

Grandma was at the top of the steps. With a shotgun.

She had it braced against her hip and pointed at them. "Where do you think you're going with my granddaughter?"

Her little dog, which was some kind of fuzzy white terrier-demon hybrid, snarled at them.

Carmella squirmed and squealed like there was a prize for most obnoxious hostage. Not that she was a hostage, exactly.

"I can take her," Neo said softly.

But Donna honestly didn't want the woman to get hurt. "Ma'am, your granddaughter shot an FBI agent. And this man that she's brought into your house is a mobster. Joseph Barrone. He's a very wanted man."

Grandma hoisted the gun a little more in Donna's direction. "He's also my meal ticket, toots. Now put them both down, or I'm gonna blow a hole in Ninja Barbie here."

Neo squinted and gave Donna a look. "Am I Ninja Barbie?"

"I guess so," Donna said. "You are dressed all in black."

"So are you."

"Shut up," Grandma yelled.

Donna had had enough. There could be fae swarming outside the house, for all she knew. "Temo. Drop her."

"You got it, boss. Hang on."

Donna hooked her free arm around the stair railing. Neo quickly did the same.

Temo pounded his foot against the tread and gave a loud, "*Tofa.*"

Grandma went flying back with the shotgun, pulling the trigger as she went and taking out a good portion of the stairwell ceiling. Her little dog yelped and tumbled away after her. Both disappeared from view.

The boom from the gun and the quake from Temo nearly caused Neo and Donna to pull the railing loose, but everything subsided a few moments later. Everything but Joe's and Carmella's squirming.

Neo hustled up to make sure Grandma was all right. Donna and Temo, still toting their human haul, followed.

The old woman was sprawled on the kitchen floor, out cold, her floral housedress hitched up to her knees, revealing rolled-down support hose. The snarly little dog had retreated under the table and growled as they entered.

Temo growled back, and the mutt went running. Grandma's hand was still on the shotgun. Temo nudged it out of reach while Neo bent at the old woman's side.

She put her fingers to the woman's neck. "Pulse seems quick, but nothing weird. I think we're good to leave her. Cops will be here soon after that blast, but we can call 911 anyway, just to be sure."

Temo nodded. "I have a burner in the glove box. We can call from that."

Neo stood. "Then let me turn the power on, and let's bounce."

"I hate to leave her," Donna said.

Neo's mouth bent with disbelief. "Donna, she was going to blow a hole in you. And she was letting Joe hide out here for money."

Donna nodded. "And we need to get these two taken care of. I know. You're right."

Sirens wailed in the distance, and Neo tipped her head. "See?"

"I hear them," Donna said.

"Hear what?" Temo asked. "Oh, never mind, I hear them now too." He adjusted Joe so he was better positioned on his shoulder. "Let's hustle, ladies. Those sirens are still a long way off, but they'll be here soon enough."

They all headed out, Neo flipping the breaker back on as they exited.

There was a light or two on in the neighboring houses. Lights that hadn't been on before.

Temo hit the button on the key fob to open the back of the SUV, and they poured on the speed, moving quickly to get Carmella and Joe loaded.

The process resulted in more muted curses and complaints, as well as a lot of squirming from Carmella and dirty looks from Joe, but Donna couldn't have cared less. The mission had been successful.

After far too long, Joseph Barrone was truly off the streets. He wasn't going to be a menace to society—or her—anymore. And she'd done it without killing him. It was a wonderful feeling.

They got in the SUV, and Temo started driving. Less than ten seconds outside of Holiday City, two patrol cars, lights flashing and sirens blaring, flew past and into the development.

Donna exhaled, causing the wound in her side to ache a little. That was the first time it had bothered her, probably because of all the adrenaline in her system.

Neo twisted around in her seat, smiling. "You did it."

"We did it. And thank you for your help."

She shrugged. "You're the most interesting vam—I mean, person I know."

Donna snorted. Wouldn't do to have Joe knowing what she really was. "Thanks. But I'd like to be a lot less interesting for a while."

Temo looked at her in the rearview. "You going to let Rico know we're coming?"

"Yes, but I want to time it right. I don't want a big production, you know? Just dump and run."

Temo nodded. "Then I'd say text him when we're five minutes out. We can sit nearby and wait too. Make sure he takes delivery, if you know what I mean."

"I do, and that's a good plan. In fact…" She pulled her phone out of the seatback pocket. "I might just see if he's still awake."

She tapped her screen on to see several waiting texts from him, all a few minutes apart.

*Those accounts are in both L & J's names.*

*Several million each. Now frozen.*

*Not like you not to respond.*

*Promise me you're not doing anything dumb.*

*Donna. I like it a lot better when you answer me.*

She laughed. "He's awake. Or at least he was." She checked the time stamps. "An hour and five minutes ago."

She responded to his last text. *Answering you now. Still up?*

A fresh round of muffled complaints and pleading started up from the back. As much as she would have loved to tell Joe the truth about who she was now and what exactly had happened to his five million dollars, she ignored him. She didn't need to give him anything that he might use against her.

Or worse, use to defend himself. Somehow, he'd turn his wife becoming a vampire into an insanity defense. She wasn't going to risk anything like that.

Her phone chimed with an incoming text.

Rico. *I'm up. Why were you so quiet for so long?*

*Busy.* But even as she hit send on that, she knew that wasn't going to satisfy him.

*Doing what?*

*Vampire things.*

*That's what I'm afraid of.*

She grinned. *Great news about the account numbers. How's the search for Joe going?*

*We found the SUV. Dumped near the shipping yards and set on fire.*

*So no leads, then.*

Enough time went by before he answered that Donna could sense his frustration.

*No.*

*Anything I can do to help?*

*If I thought there was, I'd tell you. You sure you don't know that woman?*

*Joe had a lot of girlfriends over the years. I stopped paying attention after a while.*

*I can understand.*

Neo looked around the seat. "Awfully busy with the typing there."

Donna smiled. "Just chatting."

"With Rico?"

"Yep."

"You tell him yet?" She tipped her head toward the rear of the SUV. "About what you've been up to this evening?"

"Not yet, no." She glanced through the windshield to get her bearings, then scooted forward to be closer to Temo. "How close are we?"

He looked at his phone's GPS. "Says eight miles.

You could probably tell him to meet you. Especially because he might not be coming from home."

Neo nodded. "Plus, the clock's ticking toward sunrise. Let's not forget that. We can't exactly sit there all night and wait for him to show up."

"Right. I'll see where he is." Donna started typing again. *Are you near the office by any chance?*

*Why?*

She thought for a moment. *I have something for you. I can just leave it by the front door.*

*What kind of something?*

*The kind you're really going to want. How's Agent Cheng btw?*

*Still in surgery.*

Donna shook her head. That poor man. She touched her crucifix, praying he'd live. *How soon can you get to headquarters?*

*20 mins. Maybe 15. What are you dropping off? Can't I just get it in the morning? We have a drop slot in the door.*

*Won't fit.* She snickered. She was actually kind of enjoying this. It was like the criminal version of Twenty Questions. *And you probably don't want to wait that long.*

*On my way.*

"Pulling in," Temo said.

The SUV dipped as it went into the parking lot. Donna glanced into the back to see Joe wriggling into a seated position.

He saw the building ahead of them. And the FBI insignia on the door. Anger filled his eyes for a moment, only to be replaced by a much more pitiful expression as the indecipherable pleading started up.

She had no sympathy for him or his moll.

He inched toward her, the begging growing more insistent.

She glared at him, thinking about all the times she'd feared him. And feared for her kids. "You think this is unfair of me? You think I should set you loose and let bygones be bygones?"

He nodded vigorously.

She leaned in ever so slightly. "Maybe you should remember that I could have killed you. But didn't. Even after you put a bullet through me and left me for dead."

# CHAPTER 26

Her last couple of words stopped Joe's nodding. He went quiet, but his eyes were wild and full of questions about how Donna could still be alive.

She wasn't about to tell him. Instead, she kept prodding him. "Was it fair of you to do that to me?"

Temo parked outside FBI headquarters. "We're here."

"Thanks," Donna said without looking away from Joe. She wasn't ready to let him off the hook so fast.

"You want me to pop the back open?" Temo asked.

"Not just yet," she answered. Then she spoke to Joe again. "Well? Was it?"

Joe remained still and silent. But he was seething. She could tell by the flare of his nostrils and that twitchy left eyelid. Probably wishing he'd done a better job with that bullet.

Wouldn't have mattered. It hadn't been wood. Not that he'd have known that's what it required these days to take her down. Although...did it? Her crucifix had made her immune to the sun. Had it

285

also made her immune to other things that could hurt her?

Interesting thought. And one she'd have to pursue in more depth at a more suitable time.

But right now, she pursed her lips. "Seems to me handing you over to the authorities is a kindness you don't deserve."

More seething. She almost laughed. He could be as angry as he wanted. It didn't matter. In about ten minutes, he would no longer be her problem.

The thought made her smile.

Joe growled behind his duct tape, then suddenly lunged at her—to do what, she wasn't sure—but she reacted with vampire speed and instinct. His face met her fist. Not a punch. Just him running into her tightly clenched hand with a great deal of velocity.

His head snapped back like it was on a tether, and he went down flat in the cargo hold. Donna leaned up to peer over the seat. "You just don't learn, do you?"

Joe groaned, and his eye looked like it was already swelling up. Carmella was crouched next to him, as best she could with the restraints, and stared at Donna with new respect, which was as it should be.

Donna put her backside on the seat again and faced front. "All right. I'm going to get out and wait for Rico. Smells too much like criminals in here."

Temo laughed. "No drop and run, then?"

She shook her head. "Changed my mind. We deserve credit for our hard work. And Rico needs to know about Grandma. She was helping these two, and I'm not cool with that."

"I agree," Neo said. "Plus, she tried to kill us."

"Good point." Donna hopped out and went around back.

Neo and Temo joined her. She leaned on the rear bumper and tipped her head back to stare at the sky. The cold felt good. And not because she was having a hot flash either. Those were a thing of the past, thanks to her new life as a vampire.

In fact, it seemed she wasn't as susceptible to extreme temperatures anymore. At least not the cold, anyway. She hadn't been in hot weather since she'd been turned. If she ever got to Florida to shop for that condo, she'd see how heat-tolerant she really was.

She closed her eyes for a moment. The thought of spending some time on the beach instantly made her relax. Thankfully, because of the crucifix around her neck, she could still do that.

Probably wouldn't do any full-on sunbathing. No point in tempting fate.

Neo's laugh made Donna open her eyes. "What?"

"You're all smiley. That happy about dumping Joe off, huh? Can't say I blame you."

"Well, that is pretty much a dream come true."

"I get it. I do. Congrats on that finally happening."

"Thanks."

Neo leaned back next to her and looked at the sky. "I hope it doesn't snow for Francine's party. It's pretty, but it's messy."

"I don't know," Donna said. "I see a lot of clouds. And the air has that smell about it. We might wake up to a dusting."

A car pulled into the parking lot.

"That your FBI guy?" Temo asked.

Donna stood up straight. "That's him."

She didn't recognize the car, but she could see Rico through the windshield. She'd never seen his personal vehicle before, but the sleek, black Dodge Charger didn't surprise her. There was something slightly feral and predatory about that car, which made it perfect for a guy who was both an FBI agent and a werewolf.

He parked nearby and got out. "All right. I'm here. What do you have for me?" He looked at Neo and Temo. "I see you brought backup. Must be good."

"Why don't we just show you?" Donna looked at Temo and nodded. "Open it up."

He and Neo stepped out of the path of the lift gate. Temo pushed the button on the key fob, and the rear hatch rose skyward. Joe and Carmella writhed around inside like worms bound for the hook.

Rico put his hands on his hips and just stared into the depths of the SUV for a few long seconds. Then, his mouth set in a hard line, he shifted his gaze to Donna. "I told you not to—"

"You told me not to kill him," she cut him off. "I didn't."

Rico looked around her. "That's quite the *second* shiner he's got."

"He ran into my fist. Also? Not a fatal injury."

"Donna." Rico massaged the back of his neck.

"I kept him alive, didn't I?" Donna stepped into Rico's personal space and squared off in front of him, hands on her hips, her head tilted back slightly to better make eye contact. "That's more than I should have done after he tried to kill me. Now say thank you."

A tiny spark of amusement lit Rico's eyes. "For keeping him alive or bringing him in?"

"Both," she answered.

"Thank you."

"You're welcome." She moved to the side so he could admire her handiwork.

"How did you know where to find him? And why didn't you call us in and let us handle it?"

"I had help, and that's all I'm saying. I didn't call because, to be honest, you probably would have wanted to do things by the rules, and that's not exactly how we ran this. Doesn't matter now. My team was very efficient and got the job done."

He looked less than impressed. She didn't care. "Now, listen, there's an old woman in Holiday City who blew a hole in her house with a shotgun. It wasn't burglars, or whatever story she told the local PD, who were just arriving as we were leaving. Anyway, you need to know this because she's Carmella's grandmother, and she was aiding and abetting these two, so she needs to pay for that."

"And..." Neo stepped forward, finger raised. "That shotgun blast was meant for us. So attempted murder too. Just saying."

Rico nodded. "I'll take care of it."

"One last thing." Donna chose her next words carefully. "If Joe is *ever* out on the streets again... Let's just say there's a good chance he'll end up in another accident. One that's much more successful than the first."

Rico frowned at her. "Let's hope it doesn't come to that."

"Let's. Especially since his incarceration is up to you now."

Rico sighed. "He won't be going anywhere. Besides a holding cell. You have my word." He reached for his phone. "I'm going to call in a few more agents to get this taken care of, but I'll get him and Carmella off your hands and into custody as quickly as I can."

"We can help you get them out of the SUV and into the building." Donna glanced at the sky as if sunrise was a concern for her. Really, though, it was Neo's vulnerability she was worried about. Although it wouldn't do for word to get out that the vampire governor of New Jersey was immune to the sun, so Donna had to keep up appearances. "Our time is running short."

"Right," Rico said. He pulled keys from his pocket. "Let me get the door."

By the time they had Carmella and Joe out of the SUV and were headed back to the penthouse, time really was running short. Too short for Neo to beat the sunrise home.

Donna stared at the horizon, not sure if she was

imagining the line of pink there or not. "Neo, you're going to have to stay over."

She glanced at Temo. "It's cool."

Donna smiled. "Just means you're going to have to hustle a little to get ready for the party. Not being at your own place and all."

She shrugged. "I'll manage. Sun's down around seven, and the party doesn't start until ten, so that's plenty of time. Especially for a low-maintenance sister like myself." She turned a little to see Donna better. "One thing, though."

"What's that?"

Her grin was big and bright. "You going to let my plus-one have the night off?"

Donna smiled. "I think that can be arranged. You are talking about Temo, right, and not some other plus-one?"

Neo made a face at her. "Stop playing. You know who I'm talking about."

"I do, and it's adorable." As best as Donna could tell, Temo looked like he was turning slightly pink. Which really was adorable. "I want him at the party anyway. I'd love to have Charlie there as well. After all, I'm the guest of honor, and they're my staff, so that just seems fitting. But I don't know what to do about Rixaline."

Temo looked up, seemingly happy to have something new to discuss. "Don't you think seventeen is a little young for a grown-up party?"

"I do, and I wasn't planning on taking her. Not just because of her age, but it's too dangerous for her to be so exposed. Having her out for a short amount of time in the car while hunting Joe is one thing, but all night at a crowded party? The risk of the fae trying to grab her again is just too much. What I mean when I say I don't know what to do with her is, I don't want to leave her alone in the penthouse."

Neo nodded. "You don't trust her?"

Donna sighed. "I do, but not entirely. I hate to say that with the help she's given me, but the situation is still so new, and although she hasn't given me any reason not to trust her, this is one of those cases where I am going to err on the side of caution for a while."

"I think that's wise, boss."

"Thanks, Temo." Donna sat back. "I just don't know what else to do but ask Charlie to stay with her. Which feels like punishing Charlie. Maybe not punishing, exactly. But it's certainly not fair for her to be the one who has to be the stay-at-home chaperone."

Temo looked up. "Why don't you let my cousin Penina take that job? She's one of the two new security people I hired. She has the same skill set I do with a little fire magic thrown in. That seems to be standard with the females in our family. I'm sure she'd do it."

"You think?" Donna nodded. "That would be great. Call her and see."

Temo nodded as they pulled into the parking garage. "She'll do it. But I'll call her to confirm."

He let Neo and Donna off at the elevator, then went to park.

They went straight to the penthouse. Charlie and Rixaline were at the big table in the kitchen, putting a puzzle together. Lucky was lying on the far end of the table, supervising the action. Donna took a seat next to Rixaline.

Was she being too cautious? The girl hadn't done anything but be helpful. Maybe she was just paranoid because of her life with Joe.

Both looked at her with questions, but Charlie was the first to ask hers. "How did it go?"

"Mission accomplished, and no one died."

Rixaline grinned. "Is that a good thing?"

"Yes and a little no." Donna laughed. "No, it's good. I just hope this is truly the last time I have to face my husband."

Pierce walked into the room. "I thought I heard you. Everything okay?"

"Everything's perfect." Donna reached over and took Rixaline's hand. "Your help was invaluable tonight. I am truly grateful. Thank you."

Rixaline bent her head. "I was happy to do it."

"Well, again, thank you." Donna squeezed the girl's hand before letting go. She looked at Pierce. "I think you can safely file those divorce papers now."

"First thing Monday."

"Thanks." She stood. "About tomorrow night and Francine's party. Temo's cousin Penina is going to stay in the penthouse with Rixaline. Charlie, I certainly hope you'll be able to accompany Pierce and me to the party. Do you have something to wear?"

Charlie nodded, smiling. "I do. Thank you."

"If you want to bring a date, you're more than welcome to, but I'll probably need you there professionally in some capacity. Sorry. I know that's not the best way to enjoy a party, but I fully expect there to be all kinds of vampires there that I should know."

Charlie put her hands up. "Of course. I will be sure you know who's who and make all the necessary introductions."

Neo snorted. "You better believe there will be all kinds of vampires there you should know. The crowd is legit at Francine's parties. Just keep an open mind and be prepared to realize you were not prepared."

"Really?" Donna pondered that. "Little old Francine? I mean, I know she's a vampire and a very cool one, but—"

"Donna, you have no idea." Neo shook her head. "None. The last party she threw, Count DeLaRossi ended up superglued to her ceiling."

Donna's mouth fell open.

Neo nodded. "Yep."

"You're right," Donna said. "I may not be prepared for this."

Pierce laughed. "I have to say it doesn't sound that much different than some of the attorney parties I've been to."

"Should be interesting," Charlie said.

Temo came in from downstairs. "Penina's all set. She'll be here tomorrow around five."

Donna clapped her hands together. "Perfect. Now I'm going to turn in. I'm too tired to even have pie. Tomorrow night is going to be fun but hectic. Besides, I can feel the sun inching higher."

"Me too," Neo said. She looked at Temo. "You want to show me that guest room?"

"Yeah, come on." He waved at the rest of them. "Night."

He and Neo left.

Rixaline got up from the table. "Can I leave the puzzle here to finish tomorrow?"

"Absolutely," Donna said. "Lucky might have other thoughts, though."

She laughed. "Can I take Lucky to bed with me, then?"

"Sure," Donna answered. "Just don't trap him in there, or you'll be woken up by a lot of yowling. He's his own man and likes his freedom."

Rixaline grinned. "Okay." She scooped the big animal off the table and cradled him in her arms as she went down the hall.

Charlie smiled. "I'm really glad everything went well this evening."

"Me too." Donna took a breath. "I am really ready for things to calm down, you know?"

"I'm sure." She tipped her head toward the stairs. "I should go. I'm not sure Temo knows where the extra toiletries are."

"Thanks, Charlie."

She nodded. "You're welcome, Governor."

She left, giving Pierce and Donna a moment

alone. She looked at him. "I'm going to have to call the kids and tell them about their father. And soon too. I really don't want them to hear about it on the news."

He looked at the time. "Joe Jr. is probably up."

"You're right. I'll call him before I crash." She pulled the elastic off her ponytail, freeing her hair so she could massage her scalp. "I guess I'll have to set my alarm to make sure I'm up to call Christina."

"Do you want me to do it? I realize that's kind of impersonal."

"Thank you, but better she hear it from me."

He nodded. "Understand. Sleep well. See you in the afternoon."

"Thanks. Good night." She drifted toward her bedroom, pulling off her leather jacket and tossing it on the chaise before closing the door. She was suddenly bone-tired and more ready for bed than she'd realized.

But she had one more task to do before that could happen. She took her phone from her back pocket and dialed her son.

"Hey, Mom. Should you be up right now? The sun's out and all."

"I'm inside, but your concern is noted and appreciated. I won't keep you. I know you have to be on base shortly, and I'm about to go to bed. I just needed to tell you that your father didn't die in that car accident. He faked his own death."

A rare curse slipped from her son's lips. "Sorry. I meant, what the fudge?"

She laughed. "No, you didn't. And trust me. I understand. But the good news is he's in FBI custody and won't be a problem for any of us anymore."

"I'm glad about that. But don't you have to get divorced now?"

"I do. And it's already being worked on."

"You want me to tell Christina?"

"No, thank you, honey. I'll call her in a few hours."

"Okay. Sorry about all this. He's certainly caused you a lifetime's worth of problems."

Donna smiled. "Yes, he has, but he also gave me you and your sister."

"You always could see the bright side. Love you."

"Love you too. Have a good day at work."

"Thanks."

They hung up, and still smiling, she stripped off the rest of her clothes, took a quick shower, then fell into bed, exhausted.

She was instantly asleep and stayed that way until her phone rang.

# CHAPTER 27

With the fog of sleep making her movements clumsy and her eyes bleary, she somehow managed to grab her phone and answer it. "Hello?"

"Mom? Is Dad alive? What is this on the news? It says the FBI has arrested him? What's going on? Is he? How is that possible?"

Donna sat up and shoved her hair out of her face. "Christina, honey, take a breath."

"Mom, it's on Twitter and Facebook. People are reposting the articles and tagging me. Plus, my texts and PMs are blowing up. Tell me it's not true."

"I'm sorry, sweetheart, but it *is* true. I was going to call you earlier, but I figured you'd still be asleep, so I—"

"Okay, from here on out? Anything like this? You call me and wake me up. Got it?"

Donna nodded. "Got it."

"So how is he alive?"

"He faked his death. It was all a big ruse." Donna thought about the Ukrainian who'd taken Joe's place in the car. She wondered if Rico would be able to identify him.

Christina hadn't said a word while Donna had been thinking. Finally, she broke the silence. "So…he was going to just leave us? Why would he do that? Why would he leave his family? I thought he loved us."

Donna could hear the pain in her daughter's voice. Joe might have been a criminal and a terrible husband, but she understood that, despite all that, to Christina, he was always going to be her father.

He'd doted on her when she'd been little. Treated her like his princess. Wasn't until she'd gotten older and wiser that the rift between them had grown.

Donna wished she could hug her child. "I wish there was an answer that wouldn't hurt, but the truth is, there is every indication he was planning on starting a new life. Without us."

No need to mention Carmella. Christina was already hurting.

A soft, muffled sob came through the phone, followed quickly by the harsh clearing of Christina's throat. "Too bad he didn't get to do us that favor."

Donna's smile was sad. Christina's response held so much anger, but Donna understood. Joe had that effect. "I know."

"Are you okay, Mom?"

"I am. Better now that he's in custody. I'm really sorry you have to go through all this with it being on social media and all that. Hopefully, it'll fade away fast."

"Yeah, me too. What should I say to people?"

"You don't have to say anything."

"It's not that easy. People expect an answer."

"Then just tell them you don't wish to discuss it."

"Mom. A reporter from CNN called me."

Donna blinked, more awake than she'd been a few minutes ago. "Are you serious?"

"Yes. There was a voicemail on my phone this morning, asking me to call back. The woman identified herself as a reporter from CNN."

The nerve. "So you didn't actually talk to her? Good. You know what? How'd you like the name and number of an attorney to refer them to? You could tell them all inquiries have to go through your lawyer."

"For real? That would be good. Yeah, I would like that very much."

"Okay, I'll text you Pierce's information as soon as we hang up. We're going to get through this. And next Friday night, you'll be here." Which meant Donna was going to miss her First Fangs Club meeting, but that couldn't be helped.

"I can't wait. Thanks, Mom. Hey, are you still... you know."

"A vampire? Yes, honey. It's not a temporary thing."

"Just checking. Okay, gotta run to class. Love you."

"Love you too. Have a great day. Bye!"

As the call ended, Donna laid the phone against her chest and stared at the ceiling. That hadn't gone too terribly. The fact that a major news outlet was interested didn't surprise her that much. The Mafia was always interesting. At least for five minutes.

Hopefully, that would be how long the renewed attention on Joe would last too.

She looked at the closed blinds. The room was pitch-dark, but she could imagine the sun gleaming on the river. She missed the sun. The feeling of warmth on her face. How calming that was.

Maybe she could sneak up to the roof for a few minutes. What were the chances that anyone else was up? Last night had been a late one. Really, it had been morning when they'd all turned in. Everyone had to be asleep. She should be, too, but the call had wound her up a bit.

She sent Christina the promised text with Pierce's info, then pulled on her robe and cautiously opened her bedroom door. The penthouse was dark, as the rest of the blinds were closed.

Didn't matter. She could still see. Vampire eyes were amazing like that.

She tiptoed through the kitchen and down the hall toward the stairs that led to the roof. She hadn't been up to that area yet, and she was eager to see what it was like. She put her hand on the knob, then said a little prayer that the door was unlocked and wouldn't squeak when she opened it.

Thankfully, it was and it didn't.

Barefoot, she padded up the stairs to the door that led outside. Again, she eased it open, waiting for a squeak, but there was no sound.

Just an explosion of light that nearly blinded her. She blinked hard, squinting against the onslaught of sun.

But it was glorious all the same.

As her eyes adjusted, she closed the door carefully, making sure it didn't close all the way and lock her out, in case that was a possibility.

Then she turned to survey the rooftop before her.

The half she could see was a paradise.

On one side, it was all open space with a large, weathered wood dining table and big padded chairs. It was the kind of arrangement that invited hours of lingering over good food, better wine, and stellar company. She imagined it with lots of little candles twinkling and bunches of wildflowers in mason jars down the center of the table.

Summer evenings were going to be amazing up here.

On the other side, a pergola of the same weathered wood partially covered a large seating area. White sailcloth drapes, tied back for the winter, could turn the space private very easily. Long padded benches and several chairs surrounded a grouping of low tables.

Lots of big ceramic pots and planter boxes indicated that during warmer months, greenery abounded. She could kind of imagine it too. Lots of fairy lights and some soft music playing, the delicious summer breezes and the scents of whatever flowers were grown up here. It would be an oasis.

If Christina spent the summer here, she'd probably just live on this rooftop.

With a smile, Donna closed her eyes to enjoy the sun on her skin and the thoughts of more peaceful days to come. She'd expected it to be windy this high up, but it was surprisingly calm.

"Who are you?"

Donna jumped and let out a little squeak. Pre-turning, she probably would have peed a little too. Thank heavens those days were over. "Sorry?"

A woman stood in front of her. Her wild red hair was liberally streaked with silver and tied back with a yellow bandanna. She wore denim overalls and a barn coat and had a trowel in one gloved hand. She might have been Donna's age. Or maybe older. Or younger. She had a few wrinkles, but she had a glow about her too.

And a greenhouse was behind her. On the other side of the rooftop entrance, opposite all the recreational space, was a glass enclosure filled with plants and trees. At least it seemed like that was what was inside as best as Donna could tell through the fogged glass.

"I said, who are you?" the woman repeated.

"I'm Donna. Who are you?"

The woman didn't move. "I'm Jerabeth."

"Hi, Jerabeth. Are you...gardening?" She must live in the building. Donna hadn't realized other people had access to the roof. But hadn't Charlie said it was the exclusive property of the penthouse? Donna couldn't remember.

Jerabeth's gaze was full of suspicion. "You could say that. I'm in charge of the governor's greenhouse.

Do you have permission to be up here, Donna?"

"The governor's greenhouse?" Donna grinned. How about that? "As it happens, I'm the governor." She stuck her hand out. "Belladonna Barrone. Nice to meet you, Jerabeth. I didn't even know there was a greenhouse."

Jerabeth's eyes narrowed, and she dropped her trowel to thrust a hand at Donna and bark out a word. "*Glacio*."

Donna frowned. Or rather, she tried to. Her face wasn't moving. None of her was. It was like she'd suddenly been given a full-body Botox shot. Mary and Joseph, what was going on?

Jerabeth picked up her trowel and pointed it at Donna. "Nice try, but there's no way you're the governor." She jabbed her trowel at the sky. "If you were, you'd be on fire right now. That's what the sun does to vampires. Maybe remember that the next time you try to impersonate one."

Crap. Crappity crap crap. Donna would have groaned if she'd been able. In her enthusiasm, she'd forgotten about the whole no-sun thing. The best she could do was grunt.

So ladylike.

Jerabeth stuck her trowel in the side pocket of her overalls, pulled off her gloves, and dug a phone out of her barn coat. She dialed, then put the phone to her ear, all while keeping a close watch on Donna. "Hello, Charlene? Sorry to wake you, but I caught an impostor on the roof. Some chick who says she's the governor. Beats me. Must have come up the service elevator."

Jerabeth nodded. "Sure, I'll hold her. She's hexed right now and not going anywhere. All right."

Hexed? Was Jerabeth a witch? Seemed like the only logical explanation. Unless there was another kind of supernatural that used hexes.

The call ended, and Jerabeth stuck the phone back in her coat. "Whatever game you were going to play, it's over. Security's on the way up."

Donna let out another grunt.

"Save it."

The rooftop door burst open. Donna couldn't turn to see who'd come through it, but she recognized the fresh, clean scent of Charlie's bergamot perfume and the sweet, beachy aroma of Temo's coconut shampoo.

She sighed. Internally, anyway.

"Boss?" Temo walked into her sight line.

She couldn't answer him. Couldn't even blink out *help* in Morse code.

Thankfully, Charlie took over. "Jerabeth, unhex her. Instantly." Then she pointed. "Temo, get a tarp from the greenhouse. I don't know how she's not ashes already, but we need to protect her."

Temo rushed into the greenhouse.

Jerabeth raised her hand at Donna. "*Solvo*."

Donna gasped as movement returned to her in a rush of sensation. It was like a hard jolt of pins and needles. She rolled her shoulders, happy to be free, but not loving the prickly feeling that remained. "I don't need a tarp, you guys."

Charlie looked at her. "With all due respect,

Governor, you absolutely do. I don't know how the sun hasn't already—"

"I'm immune." Donna hadn't intended to share that secret, but what was the other option? Make up some new story to explain why the sun hadn't set her on fire? What explanation could there be, anyway? The truth was easier. And she'd had enough lies in her old life. There was no place for them in this one.

Charlie blinked a few times. "How is that possible?"

Temo returned, tarp in hand and looking very ready to toss it over her.

Donna stopped him. "Temo, I don't need that."

"You sure, boss? Sun's awful bright."

Jerabeth was still giving her a weird look. She finally shifted her gaze to Charlie. "She's really the governor?"

"Yes," Donna said. "I'm really the governor."

Charlie nodded. "She is. And a good one too." She sighed and shook her head. "Governor, I apologize for not introducing you to Jerabeth sooner, but things have been busy—"

"Yes, they have been," Donna said. She didn't fault Charlie. After all, none of them had expected Rixaline's appearance or Joe's return from the dead.

"And you two tend to keep different hours," Charlie added. "Or I thought you did. Anyway, let me rectify things. Governor Barrone, this is Jerabeth Smalls, keeper of the greenhouse and garden, which is what we call the rest of the area up here.

Obviously, due to the time of year, it's not planted other than the greenhouse."

"Jerabeth."

Jerabeth nodded. "Sorry about freezing you."

Donna smiled but still had deep reservations. "We'll put that behind us."

Charlie made a face. "I still don't understand how you're able to withstand the UV rays."

"Yeah, boss," Temo said. "How is that?"

Donna didn't want to get into it. At least not in front of Jerabeth, who didn't seem ready to accept who Donna was. "We can discuss it later, but please don't say anything to anyone. For now, I think I'll just go back to bed. I didn't intend to be up here that long anyway."

"Of course. And we won't say a word." Charlie nodded in understanding. "You really should see the hothouse, though. Jerabeth is a talented elemental witch. There's not much she can't grow in there when it comes to fruits, vegetables, or flowers. She grows herbs and medicinal things too."

Temo's brows lifted. "Great papayas."

"That does sound interesting. Couldn't hurt to take a quick peek inside." Maybe complimenting some of Jerabeth's work would warm the woman up. Donna would much prefer having the witch on her side.

Especially when the witch in question could stop a vampire in her tracks.

# CHAPTER 28

The flowers, fruits, and vegetables were indeed impressive, and the place smelled incredible, rich with the perfume from all the blossoms, the tang of the herbs, and the sweet earthiness of the soil.

But it was the area at the very end of the hothouse, the part sectioned off from the rest with a full panel of wrought iron painted white, that captured Donna's attention. The door in the center of that panel, also white wrought iron, had a shiny brass lock on it. On the other side of the iron was more glass, completely dividing the space off. The glass was steamed up, just like the rest, making it impossible to see inside.

When the tour of the main area was over, Donna pointed to the far end. "What's all that about? Growing something fun for recreational purposes?" She meant it as a joke, of course.

But Jerabeth didn't laugh. "That's my poison garden."

That wiped the smile off Donna's face. "Seriously?"

"Yes."

Donna looked at the locked gate again. "Can I see it?"

Jerabeth answered, "No," at the same time that Charlie said, "Of course."

Both women looked at each other, but Charlie spoke first. "Jerabeth, you might be the gardener in charge of all this, but the governor is your boss, making her in charge of you. If she wants to see the poison garden, it's your job to show it to her."

Donna could have sworn Jerabeth growled in response. It was like Lucinda all over again. But this time the woman in front of her was an actual witch. Well, Donna had already had enough of that noise. She wasn't about to have the same kind of toxic relationship with someone who was essentially an employee. "Listen, Jerabeth, we're not going to do this. I can't do this. I won't."

"Do what?" Jerabeth asked.

Like she didn't know. "This whole back-and-forth between us. The snippiness. Let's get it out now. What's your problem with me? Why don't you like me?"

Jerabeth reeled back slightly, obviously unprepared to be called out. "That's not...that is... I—"

"Oh, come on. It's obvious there's more to your behavior than you just thinking I was an intruder. That's behind us, and you're still giving me attitude. Why?"

Jerabeth glanced at Charlie, who shrugged as if to say, *You started this*.

With a little sigh, Jerabeth crossed her arms. "Claudette was my friend. And you got her removed from office. And then took over her job."

Temo grunted. "That is not how it went down."

Donna frowned at the witch. "Are you kidding me? No, clearly, you're not. I don't know when you talked to Claudette last, but you obviously didn't get the whole story from her. Is that what she told you? Because Temo's right. That's not what happened. Not really."

Jerabeth held her defensive stance. "She told me you were the reason that she was no longer governor. But she didn't have long to talk and said we'd catch up more later."

"Just a guess, but that catching up hasn't happened yet."

"No, but—"

"Let me enlighten you on the rest of the story she hasn't told you. At the trial, after the council deemed her unfit to continue as governor and they passed their sentence upon her? I saved her life. I'm the reason she's not filling an urn right now."

Jerabeth looked at Charlie. She nodded. "It's true. I wasn't there, but I heard it from Claudette herself when she returned to the penthouse afterwards. Donna's first act as governor was to pardon Claudette, which spared her life. The council had other ideas. Why do you think Claudette left so quickly and without any fuss?"

"I just thought she wanted to get out."

"She did," Charlie said. "And as far away from the council's grasp as possible."

Donna tipped her head. "So what do you say? Can we move past this now?"

Jerabeth closed her eyes as she nodded. When she opened them, she looked genuinely contrite. "I'm sorry. And I'm embarrassed by my assumptions. Thank you for saving Claudette. I know she's an acquired taste, but so am I. I suppose we bonded over that. Please forgive me for my rudeness, Governor."

Donna smiled. "Absolutely. Anyone who can grow plants like this deserves a second chance."

"Thank you. It won't be wasted on me, I promise."

"Good. I am curious about one thing."

"Sure," Jerabeth said. "Anything."

"How did you freeze me back there?"

"I didn't really. Well, I didn't freeze you. Like Charlie said, I'm an elemental witch. My element is air. I froze the air around you."

"So that word you said wasn't a spell?"

"I suppose it was in a way. But really the word was just a means of focusing my power."

"Freezing the air around me doesn't explain why I couldn't talk."

Jerabeth nodded. "I also froze the air in your throat."

That sounded...more serious. "Could that have killed me?"

"If you were human, maybe. Given enough time. If I'd meant to kill you, I would have frozen the air in your lungs."

"I see." So Jerabeth was both a gardener and a potential killer. Donna made a mental note of that and then mentally highlighted it as well. That wasn't something she wanted to forget. Ever. "What other magic do you have?"

Jerabeth's expression took on a slightly proud air. "Did you notice how calm it is on the roof?"

Donna nodded. "I did. I expected it to really be pretty breezy up here, given how high we are."

For the first time, Jerabeth smiled. "That's me. One of my spells. More of a wind ward, actually, because it's a fairly permanent thing."

"Wow, that's very cool. Not that freezing air isn't cool, too, but keeping the wind to a minimum is probably what makes this space so useful. Without that, I don't think the rooftop would be half as pleasant."

Now Jerabeth looked pleased. "I think it contributes, yes."

Temo was peeling an orange he'd picked from one of the trees. He really did have the appetite of three people.

With a smile, Donna canted her head toward the poison garden. "So, what do you say? Will you give me a quick tour?"

"Sure, come on." Jerabeth led the way, pulling a brass key from her coat pocket as she went. She got the gate unlocked, then pushed it open, but didn't move out of the way. "A word of warning. Don't touch anything. And don't let anything touch you."

"Whoa," Temo said. "I'm out. If it's okay with you, I'm going back downstairs for coffee and some breakfast."

"That does sound good," Donna said. "But when I get back downstairs, I'm hitting the sheets for more z's, or I'm going to be a zombie at the party tonight. Wait. Are zombies real?"

Charlie started to reply, but Donna put her hands up. "You know what? Don't answer that. I don't need that information in my head when I'm about to be dreaming again. Temo, see you later."

With a laugh, he took off, leaving the three women.

"All right," Donna said. "No touching, no being touched. Got it."

Jerabeth moved out of the way. "Good. Have a look."

Donna glanced at Charlie. "Have you ever been in here?"

"Nope."

They moved slowly through the gate, mindful of everything around them.

Jerabeth pointed to a murky corner where a bushy plant with dark green leaves and inky purple flowers grew behind a cage. "This is the deadly nightshade, or your namesake, Madam Governor. *Atropa belladonna*."

Donna smiled and started to reach out, then remembered she wasn't supposed to. "I've never seen one in person. What part of it is poisonous?"

313

"Pretty much all of it. Just touching it can cause your skin to blister."

Donna stuck her hands in the pockets of her robe. "Wow. Okay."

"Would you like to know more?"

"Sure. We share a name, so why not?"

Jerabeth's smile was that of a teacher, and she truly seemed to be in her element. "The roots are the most poisonous, followed by the leaves and then the berries. Those form where the flowers are now. They're black and shiny and look good enough to eat, but just two or three contain enough poison to kill a child."

Donna grimaced. "I'm glad you have that thing behind a cage and locked up. And that there are no children here."

Jerabeth stopped smiling, her expression suddenly serious. "I agree. Nightshade has been used recreationally, but it's not something I'd ever recommend."

"And not something I'd ever try," Charlie said. She had her arms wrapped around her torso.

Donna eyed the other plants with rising curiosity. "These plants are all beautiful, but why grow all these things if they're so dangerous?"

Jerabeth's gaze held the earnestness of someone who loved what she did. "This is a dangerous world, Governor. More so for people like us who aren't completely mortal. The enemies we face don't always respond to human weapons. Sometimes, we need other tools to use to protect ourselves. To fight back. To save ourselves and those we love." She spread her hands out. "These are those tools."

"Every day," Donna said, "my education grows. You know how to use all these plants for those sorts of purposes?"

"I do." Jerabeth's pride was evident. "My mother was a green witch. Far more talented with plants than I am, but she taught me everything she knew."

"I'm really glad you're part of my team."

At Donna's words, Jerabeth beamed. "Thank you. I am very happy to be a part of it. And just to be really clear, these plants are not only killers. They almost all have other uses too. Medicinal or magical uses. It's a common truth that what kills in large quantities can often help in small ones."

"Fascinating," Donna said.

Charlie nodded. "It really is. You should teach us more, Jerabeth. Maybe once a week, we could meet up here, and you could—" She suddenly shook her head. "That is, if the governor would like something like that."

"Yes, totally. I'd love that," Donna said. "Let's do it. What do you say, Jerabeth? Teach us?"

Jerabeth blinked in shock. "You really want me to? I'd be happy to."

"Yes, definitely," Donna said. "Information like that can only be beneficial to all of us."

"That's very true," Jerabeth said. She shook her head. "I really misjudged you, and I'm sorry. I tried to teach Claudette about the plants once, but she said she didn't need to know about them when she had me, but I'm not always here." She was silent for a moment. "Thank you again for giving me a second chance."

"You're welcome." Donna stifled a yawn. "Now I really need to get back to sleep. I'm so glad we could meet, even if it wasn't under the best of circumstances."

Jerabeth nodded. "The same goes for me. I'll talk to you soon, Governor. Sleep well."

"Thank you." Donna carefully made her way out of the poison garden and back to the stairwell.

Charlie was right behind her.

As the door closed and they descended, Charlie softly cleared her throat. "Are you going to tell me now how you can daywalk? Because that's the kind of information your admin should know."

Donna stopped short of entering the penthouse. "The thing is...I don't think it's information anyone should know. I understand the kind of threat a daywalking vampire poses. Or at least the perceived threat. Can you imagine what the council would do if they found out?"

Charlie grimaced. "I can. But you can trust me. How else can I adequately serve and protect you if I don't know things like this?"

Donna sighed. "I really didn't want anyone to know."

"With all due respect, you went out on the roof in broad daylight."

"I know, but I had no reason to believe anyone else would be up there at this time of the morning. In my defense, if you'd told me about Jerabeth, I probably *wouldn't* have gone up there."

Charlie took a deep breath. "You're right. I'm sorry."

"Look, there's no putting the cat back in the bag. Besides Jerabeth, you know, Temo knows, and Pierce knows. But that has to be it."

Charlie nodded. "I'll talk to Temo, not that it's even necessary. I promise he already understands that things like that need to be kept private. So does Jerabeth, I swear."

"Good. But not within earshot of Neo. I trust her, but again, it's just not information I want out there."

"I understand. And I'll handle it."

"Thank you. As for why I'm immune, I just am. One of those rare things, I guess. Now I really need to go back to bed." Donna opened the door, went into the penthouse and straight to her bedroom. She closed the door, crawled under the covers, and tried to sleep away her massive screwup.

She was mad at herself. Going onto the roof had been a dumb move. She had to make better decisions and not allow her impulses to push her into rash actions.

Her eyes started to close, heavy with the need for rest.

But even as she drifted off, her last thoughts were of the party to come. And how desperate she was not to do something dumb there.

She couldn't afford to become someone's target. And she certainly didn't want to arouse the interest of the Immortus Concilio again. One meeting with the vampire council was all she needed in her lifetime.

Which was saying something, considering she was immortal.

# CHAPTER 29

Donna woke to the muted sounds of conversation. It was a happy sound, the sound of her new family. Didn't mean she didn't miss her own children, but it was good to be surrounded by people she could trust. People who had her best interests at heart.

That had never been the case in her marriage to Joe. She took a deep breath and let the feeling of peace and contentment wash over her. That life was really done with now that Joe was in custody.

It made slipping up and accidentally revealing her immunity to the sun seem like a small thing now that she had some distance from it.

There was no chance Temo, Charlie, or Pierce would let her secret out. Her safety affected them all, but more than that, they were her people. Her team. Hopefully, she could include Jerabeth in that.

Donna might need to mention that to Charlie. But not until she'd had some coffee. Ohhh, and pie. Then she'd be conversational.

She flipped the covers back, looking at the time as she sat up. She'd slept nearly eight hours. That was more than she'd expected, but it was good. She had a long, busy night of being "on" ahead of her.

She threw some leggings and a sweatshirt on and padded out to the kitchen.

Temo was making a sandwich. He smiled at her. "Morning, boss. How'd you sleep?"

"Good. Longer than I thought I would, but I suppose I needed it." She went straight to the coffeemaker. "Where's everyone else?"

"Charlie's in the office, Pierce went to the pool, and Rixaline is still sleeping." He shrugged. "Teenagers."

She got a cup brewing, then opened the fridge and took out the chocolate pie. "Yep, I remember those days. I think Christina still sleeps in as much as possible. Joe Jr. has to be up pretty early, though. He's in the Air Force and has to be on base by seven."

"That's pretty much when you're going to bed."

She laughed. "True. Has Lucky been fed? I can't believe he'd sleep through breakfast and lunch."

Temo nodded. "Pierce fed him before he went to swim laps, but I'm pretty sure that cat went right back to Rixaline's room after he ate."

Donna added sugar and creamer to her coffee, cut a slice of pie, then took a seat at the counter and dug in. "I can't believe he abandoned me, but then, he always was more Christina's cat than mine."

Charlie came in. "Hey, I thought I heard you. Good morning. Is that pie for everyone? I hope so, because I've been wanting a slice since I saw it in there."

"Morning, Charlie. Help yourself. What's my schedule like for today?"

"Hair and makeup are arriving at seven." Charlie grabbed a plate and fork. "That should give them plenty of time to do their thing, then for you to get dressed and us to make the party by ten. Oh, also, I've been in touch with Van Marten's about some jewels for this evening."

"Jewels? You mean like for me to borrow? Or to buy?"

"Borrow, but if you like them, I suppose you could buy them. I didn't know which dress you were going to wear, so they're coming by at six with a selection of things. Any idea which gown you're leaning toward?" She took a seat next to Donna and had a bite of pie, instantly making a very happy face.

"I need to make that decision, don't I? It's going to matter for hair and makeup too." She drank a little more of her coffee. "Tell you what. Let me finish this cup and this slice, and I'll figure it out."

"Sounds good. And this pie is amazing."

"I know, right?" Donna leaned in a little. "Did you and Temo talk?"

"We did," Charlie answered around a forkful of chocolate silk.

Temo picked his sandwich up. "It'll go to my grave, boss. I swear."

"Thank you. I know I have nothing to worry about. So long as Jerabeth is on the same page."

"She is." Charlie smiled. "It's kind of nice to know we don't have to worry about that aspect of things, though. I mean, with you and the sun. Not with Jerabeth."

Temo snorted. "Don't let Charlie fool you. She does worry about it. Or did. Every time I drive you anywhere, she texts me the time of sunrise."

Donna laughed softly and looked at her admin. "Do you really?"

She lifted one shoulder. "I can't help it."

"That's very sweet." A door opened downstairs. "I think Neo's up."

A few moments later, soft footsteps coming up the stairs caught everyone's attention.

Neo appeared, wearing a large man's T-shirt as a nightgown. Undoubtedly Temo's, which just added to the warm fuzzies Donna was already feeling.

Donna looked at her friend over the rim of her cup. "How'd you sleep?"

Neo smiled lazily. "Not bad. It's a lot quieter out here than my place in the city. I don't think I heard a single siren or car horn."

Donna hadn't considered that. "Maybe you should see if there are any vacancies in this building and buy a place."

Neo's grin took on a new shine. "Not sure I could afford a crib in this joint, but I'm not opposed to the idea."

"You want some coffee? Or pie?"

"I had coffee downstairs. And what I really need isn't pie, although that does look good."

"We have what you need." Donna tipped her head toward the fridge. "Help yourself. I'm going to feed right before the party."

"Pierce?" Neo asked.

Donna nodded.

Neo shook her head. "I need to get myself an assistant."

"No, you don't," Temo said quietly.

Neo's brows rose. "Oh?"

He suddenly seemed to realize what he'd said. "I mean, for tonight. If you want..." He looked at Donna like he was asking for permission.

She shook her head. "What you do with your body is up to you. You're both consenting adults."

Neo took a deep breath as she faced Temo, the most curious expression on her face. Like someone had just given her a cake and said every slice was hers. "I'd be up for it. I've never had the blood of another supernatural before. I hear it can kind of supercharge you."

Temo's smirk said it all. "I guess we'll see."

Donna drained the last of her coffee. She thought about a second cup to go with a second slice of pie, but she'd already told Charlie she'd figure out what dress she was wearing. "Try to behave while I'm gone, all right?"

Neo laughed. "No promises."

Donna put her cup in the sink and the pie back in the fridge and returned to her bedroom. First thing she did was open the drapes and let the light in. The rack of dresses was against the wall closest to the closet, the dresses she was still deciding on at the very front.

Taken as a whole, the rack looked like a peek into a showgirl's closet. All glitz and glitter.

She sat on the chaise and stared at the gowns. What mood was she in? She wasn't awake enough to really answer that, but she'd be lying if she didn't admit to the nerves she was feeling.

It wasn't the party. She'd been to plenty of them over the years where she'd had to put on a happy face and make small talk. And this one she actually wanted to go to. After all, Francine, Bunni, Dr. Goldberg, LaToya, and Meghan would be there, along with Neo, Pierce, Charlie, and Temo.

No, her nerves were because this was her first foray into vampire society as the new governor. She wanted to make a good impression.

The right impression.

So what was that?

She wanted people to like her. To think she was capable. Smart, intelligent. A good choice for the job. Unlike her first meeting with Fitzhugh and the Russians, she didn't want to come off as intimidating. What was the opposite of that? Warm. Fun. Approachable.

Which of those dresses said all that?

Her gaze kept going to the red one. She hadn't even shown that one to the girls when she'd been trying on dresses. Had seemed too much somehow. Too bold. Too over the top. Too exuberant.

She got up and walked to the rack, her hand caressing the gown's silky fabric. This wasn't the kind of dress a woman wore to disappear, that was for sure.

She didn't want to disappear. Not now. Not ever.

She wanted to make a statement. She was here to stay.

She pulled the gown off the rack and hung it so it faced forward.

The dress wrapped the body until the hips, where the skirt suddenly became an abundance of fabric. The slightest breeze would send that skirt into a dance of its own.

Everything about the dress made Donna think about the glamour of old Hollywood. It was an aesthetic she admired. A little vampy, but sexy in a way that had class. It was the dress of a powerful woman.

She quickly tried it on and looked in the mirror.

Tonight, it was Donna's dress.

With a smile, she changed and went back out to the kitchen. "Charlie, I'm wearing red."

Charlie looked up from her laptop. "You mean that wine one?"

"No, it's a different dress. I didn't show it to you guys because I thought it was too much. But now I think it's just enough." Donna grinned. "I'm wearing red."

"Sounds good. Can't wait to see it."

"Me either," Neo said. "I'm wearing purple. Not that you asked."

"You're going to look amazing," Donna said. "But you always do. You have great style."

Neo touched her chest with her fingers. "You really think so?"

"Absolutely. It's edgy and funky and completely your own. You are a woman that knows who she is."

With a sly smile, Neo leaned back on the counter. "What about Bunni?"

Donna hesitated. Neo and Bunni went together like peanut butter and glass shards. "I don't think Bunni's really found herself yet. But she's young and—"

"So am I," Neo said.

Donna nodded. "But you have more maturity than she does. And a lot more self-confidence. When a woman finds the self-confidence to do hard things in life and to stop caring what others think—and what society thinks—that's when you level up as a woman. Bunni hasn't gotten there yet."

Neo smirked. "I don't think she ever will."

"She might not," Donna said. "Not every woman does. But good friends, encouraging friends, they can help. And Bunni has those." Donna gave Neo a pointed look. "She could always use more."

"Yeah, yeah. What about Francine?"

Donna rolled her eyes good-naturedly. "You already know the answer to that one. Francine is the epitome of a realized woman. Look at her. She's not only living her best life, she's living it large enough for several women."

Neo snorted. "And you haven't even seen her place or met Lionel."

Charlie hugged her laptop to her chest. "I can't wait to meet Francine."

Neo glanced over. "She is something else. There is no one like her. Certainly no other vampire like her."

"What's Lionel like? I'm pretty interested to meet him," Donna admitted.

"He's very handsome in that kind of European playboy who had money but lost it all because he's too generous sort of way. Like Francine said, he's a musician. I'm sure he'll play tonight. He usually does. Maybe with his band, maybe just him at the piano or with his acoustic guitar. Hard to say. But he's so incredibly sweet to Francine."

"Well," Donna said, "he saved her life."

"He did," Neo agreed. "But he'll tell you that she saved his. That's just the kind of guy he is."

Charlie's brow crumpled. "How old did you say Francine was when she was turned?"

"Eighty-four," Donna answered.

"And how old is Lionel?"

Neo shrugged. "He's been around awhile. He was probably in his mid-thirties when he was turned, and that was a couple hundred years ago."

"Has he been in a band long?"

"Since the sixties, I think." Neo gave her a look. "Why?"

Charlie narrowed her gaze. "What's the name of his band?"

"Well, he reinvents himself every couple decades. The current band is called Bittersweet."

Charlie swallowed, and her mouth fell open. "Bittersweet?" The word came out on a breathy mumble.

Neo nodded. "Why? What's up? You have some issue with them?"

Charlie fanned herself. "His stage name is Leif Harker, isn't it?"

"Yeah," Neo said. "I think so. I'm more of a Kanye girl myself."

Charlie slumped a little, leaning hard on the counter. "Oh. Oh my. I'm going to be in the same room as Leif Harker? I…I…I have to wear something different."

Donna stared at her admin. "I've never seen this side of you, Charlie. Actually, I didn't know you had this side."

Charlie suddenly straightened. "I'm sorry. Please forgive all that." She tugged her sweater down. "I will be absolutely professional this evening. You don't need to worry about that. I will not—"

"Go all fangirl on him?" Neo suggested.

Charlie frowned. "I would never embarrass the governor that way." She sniffed. "Maybe I shouldn't go."

"Nonsense," Donna said. "You're going. Does he have any albums out? You should take them. We'll get him to sign them."

Charlie gasped. "You think—no, I can't do that. That wouldn't be professional."

"Really?" Donna made a face. "Because I happen to know Christina loves Bittersweet, and if I can get her something signed, I'm doing it. If you don't want in on that, then—"

"No!" Charlie almost shouted. "I'm in. I'm so in."

Donna grinned. Tonight was going to be more interesting than she'd imagined.

# CHAPTER 30

Donna peered through the SUV's window at Francine's house.

A lot of the brownstones in Manhattan had been broken up into smaller apartments and only retained the ghosts of the great houses they'd once been.

Francine's was not one of those, despite the basement apartment that had been her introduction to Lionel. No, this brownstone was a home in its entirety, all five floors of it.

The façade wasn't as ornate as some of the other brownstones on the street, but it was distinctive. The brick was laid in such a way that it created arches and cornices over the windows. In other spots, a herringbone pattern was used for accent.

White marble sills and trim—or maybe it was limestone, Donna wasn't sure which—stood out in sharp contrast to all the deep red along with black wrought-iron balustrades across the windows that formed decorative, shallow balconies. The only true usable balcony was on the second floor. It jutted a few feet from the house but ran the whole width.

Two wrought-iron chairs and a café table sat at one end.

The building had a clean, charming, 1920s deco vibe that Donna immediately loved.

But what Donna liked best was how the interior was so lit up that every pane in every leaded-glass window sparkled with the warm, golden glow of celebration.

Music spilled out of the place, and black-capped valets stood at the ready to park cars for those who'd driven. Temo pulled up, then jumped out and handed over the keys. When that was taken care of, he opened the car doors for the rest of them.

Pierce got out first, offering Donna his hand, then he helped Charlie. She walked ahead to go in with Temo.

Donna took Pierce's arm, and he leaned in. "Have I said how gorgeous you look this evening?"

"Only a handful of times." She smiled. She knew she looked good, and she was happy about it. Looking good made her confident. She imagined that was universally true for most women.

India had done her hair in soft, flowing waves, and her makeup was appropriately dramatic for the evening. She felt like she'd just stepped out of a movie. Even more so with her very own Cary Grant beside her.

Pierce wore his tux, of course. Temo in a charcoal suit, and Charlie had gone with an off-the-shoulder black gown that was simple but stunning. Donna had insisted she borrow a diamond bracelet and earrings from the selection of things the man from Van Marten's had brought. With his approval, of course.

He hadn't given it a second thought.

The eye-popping piece Donna had borrowed helped her Hollywood vibe. The ruby and diamond necklace was impossible to miss. The Van Marten's rep had told her it was appraised at half a million dollars and had been worn to the Oscars.

She didn't know which celebrity neck this dazzler had graced, but she had a feeling the parties it had been to on Oscar night had been nothing compared to the one they were about to walk into.

Her crucifix and chain were discreetly tucked into her bra. She hoped that qualified as wearing it if a UV situation arose, which she couldn't imagine it would. But still.

As they entered the foyer, a luxurious space paneled in green malachite and more white marble trimmed in gold, Francine met them.

She held out her arms. "Belladonna!"

"Hi, Francine."

Pierce let her go to greet the older woman.

Francine wrapped Donna in a hug. "Don't you look like the bee's knees. So beautiful. I think you're the best-looking governor here."

Donna laughed. "Aren't I also the only governor here?"

"Heavens no," Francine said. "There are three others. Plus the vampire ambassador from France. Renard and his wife happened to be in town, and his people got in touch with my people, so I said why not. They all want to meet you."

"Oh." That was unexpected. But then, Neo had told Donna to expect just that. "You look incredible, too, Francine." She was dressed in a cream-colored pantsuit and dripping in diamonds and cornflower-blue sapphires that made the color of her eyes pop.

"Thanks, honey." Francine smiled up at Pierce. "Hello there, handsome."

Donna grinned and waved Charlie and Temo over. "Francine, you know Pierce, of course, but let me also introduce my admin, Charlene, and the head of my security, Temo."

Francine stuck her hand out. "Hi. So glad you could come."

Charlie shook her hand first. "It's a pleasure to meet you. Please, call me Charlie. And thank you so much for opening your home to honor the governor. It's so generous."

Francine winked at Donna. "She's good." Then she offered her hand to Temo. "I've already heard about you from a mutual friend. She's upstairs, by the way, with Bunni, LaToya, and Meghan. Probably already surrounded by men, with that dress she's almost wearing."

Temo shook Francine's hand. "Pleasure to meet you." Then he looked at Donna. "Do you need me, or, uh…"

She tipped her head toward the stairs. "Go. Before there's an incident."

He nodded. "Thank you."

As he dashed up the steps, Donna turned back to Francine. "Who are the other governors here?"

She ticked them off on her fingers. "Fitzhugh, of course. Can't have a party like this in his state without inviting him. Greene. She's the governor of Ohio. And Showell, the Maryland governor. But listen, we have all night. There's no rush. Besides, I want to introduce you to Lionel."

Charlie let out a little *meep* but covered by coughing.

Francine hooked her arm through Donna's. "We should get you a drink too. Do you like champagne? I adore it. And as circumstance would have it, Renard insisted on sending over ten cases of Dom as a thank-you for the invite."

"Ten?"

Francine patted her arm. "That's only sixty bottles. Well, fifty-four." She laughed. "I put one case away for myself."

Donna glanced back at Pierce and Charlie. "What do you say? Champagne?"

They both nodded. Donna raised her brows. "We're all in for bubbly."

The crowd meant it took a few minutes to navigate the stairs to the second floor. It opened into a beautiful, light, airy space of cream walls and a white marble floor accented with tiny black squares and matching black marble trim around the perimeter.

In the center of the room were two shiny black platforms. Each held a performer dressed in a Harlequin bodysuit. The woman, in black and purple, was a contortionist and continually bent herself into a variety of shapes. The man, in black and green, juggled glass orbs, occasionally taking a break from the juggling to wind them around his hands and body in such a way that made them appear to float.

All around them mingled one of the best-looking crowds Donna had ever seen. Her nerves, which had disappeared while talking to Francine, suddenly returned. "You've really outdone yourself, Francine."

She grinned. "Wait until you see the fire-eater in the garden. He's really something. And not just because he's shirtless." She laughed. "I've even got mermaids in the pool. You'll see. Let's get some champagne, and then I'll give you the tour."

"I can't wait."

Suddenly, Francine stuck her hand in the air and waved. "Lionel, honey, over here."

The crowd seemed to part, and Francine's sire appeared. He strode toward them in black leather pants and a sapphire velvet smoking jacket with no shirt underneath. He looked every inch the rocker with his jewelry and guyliner and chiseled jaw covered in a few days' worth of dark stubble that paired well with the dark curls brushing his shoulders.

He was very handsome. But Donna was drawn to the fact that his eyes were on Francine and Francine alone.

As he joined them, he reached for her hands. "Frankie, my love." He brought her hands to his mouth and kissed them. "Where have you been? I've missed you."

"I've been greeting our guests at the door, you silly goose." She tipped her head toward Donna. "Our guest of honor has arrived. Lionel, meet Belladonna Barrone, governor of New Jersey."

He hung on to Francine's hands but broke eye contact with her to look at Donna. "Ah, the one and only Belladonna. Frankie speaks so highly of you. Anyone she approves of is good with me." He finally let go of one of Francine's hands to extend his to Donna. "It is my pleasure to meet you."

Donna shook his hand. For all Francine's talk about how they had an open relationship, Lionel certainly seemed devoted to her. "It's my honor to meet the vampire who saved Francine's life."

His hand went to his bare chest, and he shook his head. "In all fairness, she saved mine. She is the best thing that ever happened to me."

Donna smiled at Neo's prediction coming true.

Francine giggled. "You're so silly. You know that's not true."

"Hush, pet." He kissed her temple before looking at Donna again. "I need to meet your friends, and then we need drinks. I assume Frankie told you we have a large quantity of good champagne that needs consuming?"

"She did," Donna answered. "This is my assistant and the man who saved my life, Pierce Harrison."

Lionel shook his hand. "Yes, the attorney. Frankie told me all about you. What a wonderful thing you did for the governor. Say, how are you with living trusts?"

"They're not my area of expertise, but I know someone if you'd like a recommendation."

"I would, thank you. Let's talk some more about that."

"Happy to," Pierce said.

Donna put her hand on Charlie's arm. She was trembling. "And this is my admin, Charlene Rollins. I believe she's acquainted with your music."

"Are you a fan of Bittersweet?" Lionel asked.

Charlie nodded. "Yes," she managed.

"I'm flattered." He held out his hand. "Always lovely to meet a fan."

As Charlie took his hand, Donna leaned in a little. "She wouldn't be opposed to a signed something or other."

"Governor," Charlie growled. She shook her head at Lionel. "I couldn't possibly...that is, I wouldn't dream of—"

Lionel laughed as he released her hand. "Think nothing of it. I'll have some things sent over to the penthouse tomorrow. How's that?"

Donna smiled. "Would you mind terribly sending some things for my daughter, Christina? She's a huge fan, too, and it would earn me a lot of mom points. I'm happy to pay for them."

"Nonsense," Lionel said. "For a friend of Frankie's? Not having it. Come on, now. Let's go see about that champagne."

In short order, he waved over one of the servers

walking around, and they emptied her tray of flutes.

When they all had a glass, Francine lifted hers. "Here's to Donna. May your time as governor be successful and uneventful."

Donna laughed. "Too late, but I'll drink to that anyway."

They all took sips of the bubbly, then Lionel kissed Francine on the cheek. "Time for me to sing, my love." He looked at Charlie. "Care to join me? We play on the third floor. Better acoustics."

"Go on," Donna said to Charlie. Why not? It was a chance for Charlie to hear one of her favorite musicians of all time. Donna couldn't let her pass that up.

"But I should be with you," Charlie said. "Working."

"And you will be. Right after you hear some music."

"You're sure?"

"Go," Donna insisted. "I have Pierce with me. And Temo's around here somewhere."

"Thank you." She took off with Lionel, the smile on her face transcendent.

Francine laughed. "She's really a fan, isn't she?"

"Huge," Donna answered.

A short, portly man with an enormous but well-groomed mustache approached them. At his side was a terribly chic woman in a black slip dress, wearing her weight in Chanel pearls.

Whoever she was, his wife or his mistress, her dour expression seemed to indicate this was not how she'd wanted to spend her evening.

"Francine," he exclaimed. "Is this the governor?"

By his accent, Donna assumed he had to be the French ambassador.

Francine nodded. "Monsieur Renard, come join us. Yes, this is Belladonna Barrone. Belladonna, this is Ambassador Hubert Renard and his wife, Sylvie."

Donna smiled at them. "How nice to meet you." She gestured to Pierce. "This is my assistant, Pierce Harrison."

"*Bonsoir*," Pierce greeted them. Then he proceeded to rattle off more French that proved Donna's two years of high school language classes useless.

Sylvie Renard, however, cracked a smile for the first time since joining them, showing off a petite set of fangs. She suddenly became animated, or at least as animated as she seemed capable of, and engaged Pierce in conversation in French.

Hubert, however, seemed as happy to be at the party as a person, or vampire, could be. He nodded at Donna's glass. "I see you are enjoying some champagne?"

"Yes." Donna lifted her flute. "What a generous gift. And it's delicious."

His smile widened, revealing a pair of short fangs. "It was the least I could do to repay Francine's generous invitation. Say, Madam Governor, have you been to France? We are always happy to host other dignitaries. We find that makes travel for them so much easier."

"I haven't been, but that is a very kind offer. I'll definitely keep it in mind."

Sylvie finally joined them in speaking English. "You are a lucky woman to have such a wonderful man as this as your assistant. You both must come visit us in Paris."

"Your husband was just saying the same thing." Donna looked at Pierce. "We will certainly consider it once my schedule lightens up a bit."

Pierce slipped his arm around her waist. "A little travel would be nice."

She nodded. "It would be." How different would it be to see the world as the person she was now? And with a man like Pierce? The thought was more intoxicating than the champagne in her hand.

Music filtered down from upstairs, the low thrum of a bass guitar followed by the melancholy sounds of a ballad.

Francine looked up. "Lionel's doing his best to impress your admin. That's his most popular love song, *Cry For Me*."

Donna suppressed a laugh. "We may have to mop Charlie off the floor when he's done."

Then a familiar voice came from the crowd behind her. "Well, well, well. If it isn't Governor Barrone."

Donna's mood shifted suddenly, and with great reluctance, she turned. "Good evening, Governor Fitzhugh."

# CHAPTER 31

Fitzhugh's tux was impeccable, although the silk opera scarf around his neck and the enormous diamond studs on his shirt were a bit much for Donna's taste. He raised the glass of champagne in his hand, revealing matching diamond cufflinks.

He emptied the drink, then deposited the flute on the tray of a passing server and picked up a full one.

He was showy. And obnoxious. And thought he ruled the world.

She reminded herself that she'd been dealing with men like him all her life. And she'd just punched one of them yesterday. Twice.

He strode over to their little group. "Good evening, Governor. I see you've arrived with your staff. Interesting that you wanted nothing to do with my event, and yet here you are, at a party in your honor, in *my* state."

To Donna, he sounded ever so slightly inebriated. How much had he had to drink already?

341

"Now, Hawke," Francine started, "you promised me you were going to be on your best behavior this evening."

He had the nerve to look aghast. "I haven't done anything other than state the truth."

Donna couldn't help but laugh. This guy was nothing but a toddler with hurt feelings. "Your event was all about you. And really, how can you be put out that I would choose my lovely female friend's invite over a man with his own best interests at heart? You really are a politician, aren't you?"

He frowned at her, while Francine snickered and Pierce snorted. Hubert and Sylvie seemed a little unsure of what to do.

Donna stepped closer to Fitzhugh. The smell of alcohol filled her nose. Keeping in mind he wasn't entirely himself, she lowered her voice and tried to talk reasonably to him. "Let's not do this tonight. This is Francine's party. The fact that I am her guest of honor is really secondary, and I can assure you, if you ruin this party for her, you and I will never come to terms on anything. Ever."

He stared at her without speaking for a few long seconds, then downed his champagne. Once again, he dumped the empty glass on a server's tray, but this time, he grabbed the bottle of champagne the woman was carrying and yanked the cork out. "You're making a mistake."

"By choosing my friend over political opportunity? I'm not sure you know the definition of the word mistake. Or loyalty, for that matter. One thing I am sure of is that you have no idea how little political opportunity means to me."

His gaze stayed sharp and appraising, even while he seemed to waver on his feet. "That will change. You'll see. And then you'll wish you'd done things differently. But it'll be too late then."

"How dare you?" Pierce started.

Donna reached back to put her hand on Pierce's arm. She knew his instinct was to protect her, but she didn't want this to become a bigger scene than it already had.

Despite that thought, Fitzhugh's impending drunkenness was no excuse for his attempt to intimidate her. She returned his gaze with a hard glare of her own. "Do *not* threaten me, Governor."

He stepped back, suddenly casual and amused, lifting the bottle to his mouth for a drink. "I would never dream of such a thing. Merely offering you some words of advice."

"When I want your advice, I'll ask." She was vibrating with righteous indignation now. She turned her back on him to face Francine and Pierce. "Let's go find Neo and the First Fang girls. I want to see my friends."

"Good idea," Pierce said while staring Fitzhugh down.

Donna smiled at Hubert and Sylvie, schooling her voice into a calmer tone. "Such a pleasure to meet you both. I hope you have a lovely time this evening. I look forward to speaking with you again."

Francine took Donna's arm. "Neo's probably in

the library by now. I always set up a great blood bar back there. Dr. Goldberg hangs out in there, too, sometimes. Not sure where the rest of them might be. Upstairs enjoying the music or in the garden, maybe. Where would you like to go? The library? It's quieter if you want a break."

"Sounds perfect." Donna let herself be led. She could feel Pierce behind her and knew he was angry about Fitzhugh.

When they were deeper into the crowd and had distance from Fitzhugh, Francine leaned in. "I'm sorry about Hawke. There was no polite way to keep him from coming, and since I live in his state—"

"You have nothing to apologize for."

Francine shook her head, clearly unhappy. "I did *not* know he'd drink so much. Or that he'd show up half drunk to begin with. Or that he was going to be so cross with you. I should have known he'd cause trouble."

Donna laughed softly. "That wasn't trouble. That was posturing. He's mad because I won't play his games. He'll get over it."

"I don't know. But you're being very gracious about it, so thank you." Francine looked up at her. "If I'd had a daughter, I would have wanted her to be just like you."

The sweet compliment made Donna feel a little weepy. "If I'd had a mother like you, I probably never would have married Joe. Which isn't to say my mom didn't do her best, but she wasn't around much. And I think because of that, I was looking for someone to pay attention to me, you know?"

Francine patted Donna's arm. "You're a good girl. You just keep your head up and focus on what matters, and you'll do fine." She laughed. "You're already doing fine."

"Thank you. I really appreciate that."

Getting through the crowd with Francine was like walking with the queen. Everyone had to talk to her, telling her how fantastic the party was, how beautiful her home was. How good, how great, how wonderful. They gushed over her.

Donna found it very entertaining, but by the time they reached the library, which appeared to be a kind of VIP area based on how few people were in it, she was ready for a break from the crush.

It was a good-size space but made cozy by the wood paneling and leather furniture. The walls were bookshelves stuffed with books. Dr. Goldberg was standing in front of one, chatting with a few people Donna didn't know. At the back was a long bar with two bartenders behind it.

That's where Neo was with Temo, and just as Francine had suggested, her dress was more skin than fabric. Donna was slightly jealous because she was sure she'd never looked that devastatingly beautiful in her life.

While Pierce and Francine settled in on one of the big couches, Donna gave Dr. Goldberg a little wave of greeting, then walked over to Neo, shaking her head as she went. "Wow."

Neo grinned. "You like?"

The dress was deep-purple silk and cut down to Neo's belly button and up to her hips. "Not only do I like, but I can't figure out how you're keeping it on."

Neo leaned in and whispered, "Magic."

"No, seriously."

"No," Neo said. "Seriously. It's a spell. Cost me a couple bills and a firewall."

Donna blinked. "There's fashion magic? I didn't even know such a thing existed."

A bartender appeared on the other side of the bar. "What can I get you? We have every blood type."

"I'm good," Donna said. She'd had her fill from Pierce before they'd left and made sure he'd had his fill of her too. She needed him at his best tonight. Not that she suspected anything bad was going to happen, but Neo had told her to prepare to be unprepared.

Having herself and Pierce at full strength and having Temo here were the best ways she knew to do that.

"Quite a party," Neo said.

"It is. I haven't made it past this floor yet."

Neo looked over Donna's shoulder. "I see Pierce. Where's Charlie? Or should I even ask?"

Donna smiled. "Upstairs. Listening to Lionel. He's going to send a bunch of signed Bittersweet stuff to the penthouse for her and Christina."

"That's sounds just like him. He's a good guy."

"And the way he idolizes Francine." Donna let out a little groan of joy.

"I know," Neo said. "Is he even real? But you know, vampires tend to get *more* as they age. More dramatic, more sensitive, more cruel, more introverted. Whatever your strongest characteristics are, age tends to distill them down to their essence. Of course, we're talking centuries here, not decades."

"Interesting. That might explain a certain governor I ran into."

"No way. Fitzhugh?"

Donna nodded. "Yep. And he was in a whole mood."

Neo leaned into Temo, who'd moved to stand behind her. "What a tool. Francine's party is not the place to work out your issues."

"You can say that again—"

Behind her, the library doors burst open, accompanied by the rush of sound from the party.

Temo's stance changed instantly, and Neo frowned.

Donna turned to see Fitzhugh had joined them. He was leaning slightly and still had a bottle of champagne in one hand, although there was no telling if it was the same one. He seemed less stable than he had before, and Donna knew one bottle wasn't enough to cause that in any vampire. But then, Francine said he'd arrived already half in the bag. Just how long had he been drinking? And how much?

He scowled at her. His eyes glowed like reflectors. "You."

Donna squared off toward him, putting Neo behind her. "What about me?"

The doors opened again, and LaToya, Meghan, Bunni, Lionel, and Charlie came in, a chatty little group that seemed afloat with happiness. They quickly quieted as they realized they'd interrupted something.

Fitzhugh whipped around to look at them, a move that forced him to take a few extra steps to stay upright. "The whole lot of you make me sick. You're all here for what?" He turned and pointed the bottle at Donna. "For her? To celebrate that gangster's moll? She's a glorified reality TV star, and you all treat her like she's—"

Pierce abruptly stood. "You don't want to finish that sentence."

Fitzhugh glared at him. "Don't you dare tell me what to do, *assistant*."

This time, Francine got to her feet. "Hawke, that's enough now. Why don't you have some blood and sober up?"

Fitzhugh wavered, like he was considering it. Then his scowl deepened. "You should be ashamed of yourself, old woman. Throwing this party for that interloper. She's trash, don't you see that? The trophy wife of a criminal. Probably a criminal herself and—"

Pierce took a step forward, and his fist landed on Hawke's jaw with a loud crack. The impact twisted Fitzhugh like a corkscrew. He dropped the bottle, causing a geyser of champagne to erupt when it hit the floor.

No one moved. No one said a word. It was like someone had pressed pause.

Fitzhugh wobbled, arms out in the corkscrew shape for a moment, then he slowly, carefully unwound himself and started laughing. The sound was shrill and maniacal. Blood trickled from his lip, but the split had already healed.

Eyes aglow, he pointed at Pierce. "You're a dead man. How dare you, a human, strike me? I'm the vampire governor of this state."

"We know who you are," Francine said. "And frankly, you deserved that punch." She looked at Lionel. "He needs to go."

"Agreed, pet. Your invite is rescinded, Fitzhugh. If only I were human and that was enough to remove you immediately from my home." Lionel then simply spoke the words, "Security. Library."

A split second later, the doors opened yet again, this time to give entry to four large men, one or two who were not vampires. Two of them took hold of Fitzhugh and, with another man in front and one behind, removed him from the room.

It was done so quickly and efficiently that Fitzhugh didn't even have time to protest. All that remained was the champagne bottle in its puddle on the parquet floor. One of the bartenders hurried over with a rag to clean it up.

Donna rushed to Pierce. "Are you okay?" Frowning, she took his hand in hers to inspect it. The knuckles were already swelling. "Hitting Fitzhugh must have felt like punching concrete."

"I'll be fine," Pierce said. "Your blood has already kept me from breaking any bones."

"This is my fault," Francine said. "I should not have allowed him to come."

"You had no choice." Donna didn't want her friend to feel guilty about this. Fitzhugh was the one to blame. "He's mad at me. All because I refuse to treat him with whatever reverence he thinks he deserves."

Lionel put his arm around Francine. "Donna's right, pet. Fitzhugh's actions are his own responsibility."

Bunni came over to peer at Pierce's hand. "Nice hook for an attorney."

"Thanks," he answered with a smile.

"Hey," she said to the bartender who was still behind the bar. "Get this man some ice already."

Pierce took a breath. "I shouldn't have reacted that way. I'm sorry."

Neo and Temo joined them. Temo shook his head. "I would have done the same thing. You just got to him before I did."

LaToya and Meghan moved a little closer, plainly curious about everything that had just happened.

The second bartender brought over a clean towel filled with ice. Donna took it and held it on Pierce's knuckles. "He definitely earned that punch."

"But," Pierce said, "I still shouldn't have done it. I know I've made things worse for you."

Lionel sighed. "He's not wrong."

Donna looked at him. "What does that mean? How much angrier could Fitzhugh get?"

"It's not just that he was publicly humiliated. A human who works for a vampire and strikes another vampire…it's a bit of a gray area, but there could be consequences if Fitzhugh presses charges."

Donna felt the familiar cold chill of dread down her back. "Are you saying he could involve the council?"

Lionel nodded.

"He won't," Francine said. "He might think about it, but Fitzhugh won't want it known that an assistant drew his blood. He has too much pride to let that get out."

"I hope you're right," Donna said. She flattened her hand against her cleavage until she felt the hard metal of her crucifix. *Please let Francine be right.*

"Come on, now," Lionel said. "We can't let this derail our fun. Frankie is correct. Nothing will come of this once Fitzhugh sobers up and realizes what an ass he was."

Donna nodded and smiled, wanting to be convinced. She didn't need more bumps in the road ahead. She wanted to coast for a while. To have smooth sailing on glassy seas.

After all, her children were coming to visit soon. She didn't want them worrying that their mother's new life was more dangerous than the last.

Although she was starting to think that coasting would not be possible. It hadn't been in her old life. Why would it be any different now?

# CHAPTER 32

Francine clapped her hands. "Why don't I take you on that tour I promised? Unless you're not up to it, Pierce?"

He smiled. "I would love to see the rest of your beautiful home."

"Then follow me, kids."

Francine was a marvelous tour guide, and because of the party, she seemed to pick up with each step more guests who wanted to hear all about the brownstone. On every floor and in every room, she had a story to tell, often involving her late third husband, Artie, and some celebrity he'd gotten to know from his life as a movie producer.

The fame of the stars who'd been guests for dinner and overnight was jaw-dropping, so it was no surprise that the home was filled with Hollywood memorabilia too.

Donna found it all fascinating, and in no time, she'd forgotten enough about the dustup with Fitzhugh to have fun again.

They worked their way to the top, then back

down to the basement and the pool—complete with mermaids—and then out to the garden, which was a space so well done it was hard to imagine they were in the heart of Manhattan.

As they stood in the garden, with lanterns setting the area aglow, tiny flakes began to fall.

Neo looked up. "There's the snow they promised."

"It's kind of magical," Donna said.

LaToya held her hands out to catch the flakes. "It is pretty."

Donna looked at Francine. "Thank you again for doing this. For opening your home. It's been a wonderful evening."

Francine's joy was evident in her face. "I'm so glad you still think that despite what happened."

Donna waved the words away. "It's forgotten. You're right about Fitzhugh. He's too proud to want to make it public. He and I will never be friends, but that's okay." She smiled at all the familiar faces around her. "I have all the friends I need."

She lifted her champagne flute, which had been refilled just a few minutes ago. "To the First Fangs Club, new friends, and new experiences."

Everyone raised their flutes as well, then much clinking of glasses followed. As everyone drank, Charlie joined Donna.

"I hate to be the bearer of bad news…"

"I know," Donna said. "Dawn approaches."

"It does, Governor."

"Thank you for the reminder." Donna went to Francine. "We're going to head out. I hope someday

I can repay you for this wonderful evening. Not sure I can do it with the same style and panache you've managed, but we'll do something. I promise."

Francine bubbled over with happiness. "Honey, I'd go bowling with you if that's what you wanted to do. You just tell me when and where. Have a safe ride home. See you next group?"

"You know it." Maybe she could take Christina along. That would be all right, wouldn't it? She gave Francine a hug, said goodbye to Lionel with a kiss on the cheek, then goodbye to Bunni, Neo, Meghan, and LaToya with hugs as well.

The rest of the group said farewell, and at last, they departed. Not without Donna noticing a sly, hastily exchanged kiss between Temo and Neo.

When they were settled in for the drive home, Donna checked her phone for the first time that evening and found a text from Rico that had come in hours ago.

*Prints from the gun are Big Tony's, and the gun matches an unsolved murder. Nicely done. Oh, and get this. Carmella is a dental hygienist. She switched Joe's records.*

Big Tony could join his brother-in-law in prison. And Carmella would probably get additional charges for helping Joe fake his death. Wasn't that nice? She smiled. There was a lot to smile about. Tonight had been a good night. Even with Fitzhugh's nonsense.

"Pierce?" she said softly.

"Yes?" he answered from the front passenger seat.

"How's your hand?"

He flexed it. "Not bad. Nothing broken. I'm sure it'll be sore tomorrow."

"Thank you for defending me."

"It was my pleasure." He laughed. "It really was. I've never met anyone more punchable than Fitzhugh."

Temo snorted. "Ain't that the truth."

"That's only because neither of you ever met Joe."

After much laughter, Charlie sighed. "I just hope it doesn't come back to bite us."

"If it does," Donna said, "we'll deal with it. There's no problem so great that you cannot find a solution."

They all went quiet again until they were home and on their way up in the elevator. They all went to the penthouse, Temo included, to see how Penina and Rixaline had done. The two were watching a movie in the living room, a pizza box on the coffee table and the scent of popcorn in the air.

Rixaline greeted them all with a big smile. "How was the party?"

"Very nice," Donna said. "How were things here?"

Penina answered. "Uneventful. We had a good night."

Rixaline nodded. "Penina taught me a haka. It's a Samoan war dance that intimidates your enemies."

"Maybe I should learn that," Donna said.

Penina smiled. "Anytime, boss, but my cousin says you do intimidation pretty good already."

Donna laughed and glanced at Temo to find him smiling.

Something chimed, and Charlie pulled her phone from her evening bag. Then the chime sounded again, and they realized it was all of their phones. Donna's, Pierce's, and Temo's.

Donna took hers out to check the screen. "Incoming video message. Are we all getting this?"

"I think so," Charlie said.

"Is it some kind of countrywide alert?" Pierce asked.

"Wouldn't that just be a text message?" Donna pressed the arrow to play the video. A dimly lit holding cell of some kind appeared in shades of bluish gray. A man was bound to a chair in the center, head down.

Temo shook his head. "I don't like this."

"Me either," Donna said.

Just the same, they all watched as the footage played on their phones.

A fae walked into view and grabbed the man's head as he spoke into the camera. "We know you have the dhamfir. Return her to us, or your friend dies. You have forty-eight hours."

He yanked the man's head back.

And Donna looked into Rico's face.

Want to be up to date on all books and release dates by Kristen Painter? Sign-up for my newsletter on my website, www.kristenpainter.com. No spam, just news (sales, freebies, releases, you know, all that jazz.)

If you loved the book and want to help the series grow, tell a friend about the book and take time to leave a review!

# Other Books by Kristen Painter

COZY MYSTERY
*Jayne Frost series*
Miss Frost Solves a Cold Case: A Nocturne Falls Mystery
Miss Frost Ices the Imp: A Nocturne Falls Mystery
Miss Frost Saves the Sandman: A Nocturne Falls Mystery
Miss Frost Cracks a Caper: A Nocturne Falls Mystery
When Birdie Babysat Spider: A Jayne Frost Short
Miss Frost Braves the Blizzard – A Nocturne Falls Mystery
Miss Frost Chills the Cheater – A Nocturne Falls Mystery
Miss Frost Says I Do – A Nocturne Falls Mystery

*Happily Everlasting series*
Witchful Thinking

PARANORMAL ROMANCE
*Nocturne Falls series*
The Vampire's Mail Order Bride
The Werewolf Meets His Match
The Gargoyle Gets His Girl
The Professor Woos the Witch
The Witch's Halloween Hero – short story
The Werewolf's Christmas Wish – short story
The Vampire's Fake Fiancée
The Vampire's Valentine Surprise – short story
The Shifter Romances the Writer
The Vampire's True Love Trials – short story
The Dragon Finds Forever
The Vampire's Accidental Wife
The Reaper Rescues the Genie
The Detective Wins the Witch
The Vampire's Priceless Treasure

*Shadowvale series*
The Trouble with Witches
The Vampire's Cursed Kiss
The Forgettable Miss French

*Sin City Collectors series*
Queen of Hearts
Dead Man's Hand
Double or Nothing

STAND-ALONE PARANORMAL ROMANCE
Dark Kiss of the Reaper
Heart of Fire
Recipe for Magic
Miss Bramble and the Leviathan

URBAN FANTASY
*The House of Comarré series:*
Forbidden Blood
Blood Rights
Flesh and Blood
Bad Blood
Out For Blood
Last Blood

*Crescent City series:*
House of the Rising Sun
City of Eternal Night
Garden of Dreams and Desires

*Nothing is completed without an amazing team.*

Many thanks to:

Cover design: Janet Holmes
Interior formatting: Author E.M.S
Editor: Joyce Lamb
Copyedits/proofs: Chris Kridler

# About the Author

*USA Today* Best Selling Author Kristen Painter is a little obsessed with cats, books, chocolate, and shoes. It's a healthy mix. She loves to entertain her readers with interesting twists and unforgettable characters. She currently writes two best-selling paranormal romance series: Nocturne Falls and Shadowvale. She also writes the spin off cozy mystery series, Jayne Frost. The former college English teacher can often be found all over social media where she loves to interact with readers.

www.kristenpainter.com

For More Paranormal Women's Fiction Visit:
www.paranormalwomensfiction.net

Made in the USA
Monee, IL
01 October 2020

43754553R00199